WAITING TO WIN

LAKE SPARK OFF-SEASON
BOOK 2

EVEY LYON

LAKE SPARK OFF-SEASON SERIES

Waiting to Score

Waiting to Win

Waiting to Play

Copyright © 2023 by Evey Lyon, Lost Compass Press

Written and published by: Evey Lyon, Lost Compass Press

Edited by: Contagious Edits

Proofreader: Rachel Rumble

Cover design: Lily Bear Design Co.

All rights reserved.

No part of this book may be reproduced in any form or by any electronic or mechanical means. Including information storage and retrieval systems, without written permission from the author, except for the use of brief quotations in a book review.

This book is a work of fiction. The names, characters, places, and incidents are products of the writer's imagination and used fictitiously and are not to be perceived as real. Any resemblance to persons, venues, events, businesses are entirely coincidental.

The author acknowledges the trademark status and trademark owners of various products referenced in this work of fiction, which have been used without permission. The publication/use of these trademarks is not authorized, associated with, or sponsored by the trademark owner.

The author expressly prohibits using this work in any manner for purposes of training artificial intelligence technologies to generate text, including without limitation, technologies that are capable of generating works in the same style or genre as this work. The author reserves all rights to license uses of this work for generative AI training and development of machine learning language models.

Author's Note: No artificial intelligence (A.I.) or predictive language software was used in any part of the creation of this book.

This book is U.S. copy registered and further protected under international copyright laws.

ISBN E-Book: 978-1-959094-17-3

ABOUT

Connor Spears is hockey royalty who most definitely never planned to accidentally marry his childhood irritation, Hadley Crews.

Connor is smug, grew up destined for his hockey career, and he's irritatingly good-looking. He was also my next-door neighbor growing up. Now we're enemies. He wouldn't give me the time of day and made it clear he would never be friends with me, the ballerina and daughter of a baseball legend. Except for that one time. Years later, waking up in a Vegas hotel room after one hazy night, and now he's apparently my husband according to the paper next to his bed. You would think we would have it annulled, but he needs to clean up his image, and I'm a sucker for his occasional glances.

So, we agree to stay married and fake it.

Rumors spread fast in Lake Spark, and the responses of our parents, who are best friends, well, uh... they're mixed. But the problem with marrying for convenience is that you discover secrets about each other. You learn things too, like how he may just kill anyone who looks my way, or how sharing a bed brings out his dominant side. The thing is, it turns out that I may mean more to Connor than he'll ever admit. When life throws me another twist, I need a real husband to support me. And it turns out that Connor may have always been offside, waiting to win...

Connor and Hadley bring heartwarming steam to this marriage-of-convenience romance with a hint of enemies-to-lovers and a dash of unrequited love. Waiting to Win can be read as a complete standalone and is the second book in the interconnected Lake Spark Off-Season *series which is a spin-off of the* Lake Spark *series that includes their parents' stories. For lovers of small-town romance with a touch of hockey.*

AUTHOR'S NOTE

Age. It's just a number. And in case you are wondering, the math adds up, just barely. It isn't Lake Spark age-defying water. Waiting to Win can be read as a standalone as I always focus on one couple. But if you've been following the town of Lake Spark then you first met Hadley and Connor in their parents' stories. Hadley is Spencer's daughter (Worth the Chance) and Connor is Brielle and Ford's son (Worth the Wait) whom they had when they were teenagers. Basically, the parents in this book are still rocking their prime, and the kids are no longer kids.

If you are already familiar with Connor and Hadley, then you are in for a treat, as their romance was always there in the making!

1

CONNOR

Arriving late because I got sidetracked, I slide into my chair and swipe my sunglasses off my eyes. I can't help but smirk at the men sitting across the outdoor table from me, overlooking Lake Spark at Catch 22, a local establishment with a decent menu. The dark emerald-blue lake is calm today, and the pines lining the backdrop are green from recent rain.

And these men? They may be embracing a casual day with jeans and t-shirts, but their seething stare has become a constant occurrence.

But I'm the golden ticket, and they know it.

"What lovely weather we're having for May in Illinois. Probably means it'll snow next week, but it's the small wins, right?" I calmly say as I cross my arms and feel a victorious grin form.

"Cut the bullshit, Connor." My Uncle Declan is the first to speak, and that doesn't really surprise me. His stake in my hockey career is a little high, considering he owns the Spinners. He's never afraid to voice his disapproval, yet he has a soft spot for me. How can he not? He married my aunt Violet, and she's the best. More like a friend since we're closer in age, plus her flower shop provides the flowers that I need to charm the female population around here.

Sitting next to my uncle is my father. Ford Spears and Declan Dash are hockey legends; they played together years ago and never left hockey behind. My father owns the sports complex nearby where the Spinners train, and these two are also true partners in crime.

Which is unlucky for me most of the time.

My dad sighs. "Why are we having this conversation yet again?" While he isn't my agent, he voluntarily took on an unofficial role as my manager and trainer without the title, lucky me. He can throw in the dad card too, yet I've never minded. My father and mother had me when they were young, which means the age difference makes it a hell of a lot easier to connect sometimes. My parents did a lot for me, that I'll never forget. So, if he wants to help guide my career, then so be it.

But right now? These two men are ganging up on me.

Uncle Declan slides his drink to the side and leans against the table, scanning the area to ensure nobody is taking notice of us. Even if they did, Lake Spark is a small town that respects keeping gossip within our bubble. "I'm begging you, for all our sakes, to cool it down with the partying," he states.

"You're landing in too many media reports and not for the reasons that make your mother happy," my father adds. He's pulling out the big guns, mentioning my mother who I buy flowers for on a regular basis because she's amazing.

Still, I roll my eyes. "We made it to the playoffs, even after our shitty season, so of course, the team was going to celebrate," I justify. What a shame we were out in the second round.

"There is a photo of you taking shots next to the goalie while lying on a bar top," my uncle deadpans.

I shrug a shoulder. "So? I'm in my twenties. What else would I be doing to celebrate?"

My father shakes his head from my answer while he slides his hand along his brow.

Good ole' Uncle Declan points a finger at me. "I swear I could strangle you." He doesn't mean it. He has to play bad cop when he's in business mode. At family events, he'll just turn off his work switch and be uncle extraordinaire, complete with a side hug and jokes.

"It's off-season now. I'm strongly suggesting that you lie low. Try to straighten up your image a bit. You want to be in the media because of your skill, not because of your off-ice antics," my dad points out.

He may present a valid point. It took years to prove I earned a spot on the team due to talent, not connections. Hockey may be family tradition, but my abilities have made me MVP for two seasons straight. I'm a damn good defenseman. And so what, sometimes media throws in the hottest bachelor title. If you have good looks, then celebrate it.

"Relax, I have one more thing, then I'll focus on sleeping in, hanging with my little brothers, and hitting the gym." My parents got back together when I was ten, and my little brothers came a few years later. When I return to Lake Spark, even though I have my own place, I'm at my parents' a lot, and the house is chaos, with kids running around and a Labrador who is enjoying his final years.

The two in front of me glance at one another with a puzzled look.

Lifting his nose, my father asks with a hardened stare, "What's one more thing?"

My grin stretches. "Vegas. The boys and I are heading

there tomorrow for Briggs's birthday. Don't worry, I'll be back for family dinner by the weekend."

Both men wince at my statement before shaking their heads in disapproval. But then my father forms a soft smile for someone who seems to be standing behind me.

"Hey, Hadley," he greets her.

My body tightens, and her name wipes my cocky grin right off my face. Keeping my eyes set on the table, I choose to ignore the fact that Hadley Crews, with her long silky hair with caramel highlights and sparkly blue eyes, is stopping at our table to say hello to my father because she's a good girl like that.

"Hi, Mr. S and Mr. D." Her polite tone makes me grip my denim-clad thighs.

Hadley is a few years younger than me, my next-door neighbor growing up, and the daughter of a former baseball star. She's also anything but polite… when it comes to me.

"Christ, how many times do we have to tell you, it's Ford and Declan. We're too young for that mister crap," my father corrects her, because our parents are best friends, down to our moms sipping a dry white on weekends together.

She chuckles softly. "I know, but still."

"Brielle, my sister, and your mom are hysterical. They go on and on about that class you teach," my father mentions.

"Ballet barre? They come every week, work up a sweat, then hit Jolly Joe's right after class for cake. Balance, I guess." Hadley can't help but gush because she loves her mom, and well, probably loves my mom also, then add my aunt to that list too. In return, they have her on a pedestal of greatness.

"Brielle keeps asking me to check out her toned body," my father reflects.

I cringe at the thought. "Get it together," I mutter. "None of us want to know what you and Mom get up to."

"Passion doesn't die, Son." He chuckles at me then turns his attention back to the thorn in my side. "Grabbing lunch, Hadley?"

"Yeah, I'm just meeting Isla for a quick bite then heading back to the dance studio. I'm teaching a group of eighty-year-olds this afternoon."

Uncle Declan interjects and speaks to me. "See? Work ethic and helping the senior population. You could learn a lesson or two from her."

I scoff a laugh. "Trust me, I'm sure underneath her heart of gold, her mouth spits out wicked things." It flies off my mouth too easily.

The men at the table stare at me blankly, and Hadley's eyes snap to me with distaste apparent on her face; I know because I glance up to catch her soft lips form a tight line. She may be an elegant ballerina that teaches dance in our little town, but her eyes have a tint of wildness, the type that can make a man come undone if he isn't careful. She's always been the ballerina who dances with her hair down to Guns 'n' Roses. And her dark polished nails? They dig into skin as if she doesn't want to let go. But that's our little secret, one she wishes we didn't share.

One of the men sitting across from me clears their throat, attempting to break the stiff tension now gracing our table.

Hadley throws on a smile for their benefit. "I hope you both enjoy your lunch despite sitting with this menace. See you around."

"Yeah, he is special, this one." My father flashes me an over-the-top grin before turning back to my nemesis. "Oh, and thanks for babysitting the boys last weekend," my father remarks.

"Maybe we can add babysitting my nephew here. I'll pay extra," my uncle adds.

"There isn't enough money in the world for that," she states dryly before walking away. She's right too. Because she hates me, and hell knows, I've given her a bucketful of reasons, which is why she'll never change her mind.

My relatives have the audacity to chuckle at her comment, which causes me to give them an unimpressed look.

My father smiles. "You two are always the same. Ever since you were kids. Not sure why. I mean, she had the world's biggest crush on you."

"And?" I can't care.

"Grow some maturity is what your dad is saying. You may actually realize that she is quite a joy to be around, and you've just been flirting with her," my uncle has the audacity to casually mention before he looks at his phone.

My face stays blank. "I'm not flirting."

"Thank God. Spencer would kill you." My dad is only half-joking. Spencer, Hadley's dad, probably would. I'm like 90% certain that he might hate me due to my wild teenage years or the fact he doesn't like the idea of any guy around his princess… and I don't mind one bit.

Ignoring what they say, my eyes scan the room and land on Hadley with her friend Isla sitting at a table. Internally, fear forms that Isla is inviting Hadley to Vegas. These are the hazards of Isla hanging with the team, since her older brother is our winger and my best friend.

Why the fuck does Hadley have to be a vision? Even when she's wearing an oversized shirt that falls off the curve of her shoulder, then she's in those tight little dance pants, and I bet she's sporting a leotard underneath too. Nobody knows how she gets under my skin or how in another life she deserves to be my queen.

"Vegas, Connor. Best behavior," my uncle grits out as a reminder.

Memo received.

"What happens there, stays there." I turn my attention to him with an overdone smile.

"Connor," my father warns.

"Relax." I humor them, or maybe I consider their concerns… for a second.

I haven't decided because my eyes flick briefly back to Hadley, the delicate flower with a feisty tongue who is tucking a lock of loose hair behind her ear while the waiter flirts with her. I bet he would never be able to make her scowl the way I do.

My eyes pin on my uncle and father. "I hear your advice loud and clear, and I'll follow it *after* Vegas," I promise.

2

HADLEY

"I know it sounds crazy, but it felt like someone was watching me," I say as I play with the wrapper of the straw.

Isla tightens her ponytail. "What do you mean? At the dance studio?"

"Yeah. I was doing my usual self-practice. Just dancing a modern piece to music on the speakers, in my own little world, but then I swear someone was outside watching. I had the backdoor to the studio open, but when I looked, nobody was there. Maybe I'm paranoid. Then again, I also didn't feel unsafe, you know?"

She shrugs. "I mean, Lake Spark is one of the safest places to be."

"True."

I've lived here my whole life. I also grew up in that dance studio, and after my teacher Ms. Romy moved to Colorado, my father bought the place and gifted me the studio when I finished up my dance degree over at the university in Hollows nearby. I turned down a spot at a professional dance company, as it wasn't for me. I don't like rigid routine, and I love my family too much to be far. Teaching is my calling, as proven by the fact that it's been a few years and I'm still happy.

The waiter returns to take our orders. I go for a chicken salad sandwich, it's my favorite at Catch 22, and Isla orders a Caesar salad.

The moment the waiter leaves us, Isla is in action mode while I down my glass of water. "Pause your gallon-a-day hydration for a sec, we have business to discuss."

"Hydration is key for my dewy skin," I playfully defend.

Isla crosses her arms on the table and looks at me with enthusiasm. "*So,* Vegas." She flashes her eyes at me.

"What about it?"

Isla is a few years older than me, but it doesn't deter our friendship. Her brother plays for the Spinners, and she's close with the team, as she works for Ford at the training arena in project management for the summer camp that he runs.

"Come on, it's my brother's birthday. I can't not go to Vegas. But I *do* need a trusted sidekick with me."

A half-smile forms on my mouth. "As much as I love a good party, I'm not… sure."

"Because of a certain player who is sitting somewhere in this restaurant?" Isla's face screws up, and she pretends to search.

I huff out a breath, and my eyes do a quick travel to land on Connor Spears, the carbon monoxide of my air. His piercing brown eyes don't affect me, nor do his cunning grin or well-defined biceps. And so be it if his hair is the kind of shade of light blondish-brown that I like, not quite as dark as his ruthless heart.

I hate the off-season. It means I have to see his face

around town more than usual, and it exceeds my tolerance quota for the guy.

My eyes journey back to Isla. "Trust me, I could care less if I have to witness his partying antics or flavor-of-the-week puck bunny."

Isla offers me a pained look. "Did you two ever talk about—"

My palm flies up to stop her. "Please don't mention it." I groan from the pure memory of a time I should have known better.

She nods in agreement to my request. "Then it's settled. You will pack your sexiest dress and come with. The private plane that my brother arranged leaves tomorrow at lunch, and we should be back the day after."

Picking up my phone, I see my screensaver. It's my dad, mom, and little brother Ashton. It's an old photo, which you could tell because Pickles, the beagle that lived to a hundred, is in the photo. I loved that dog. He was almost the best part of my dad marrying April, except April became my mom and nothing tops that. My biological mom was never in the picture, a fling of my dad's. She even signed away her rights the moment I was born. But I don't care, because it means my dad and I ended up with the person who I consider to be my real mom, and they had my little brother one day after my ninth birthday.

I bet if I told my mom that I was going to Vegas, she'd help me pack. My parents are the kind of people that you can throw back a drink with while listening to good music. They encourage living life to the fullest.

"I guess I should get out of the house," I say. "Plus, I do want to get another small tattoo, which I could get in Vegas in the morning before we go." I already have a small pair of ballet slippers, and a baseball because my dad was a pitcher. I would like to add a few tiny shooting stars somewhere. I keep my tattoos hidden in intimate spots near my hip bone. There are great tattoo artists in Vegas, so it would be a bonus for this trip.

"That would be fun, and you should get out of the house. You live with your parents."

I give my friend a pointed look. "By choice," I correct her. Why give up a great room in a beautiful house with an indoor pool, family, and a mom who cooks to professional standards?

Isla reaches across the table to take my hand between her palms. "Please, Hadley, I don't get along with the other girls in the group. I need someone who can dance all night and tell a good joke. I think Cann has a thing for you too."

"Shawn Cann, the center?"

She nods.

"Not interested. Besides, my dad would go through the roof if I ever introduced a hockey player as a boyfriend. He witnessed too many of Connor's varsity team parties next door, and it's only gotten worse since then, and his opinion has only grown since then thanks to the asshole over there."

Isla can't help but smirk. "A party. Is that how you and —"

"You are bad. Don't bring him up. Con is his nickname, and trust me when I say it's purely fitting for his personality too." Connor is the opposite of what he seems, but few people know that, and I don't call myself lucky that I'm one of those people. "Your pitch to get me to Vegas really sucks," I tease her.

Isla sits up and clears her throat. "You're right. Okay, how about my brother is getting you and me a luxurious suite with a hot tub, full breakfast, and unlimited champagne."

My eyes slightly bug out, as I'm impressed. "You should have led with that."

"Come on, please? You know I'm not a big party girl, but this sounds like something fun and out of my norm, plus it's my brother's birthday." She brings her hands together in a pleading gesture.

I debate for a few seconds, but it doesn't take long. "Fine." A grin slowly forms.

She nearly squeals. "It will be unforgettable."

"I'm sure." I look at my phone and see the time is near one. "I'll get someone to sub my classes tomorrow. Be sure to have a glass of champagne ready the moment I walk onto that plane." My eyes sideline to Connor who is standing up from the table with his family. "I'll need it," I murmur softly.

———

Isla hands me a glass of champagne as I settle in my seat post takeoff on this private plane, and I adjust my black dress; it's casual, but I know it turns heads. Already, the party seems to be going, so I'm not sure many would notice anyhow. Shots of tequila are being poured, and a few women are sitting on hockey players' laps.

Why I signed myself up for this, I'm not entirely sure. Maybe it's growing up with professional athletes always around me, but I appreciate that these guys have an unusual life. I guess that I have more understanding than most, which is why I'm often invited to their social gatherings. Most of the guys here are good men who treat Isla and me with respect and as a friend. They're fun to hang around with too.

Well, all except one.

Connor is sitting by the window with a nice pair of jeans and a baby-blue button-down. It nearly makes me miss his glared look of steel or appreciate how baby blue brings out his eyes. But the scotch in his hand has me thrown. The image itself makes me chortle.

Scotch is a man's drink. And I've seen Connor as a boy, the next-door neighbor who made fun of my ballet costumes when I was a little girl, to the teenager whose parties I would crash and he would shoo me away. The guy who lived and breathed hockey his whole life and gave roses to girls, with a charming grin plastered on his face. God, I had such a crush on him. Made worse when I was fourteen and his uncle forced Connor to walk me home after Connor's party got busted, then he surprised me and kissed me on the cheek.

His parents are the sweetest and are good to me. They raised him well, which is why it doesn't make sense that, when it comes to me, Connor is…

Our eyes connect, and for a mere second, I could swear something underlying is there, and I hate my treacherous heart for jumping.

Isla breaks my focus by nudging my arm with hers. "Drink up. Tequila is next, and it's calling our name."

I laugh. "We should pace ourselves."

"Don't you want to be a little numb and hungover when you get your tattoo tomorrow?"

"You're getting a tattoo?" Shawn asks, having overheard as he flops onto a seat nearby. He has a sweet smile, so it's a shame I seem to be drawn to hardened looks.

I offer him a polite smile. "Yeah, I think so. I've been wanting it for a while, but I didn't have the right moment. I actually got my last tattoo with my dad, and he got one too—a baseball glove with names of everyone in the family."

"Your dad is cool like that. He comes to our games sometimes, but in truth, I used to watch him play baseball. He was a really talented pitcher. Where are you getting the tattoo?"

He swipes his hand across his jaw in a suave manner. "Let me guess, your inner thigh?"

The sound of a cough breaks our conversation, and my eyes sideline to the culprit. Connor gives his teammate a death glare. "I'm confident princess tippy-toes keeps her tattoo destinations above the waist."

My eyes roll before I down a long sip of champagne. Of course, this would happen. My favorite villain always surprises me when he decides to go possessive on me, as if he has a fucking right. He doesn't. Yet he still takes it upon himself.

"Or I enjoy very intimate locations. Hidden, private, slightly questionable for the tattoo artist," I challenge with my eyes set on Connor whose jaw clenches slightly.

"If you need someone to hold your hand, I'm there," Shawn volunteers with a grin.

Isla makes a sound of approval.

Connor, on the other hand, is quick to stand up. "Cann, now," he orders and indicates to follow him.

Shawn gives me a rueful shake of his head before he agrees and follows Connor to the other part of the plane behind a curtain.

Leaning back in my chair, I sigh and finish my champagne down to the last drop.

Isla leans in to whisper, "Remind me again, what the hell is Connor's problem?"

"Hell if I know." I puff out a breath and offer my glass for replenishment, while I attempt to fog out the memory of that one time, when his hands and lips landed on me.

But I was just a little mistake, and we've hated one another since.

Which is why I stare at my champagne flute, confused as

to why Connor Spears is berating his teammate for merely glancing at me.

For a jerk who hates me, his possessive streak is *sometimes* endearing.

Definitely infuriating, and I sure as hell will let him know. Which is why I unbuckle my seatbelt and stand.

3
CONNOR

Roughly, I pull across the curtain dividing the plane and step into Shawn's space.

"What the hell was that back there?" I grit out at my teammate.

His mouth curves. "I was just talking with Hadley, because I bet that dancer knows how to bend and—"

"Shut the fuck up." I grab his shirt near the collar from pure instinct. "Stay away from her," I nearly snarl, and I hate that I care.

Shawn squints his eyes before he smirks. "Oh yeah, someone mentioned you get a little crazy when it involves her. You should seal that deal, Con. She's sports dynasty, hot as hell, and flexible, the kind of woman that I'm sure my dick would thoroughly enjoy."

I push him against the side of a seat, enraged somewhere inside of me. "Say that again and I will gladly break something, since we don't need your arm during the off-season." Shawn just chuckles. "Listen, it was your first season with us, but everyone knows to leave her alone. It's a team rule," I attempt to rationalize, and I roll my shoulder back.

He raises a brow. "You mean your rule, and everyone just follows because they're too scared of who your daddy and uncle are."

I tighten my grip on his shirt. "Think whatever the hell you want, I'll gladly prove you wrong."

"Whatever, Connor. She's an adult, and from what I hear, she hates your guts, so let me just walk back in there and offer her a drink." Christ, this dude is pushing me. I always thought he was half-decent, but now he's just irritating me to the max.

Before I can shoot off another warning, the curtain slides open in one abrupt swoosh, and our eyes land on Hadley who is leaning against the divider with her hand over her head and hip tipped out, and her tits are perked up because of her dress. Well, this is just agony; she looks like a pinup girl full of sass. My dick stirs against the zipper of my jeans, knowing her pissed-off look is for me, and that's just exciting.

She throws an overdone smile at Shawn. "Do you mind giving your teammate and me a moment?"

Shawn looks between us and chuckles. "Sure. Body shots later?"

My muscles clench from every word this guy directs toward her.

Hadley smiles tightly. "Maybe."

With my teammate walking past her, and I'm sure as hell confident he purposely brushes against her shoulder in passing, Hadley steps into my space, and in one movement, closes the curtain again before her hand returns to her hip with her dark blue nails tapping the curve of her waist.

But I've been here before with her, and it's on.

"You're breaking the rules, Hadley," I chide as my eyes transfix on her face that doesn't move an inch.

"Ah yes, your imaginary rules that you believe I follow," she muses.

I wave my long finger side to side. "Staying away from one another is about the only thing we agree on, so why are you here?"

She steps forward and stands tall to appear unaffected by me. "To enjoy your pleasant holier-than-thou company, of course." Sarcasm suits her, damn it. "Unlike you, your teammates and my best friend find me a little more than tolerable, so here I am, because I don't give a rat's ass if you care or not." There is a little bite to her tone.

"Feisty Hadley, lucky me," I mock.

Her mouth changes shape to a sultry look. "Someone will be lucky. I didn't even offer yet, but I may let Shawn trace the spot of my new tattoo with his tongue," she rasps.

Willpower.

It's taking a ton of willpower not to snap right now. She's riling me up because she seems to think I'm affected, and she can't know her theory is true.

But I'll play her little game. I pretend to look at my watch. "You should send him my way if he needs directions, considering we both know that my tongue and hands are far too familiar with your body."

"And don't I regret it," she snipes.

In a flash, I step forward and trap her between the side of a vacant seat and my body, our breaths mingle, and her chin rises from surprise. My head lolls to the side gently, and if I were to move an inch, then her mouth would be mine. "Trust me, I'm honored that you gave me your V-card." I pretend to be touched because she can never know the real truth.

Two palms land against my chest because I delivered a low blow, even I know that. Trust me, I'm already disgusted with myself.

"Don't dredge up our past mistakes," Hadley seethes, and I notice the rhythm of her chest moving while her scornful gaze feels like fire on me. "You're the biggest asshole on this plane."

"Big and me do go hand in hand," I taunt.

She growls. "Your ego is a piece of work, and your arrogant tendencies aren't the least bit refreshing. Anything but original, actually. This is how this is going to go, Connor. You'll let me drink, dance, play blackjack, and do whatever the hell I want in peace. Watch all you want, because we both know you're like a child upset that his toy got taken away."

A deep chuckle roars in the back of my throat. "You're a toy now?"

Hadley shakes her head, clearly exasperated. She looks away then back to me, with her eyes softening. "Insufferable, that's what you are." For a second, I hear sadness in her tone, and I nearly falter because I do actually hate that she was hurt and it's my doing.

But I stay strong.

When she pivots to leave, I grab her arm, and she looks down then draws her sight up. "Just… not Shawn. He's bad news." My voice grows delicate, because as much as we're one another's despair, a protectiveness that I have no right to feel hits me when she's around.

She scoffs a sound. "No, Connor… you're bad news, and I swear, if I had it in me, then I would find a way to destroy you." It takes me a moment to digest her honesty, but then she snickers and walks a step before glancing over her shoulder. "I'll be sure to ask you to pass the salt when I decide to do body shots with your teammate."

She turns her back and leaves, so maybe she doesn't hear my growl. She's impossible, agonizing, and beautiful when she snarls.

Having her on this trip, not my choice, is the work of the devil. That's the only thing I can come up with when I decide another scotch is calling my name.

That was a near excruciating flight, but luckily, other than a few drinks, everyone kept it steady, as we all know we have a long night ahead.

Now we are in Vegas, and I'm sitting on the sofa in the luxurious penthouse that we rented, complete with a rooftop pool. After checking into the hotel and freshening up, we got straight into the celebratory mood. I'm sitting on a sofa, overlooking the Vegas skyline as the sun hangs low to the west.

My friend and teammate, Briggs Chase, hands me a fresh drink with a grin. "God, I'm having a good time. No Vaughn Madden in sight." That's his archnemesis on the ice, the guy who got Briggs a ten-minute misconduct penalty during our game with Tampa.

"You're still going on about that? He is actually quite a good guy off the ice." Briggs gives me a death stare, and I give up.

He tips his nose in Hadley's direction. "You going to survive?"

I stare into the presumably gin and tonic that he placed in my hands. "Always do. I'm feeling lucky tonight. Let's head straight to the blackjack table when we head down."

He feigns a sound of doubt. "I don't know, man, can't be late for the strippers."

I scoff. "I'll take a hard pass."

Briggs raises his brows at me. "Why? Because you want to stick around to deter Shawn from getting his own private show from a certain dancer?"

"Fuck that. She isn't my problem." I hate that there is frustration in my voice.

Choosing to ignore the giggles of the girls in our group, lining up shots near the snack buffet, I know the daggers I feel on my back can only be coming from one person on this trip.

I don't dare search for her with my eyes. Not when my mind is replaying how this all started a few years ago.

Glaring at my mother, I'm not impressed with this set-up as she sits by my side in the theater while we wait for the show to start. "Why the hell am I here again?" I ask her.

She adjusts her sunglasses resting on the top of her hair framing her face. "Because we are neighbors and friends. Everyone on our street supports one another. We go to Hudson's football games, everyone comes to your hockey games, and now we are here for Spencer and April and for their daughter."

"I come home for the weekend, and you have me watching little kids in tutus." I'm very unimpressed.

My mother leans in. "If you stay in our house for the weekend, then you follow our rules," she chides.

"I'll go stay at the Dizzy Duck Inn," I counter.

Her frown informs me that she isn't having it. "You can suck it up for an hour or two. Besides, you missed Hadley's eighteenth birthday party." She stresses the word eighteenth.

"And?" It comes out flat. She's the neighbor who has crushed on me for years. Sure, I've noticed that she's no longer a little girl. Instead, she's easy on the eyes, and I've done my damnedest to block her out of my head when she shows up to any family gathering or party I used to throw at my parents' house.

The lights flicker, indicating that the show is about to

start. I lean in to whisper to my mother, "This is my chance to escape."

She grips my arm, preventing me from standing. "No, you won't."

I begin to grumble, but the curtain rises and music starts, an alternative rendition of a song by The Police. My eyes land on the ballerina dancing solo on her pattering toes in her pointy slippers, and my lips twitch when I notice there isn't an ounce of baby pink on her like you would expect. Her shoes are blue satin, and everything else on her tight body is black. Her hair partly up and her eyeliner strong, she's beautiful and mesmerizing as her leg stretches into the air in a long line. My eyes adjust to register that it's Hadley. My breath cuts when I realize my fear has come true.

She's worth looking at, roping me in, and now is entirely legal.

Suddenly, I'm invested in this dance show.

I don't need to glance to my side, and I couldn't tear my eyes away even if I tried. My mother gently clears her throat. "Thought so," she mumbles. I hate how she can read my mind; she walked me into this trap willingly.

Hadley spins in a turn, and when she lands perfectly on her feet, I swear that for a mere second our eyes connect, with the bright stage light sparking in the corner of my eyes.

The light of a match. That's what this is.

Blinking, I bring myself into the present when someone clinks a glass. "All right, everyone, we have a birthday to celebrate and Vegas to conquer. Tequila, anyone?" The whole group erupts in cheers before someone turns up the music full blast.

It doesn't take long for things to spiral from there.

It's when I turn my head that I see, across the room, Hadley is clearly in good spirits, sucking on a slice of lime, and I realize it's near enraging that she can be the life of a party. She's laidback, doesn't try to be anything she isn't, a free spirit, complete with a kind heart—as long as it doesn't involve me. Her presence here isn't because of who's here or that she wants to be associated with a name; she's here because she wants to enjoy life.

Watching her is glorious torture.

Curiosity gets the best of me, and I stand up to walk casually in her direction, partly to annoy her and the other part giving me one hit of enjoyment.

In the process, a random woman touches my arm. "Con, you should totally go in the pool with us," she coos.

I don't even bother giving her a look. "Nah, I didn't come to Vegas to go swimming," I say.

Briggs arrives by my side and throws an arm around my shoulder as he holds a bottle of tequila in his other hand.

The woman tries not to show her disappointment. "Who knows where the night will go, right?" Her blonde hair flicks in front of me as she spins to turn her attention to a friend.

My quest leads me closer to my target. Hadley peers up to meet my eyes with disapproval. "Go away," she groans in warning.

Briggs fills her empty shot glass. "You two better get it together. We haven't even hit the club yet or sung happy birthday. Call it my birthday wish that you two call a truce."

"As the responsible one, he's right, Hadley," I say, sounding condescending.

"Spare me. Oh look, there's a stripper pole in the room. Let me go experiment with my life choices." She begins to walk, but I step in her way.

"Sure, we both know you love to make daddy proud," I say, and I don't know why.

Hadley shakes her head as she bites her bottom lip

because she's pissed and probably knows she's drawing my sight straight to her delectable mouth. Briggs awkwardly stands there with his lips quirked out while he freezes and holds the bottle up.

"What planet did you wake up on? Your family's Labrador has more manners than you," she snipes.

"You two are at it again?" Isla intercepts as she arrives and rests her hand on Hadley's shoulder. "I swear, I'm about to lock you two in a closet together."

"Maybe we should give them an ultimatum," Briggs ponders.

Isla throws her arms up. "Or just give them another shot. It will loosen them up eventually."

"I don't know, Hadley is already mentioning a career on the pole," I comment dryly, but the image inside my head is driving me nuts.

Frustrated, Hadley abruptly hands her glass to Briggs. "One more. Obviously, Prince Charming isn't going to arrive, throw me over his shoulder, and save me."

"You shouldn't have come, princess tippy-toes." I hand my glass to Briggs, with my eyes drilling in on Hadley.

In the corner of my eye, Briggs looks at Isla to double-check this is a smooth plan. Isla responds with her eyes gawking, which causes Briggs to hold up the bottle. "You guys only get another shot if you give it to one another. Call it a truce," he informs us with a smirk.

Well played, but fine.

Hadley grumbles.

I take the two filled glasses from Isla. "I'm sure Hadley can follow my lead, she has before."

"That comment just made me not care how the hell I get my shot, as long as you become a blur," she boils.

I grin, satisfied, as I step closer and hold up the glass. Our eyes lock before her lips press against the rim of the glass that I hold, and her fingers wrap around my wrist to keep me steady as I slowly tip back the liquid. The electric shock hits us both. I feel it in my bones, especially as our eyes linger for an extra second. When she swallows, I don't release the glass. I enjoy this connection that doesn't feel alcohol-infused, even though it must be. She doesn't seem to be escaping either, and that's of her own accord. Hot energy shoots down to below my navel because this woman is a curse.

When I finally bring the glass away, she instantly reestablishes contact by bringing my other hand with my shot glass up, and the corner of her mouth tugs, but she won't commit to a smile, not for me.

Our eyes stay pierced as the shot comes to my lips. She stands on her toes as she guides the alcohol to me. The shot comes to my lips, and she slowly eases the liquid into my mouth, and my free arm wraps around her middle to keep her in a firm stance, causing our bodies to press together. We stand in this embrace longer than we should, the music in the background fading away as my attention is on Hadley.

I refuse to believe that anything less substantial is causing me to feel dizzy. My current state is her doing, purely from a spark in her hazel eyes. But whatever the reason, she gets her wish, because the night becomes a blur...

Until the next morning, that is, when I feel my favorite little vixen in bed next to me.

4
HADLEY

A brick. Why does my head feel like a brick?

My stomach doesn't feel too great either.

My eyes flick open to find my face is half smashed against an admittedly comfortable pillow. This bed is warm, unusually warm for being under the covers, almost as if there is a heater next to me. From behind me, in fact. I begin to stretch out my body, but my foot hits the skin of a leg.

Not my leg.

Rolling over, my eyes widen when I see Connor groggily waking up on the other side of the bed, his eyes already in a blinking frenzy, as he is a few seconds ahead of me.

Oh no.

Instantly, I jab his shoulder, and his response is a low grumble, but he begins to stir awake.

I'm an idiot. Why am I alerting his attention? I should just sneak on out of here and ignore the fact that we…

Wait, what did we do?

"Connor," I shriek in a loud whisper.

"What?" His voice his scratchy against his throat, but

something must connect in his head because he jackknifes up to sitting. "Why are you in my bed?" Connor's tone is gruff, with an edge that would be sexy if it wasn't for the detail that it's him speaking.

We look at one another, horrified, then his eyes dip down, which causes my own attention to follow his line of sight.

I'm gripping the duvet around my body, but one glance and it appears I'm naked, proven when I lift the blanket slightly and confirm that I'm only wearing a thong... and he's wearing nothing, which is why I slam the blanket back down into position, because I don't need a reminder of his size even in downtime.

"What the hell did we do?" I begin to panic.

He scratches the back of his head. "I... did we?"

I shrug my shoulders and shriek, "We're both pretty much naked!"

He has the audacity to half-smirk. "Got a glimpse, huh?"

I growl in frustration. "I vaguely remember last night, but I'm missing moments." My eyes scan the room, and I see empty water bottles which causes me to knit my brows together. "Oh, gee, we were responsible and stayed hydrated," I deflate with sarcasm.

"Relax." His hand indicates to stay calm. "You would feel it if you decided to ride my pony again."

Shaking my head, I choose to ignore his ridiculous comment and search for my phone that I hear vibrating. Luckily, it's under my pillow.

I see Isla's name on the screen and pick up, careful to bring the phone to my ear so the devil doesn't hear.

"Hey, Isla," I calmly greet her. "What the hell happened?" My voice does a 180, pitching higher at the end.

My friend laughs. "What do you mean? You're the one not in our room. I was scared I needed to send out a search party. But then I remembered that you left the party with Mr. Nobody's Eyes Shall Ever Land on You But His, so I knew you were safe."

I glance over my shoulder and notice Connor doesn't seem stressed by the fact we're sharing a bed, with no recollection of events.

"I left the party with Connor?" That can't be right.

"You two were doing shots. It seemed to loosen you two up, you were both even laughing about childhood memories at one point, certainly didn't want to kill one another. When Shawn asked if you wanted to do a body shot, Connor threw you over his shoulder, you giggled, and you dared Connor that he wouldn't carry you out to save you. It was kind of cute."

I vaguely remember Connor carrying me out of the party and a dare… but that was when we were in an elevator. Oh no. Nope.

"You let me leave with him? I swear, I may be revoking your friend card," I huff.

"Hey! I called you twenty minutes later, and you said that Connor was taking you to get your tattoo." Strange. I have no new tattoos. "Then you sent me a text later saying not to wait up as you were having an unforgettable night."

I try to remember. "I don't recall any of that."

"Well, I'm assuming that you and him…"

"Don't even say it," I grit out and feel Connor's eyes on me.

"Okay, well, thought I'd check if you want to have breakfast?" Isla asks, and the thought of food just makes me want to heave or it's the presence of the man behind me, I'm not sure.

I roll my eyes, and a long exhale escapes me. I reach for

the bottle of water near the bed, and that's when I notice something. It's new, *very* new.

"Uh, you go ahead. I'll come to our room soon." I manage to string a sentence together, end the call, and toss the phone to the side while my sight locks on my finger that's sporting a diamond ring. A gorgeous, albeit new ring.

"Breakfast sounds good, I'm starving," Connor casually mentions as he yawns and stretches his arms over his head like this is a daily occurrence.

My head turns sharply to stare at him full-on, and I hold up my hand. "What the hell is this?"

It catches him off guard, and his jaw goes slack, but only a croaky sound escapes him before he looks down and notices a band on his finger. "Oh, shit."

My stomach drops, and a meltdown is fast approaching. "Tell me we didn't," I plead.

He gives me a sympathetic look. "I can't."

I shove him with my hands and the blanket drops slightly down my breasts before I save myself. "Do you remember last night?"

Connor gives me a funny look as he scratches the back of his head. "Parts."

"Which parts?" I'm furious.

"Not the part where you apparently got your childhood wish." He examines his finger and leans back against the headboard. "The one where I'm your husband."

I groan and quickly slide off the bed, taking the blanket with me, only allowing myself one glance at his impressive package, before giving him a glare. "We did not get married!"

He examines the scene before his eyes discover something, then he leans to the side to grab it from his bedside table. Connor chortles a sound and holds up the paper.

"According to this, we are husband and wife." Why is there a hint of a smug shade across his lips?

"No!" I look up to the ceiling.

Connor scrubs a hand across his face. "I'm sure this is not what my uncle had in mind for staying on the straight and narrow."

I could scream, but instead, I head directly for the bathroom and abruptly close the door behind me, ensuring I lock it. Walking straight to the mirror, I rub my face and attempt to calm myself down. I look like a trainwreck, yet I have a glow on my cheeks, and this ring is a blinding accessory that is somewhat flipping perfect on my finger, but no, nuh-uh, I am not Connor's wife!

"What have I done?" I whisper as my thoughts head into a memory from when I was eighteen and why Connor Spears can never be my husband.

Connor grips the steering wheel, internally preparing himself as he pauses before he starts the engine, probably because I'm sitting in the front seat. The air between us feels heightened. For the longest time, I thought the guy was neutral about me, has never given me any indication we could be anything more or less, except lately. First, when he showed up at my dance show, and then the other week when our families went out to dinner to celebrate being drafted. It was near unbearable because I kept catching that his eyes were on me, and our gaze held while his lips tugged, as though my sight on him is something he enjoys.

And here we are because we were both watching our little brothers play T-ball, and our parents wanted to take the team out for pizza and ice cream after. We love our brothers, but not a group of kids their age. Connor and I just looked at one another, agreeing on our version of hell, and made up excuses for why we couldn't go. A promised attendance at a party for him, and tired for me because I rehearsed for six hours yesterday.

So here's Connor, driving me home.

He is also my answer, and he might have appeared in my fantasies a few times too. Well, a lot. But right now, it isn't just that. Something is causing me to want to orbit around him more than usual.

Connor backs the car up and drives us away. "Come on, let's get you out of here, Sprinkles." He gave me that nickname when I was thirteen, and I hate it as much as I love it.

"Why do you call me that?"

"Because you used to bring me cupcakes when you had a ridiculous crush, and you smelled of icing and cake. Sprinkles seemed fitting."

A smile begins to stretch on my mouth.

"Can I go to the party with you?" I try my luck.

He scoffs and doesn't even bat an eye as he focuses on the road. "Not a chance."

"Why not?" I ask, defensive.

"Because that's the deal we've always had. I've tolerated you because our parents are friends, and I know your dad would want me to keep an eye on you. That means no parties because I can't watch you every second, and you're a distraction to most."

The corner of my mouth tugs that he called me a distraction. "Am I distraction to you?" I glance to him and notice the twist on the corner of his mouth.

"Yes." He's blunter than I anticipated, but I love his answer.

Silence overwhelms the car since he just admitted that I'm something.

I sigh and rest my head against the headrest. "I need a

moment, and I'm not ready to go home. I'll only think about my future there."

He glances sidelong at me for a quick second before returning his focus to the road. It feels as though the mention of my future fueled compassion inside of him. "Come on, I know a place for that."

"Okay." A giddy feeling hits me.

It's a few minutes later when he pulls off onto a side road then up a hill where he parks. It's empty and dark, but I only feel safe around him. We get out, and the engine is off but his car still plays music, and when I follow him to sit on the back of his car where he opened the hatch, a bit of light from the car highlights his face, and the sky is speckled with stars.

"I come here to think of my future all the time." He sighs.

I turn to him, and he mirrors my move. "Do you ever find it exhausting?" I begin. "The whole hockey career thing? Don't you just want to wake up and play without any pressure?"

He seems to study me for a second. "Not often. I've wanted to go pro since I first touched the ice. Why do you ask?"

"There was someone who watched my dance showcase a few weeks ago, and they offered me a spot in their company in New York, even without an audition," I admit.

Connor touches my shoulder gently, and it surprises me, but it's welcomed. "That's great... or isn't it?"

I shake my head. "I don't want to go, it's not for me. Too much pressure, but I don't want to let down my parents. I mean, I know they would support me no matter what, but it's just a thought in my head, you know?"

"I do. My uncle and dad are a constant reminder of what I need to achieve, and they don't even mean to be." He sighs.

"I guess we have something in common then. Being good

at something but struggling to fully breathe." I can't stop staring at him.

He twirls the end of my hair around his finger and attempts to focus his eyes on my hair, but they only flick up again.

This is my moment.

"Do you find me attractive?" I ask, and I'm not shy about it.

He scoffs a sound before biting his inner cheek, desperately trying to hide his entertained smirk. "Where is this coming from?"

"Answer me." My tone is short.

He avoids looking at me and instead wraps my strand of hair tighter. "Hadley, you're a beautiful girl. You don't need me to tell you that."

I smile to myself with satisfaction and confidence before I interlace our hands on the floor of the trunk, catching him off guard, but he doesn't pull away. "I thought so. Do you want to kiss me?"

"I'm not answering that." There is a hint of a grin on his mouth. "What is this about?"

"I'm no longer a kid," I remind him.

"I've noticed."

"Help me," I rasp, barely a whisper.

His eyes linger on our joined hands. "With what?" he asks softly. Maybe I make him nervous or maybe his brain is already connecting the dots.

"Kiss me because I'm too scared to." My bold declaration surprises even me.

Connor's sight rockets back up to mine, and he tilts his head slightly to the side, the light highlighting his concerned face. "You don't seem scared now."

"Kiss me," I repeat my request.

His eyes sideline, only to return to me with heat in his gaze. "Hadley, I've done a hell of a job avoiding you lately because the ideas in my head don't make me a gentleman, and here you are throwing it all at me. I won't be the guy to walk away noble, I'm too selfish."

"And?" *I'm not concerned.*

He debates for a few seconds, clearly having an internal struggle. "I've tried to warn you. Fuck it," *he seems to curse to himself right before his lips slam onto mine.*

His kiss is an explosion of my heart. A command that he leads. So damn firm and better than all of my dreams combined.

I've kissed guys before, but nothing like this. My whole body is alive, and his tongue swipes into my mouth with clear direction, causing me to melt. Then it only gets better when it turns fervent. We don't pull away nor stop.

It escalates until we're lying down in the back of his car. His hand finds my leg, and I feel it in my bones that we won't stop. I pause for a second, and his head jolts back to attempt to read my face.

"Just go slow." *My eyes gently gawk at him to ensure he understands that I want more.*

But his head gently tilts when a realization hits him. "You're…"

"Don't be surprised."

"Fuck," *he groans before swiping a hand through his hair.* "I'm the last person you should be with now. My moral standing to take you right home is non-existent." *He begins to create space between us, but I grab his wrist.*

"You're not other guys… you're…" *It trails off, and I lean in closer to him to run my hand along his arm.* "Or would you rather I find some other guy?" *I challenge, and instantly I see a sort of possessiveness roar in his eyes.*

"Hadley," he warns. "Don't do that either. It should be with someone who cares."

I bring his hand that I'm holding by the wrist and plant it on my bare thigh just below the hem of my skirt. "Like you. You care." His eyes turn tense, and his jaw tightens, but he doesn't remove his hand. "Connor, I want it to be you," I whisper my insistence.

"Don't throw this offer at me, Sprinkles." His voice has an edge to it.

I lean in to close our distance, and it can't be my imagination that I feel his pulse quickening. "Why? Because it's enticing?" I husk then brush my lips along his jawline.

"You're not just some hookup," he whispers as he brings the fingers on his other hand to splay against my throat to hold me in place. His gesture is demanding yet soft.

"How so?"

Connor lifts the corner of his mouth as the fingers on my thigh begin to swivel a lazy design on my leg, as if he is contemplating a few ideas, and my whole body tingles while his lips remain nearly touching my own. "Don't make me say it." His voice sounds desperate.

The last few minutes have proven that my attraction is not one-sided. We've grown up with one another, at a distance yet so close too. And it seems we both want the same thing.

"Fuck me, I shouldn't be doing this here with you. You deserve more." He seems to be talking to himself.

He grabs the blanket from the side, and I have a wary look.

It causes him to laugh. "Relax, it's in here because I went with some friends to the beach." Ah, so not for another conquest, except he just highlighted that I'm not just anyone. Nerves hit me, but I feel comfortable and ready.

He lies on his side while I'm on my back. "Have you

really thought about me like this?" I hear vulnerability in my voice.

A smirk forms on his mouth, but it's an earnest and natural look. "I have. Too many times to count."

I try to control my smile, and we take a few seconds of staring at one another, soaking in our realization that after years of knowing one another, here we are together in a different manner. My fingers begin to work at my clothes, but he stops me.

"You're going to have to tell me if I'm not gentle enough or I need to slow down. Don't lie to me. You understand?" He's insistent.

I nod once, and he does something that surprises me; he kisses my cheek so tenderly, like the time he walked me home once. Then he peels off his hoodie and shirt, placing his balled-up clothes near my head before digging into his wallet for a condom. He helps slide my panties off while I peel off my sweater, and I lie back across the seats.

His lips are already trailing my body, heading lower to my most intimate spot. I shiver from the thought of what he is about to do.

"I know this is only a favor." My breath shakes as I try to reassure him as he hovers over me, but I'm desperately wishing for more.

Connor glances up before he returns to a higher destination, where he hooks his finger under my chin to guide my eyes to meet his. "It's a little more than that. A lot more than that." He dips his head down to capture my lips again. "You're giving me something, and I will never let you forget it. You're not just anyone. You were always going to be more than something to me."

His words make my heart soar. I've been hoping for the moment we would confess our feelings, and now it's a reality.

Shaking my head and throwing water on my face, I do my best to forget the way he kept his promise to go gentle and slow. Urged me to look at him and claw his back when pain hit, and his answer was to distract me by kissing me deeper, to the point that I felt he had control of my breath and body. After, he ditched his party and opted to lie with me for what felt like ages. He covered me with his hoodie, stroking my hair with his fingers as he laid on his side, reminding me that I was okay, before we reminisced about many things growing up as next-door neighbors and our future careers. We unleashed a promising start with one another.

Connor told me that we should see one another again. His parents had a relationship when we were that age, and it made him believe we could have been possible. He showered me with kisses every chance he got. It felt like I was on top of the world.

But then the next morning, he appeared in my room completely different, eager to find his hoodie, and he made his thoughts clear.

"We were a mistake.

Forget last night ever happened, we will never be anything."

It's been vile hatred since then.

Patting my cheek, I blow out a breath and throw on a hotel robe. Bracing myself, I know I need to face the man in the other room.

Opening the door, I'm surprised to find Connor sitting up against the headboard with only boxer briefs on and perusing a room service menu.

Great, he wants to have the marriage talk shirtless, just freaking awesome.

"Hey there, Wifey." He smirks as he pats the spot next to him on the bed, inviting me to join him.

I cross my arms, determined not to move an inch. "I am not your wife."

He hums a sound. "Our marriage certificate and rings say otherwise, so…" It drags, and his chipper tone has me concerned.

"We'll get it annulled."

"Can we, though, considering we might have consumed our blessed union?" He's taunting me.

Why is he sitting there cool as a cucumber?

"We didn't." I would have felt it. He isn't easily forgettable, even when alcohol is involved. "Besides, we can file for a divorce," I counter.

He slides off the mattress, making a skeptical noise. I gulp when I watch him slowly take a few strides in my direction, and my sanity checks out for a second as I drink in the view of his muscles and chest. "We shall do no such thing, Sprinkles," he states.

Reality hits me again when he calls me a name I haven't heard in years, and it throws me off. "W-what?" I stammer.

Connor brings his fingers to my hair and gently tucks a few strands behind my ear, as if he is a sensitive creature, but before I can enjoy any cozy feelings from his touch, I blow away his finger.

"The thing is, I need to keep it positive in the media for a while, and I know you don't want to break dear old mom and dad's hearts by informing them that you became a Vegas cliché. Not to mention, the parents of those little gremlins you teach have a lot of opinions. Since we know what this is, then I think it's best that we…" I'm already shaking my head, and my hands form fists from aggravation. I can't muster any words. "Stay married for a while," he confirms my suspicion.

"Why would I want that misery?" I snicker, with our eyes in a standoff.

"We won't even manage to end this marriage fast enough before our parents find out. Let's not break their hearts until we mentally prepare them that our marriage was doomed from the start," he explains.

I growl because he may have a point. Plus, I'm in no clear mind right now to find a divorce lawyer. Or see the look on my father's face, probably filled with disappointment that I went away and came back in need of a divorce.

"It's the off-season, I'm sure you can fake it for the summer."

I laugh to myself that this is my life, but then I remember what this guy did to me. "You're right." I fake a sweet smile. "Being your wife sounds like a real delight. I can make your life dismal all in the name of marriage." I pat his hard chest with satisfaction at the new plan forming in my head, all because the idea of destroying him feels like a relief, and the opportunity is here.

He sneers. "I can't wait to see you try. How about you save it for after our news hits Lake Spark that you're the new Mrs. Connor Spears, okay?"

"Whatever you say, dear husband." A contrite smile hits my lips because he will not get the upper hand.

He'll see.

5
CONNOR

Sliding into the backseat of the limo that's taking us to the private airport, I notice instantly that Isla and Hadley are deep in discussion that abruptly stops when I arrive. My inkling is that I was the main topic, but married or not, I'm confident Hadley talks about me and how to use a pitchfork on a regular basis. Since they are facing me, I get a prime view of my wife. It's the first time I'm seeing my dear wife since she left my room to go change and grab her bag.

"There you are, it's been unbearable the last hour without you. Forgot how much you love backseats." A cheeky look is planted on my face, and I offer it to Hadley while Briggs slides in next to me.

"Save it," she mutters to me with a shade of disdain for my reference.

Isla looks back and forth between us. "She wasn't joking, was she?" Isla asks me, deeply concerned.

Briggs slides a glance at me. "About what?"

Isla chortles. "Haven't you heard the news? These two got hitched." She points between us.

"Funny." He doesn't believe her.

The car begins to move, and I lean forward to gently touch Hadley's knee because I can. "Go on, we're amongst friends, they can share our joy."

The glint in Hadley's eyes is pure venom, and I love it.

Did I mean to become someone's husband? No.

Do I hate that it's Hadley? Well, no.

My rule has always been to keep her at a distance for reasons that I don't care to think about today. So be it, fate threw us a wild card by making us husband and wife. I'm going to soak in these accidental nuptials that mean I get to have her close. I might as well. Call it selfish. My reasons to keep her away are still valid, but maybe I should have always kept her close with a difficult escape, à la marriage.

Hadley takes a deep breath. "Connor and I are husband and wife. Our night was unforgettable... *clearly*." Hmm, I could do with a little more enthusiasm in her tone, but we'll work on it.

"No shit." Briggs looks at me in awe. "That's what you two got up to?"

"What can I say? Sprinkles here always had her heart set on me, and I caved." I sit back with ease and satisfaction.

"But you two wanted to kill one another yesterday, so is this like... what is this exactly?" He's confused, as he should be.

Hadley crosses her arms and keeps her sight fixed on me. "Please, Con, do tell us the romantic tale of how I became your wife. It better be good, since you seemed to woo me in the span of only a few hours."

"Alcohol," Isla deadpans an answer.

I cluck the inside of my cheek with my tongue and point to Isla before I spew out a story. "Cute. But I'm positive it was Sprinkles here reliving the time I was forced to walk her home after my uncle ended my impromptu party. I was sixteen. I kissed her cheek when I said good night, to make her dreams come true, and told her she smelled of cupcakes with sprinkles, the kind she would bring me when she baked."

"You never said that," Hadley interjects with surprise in her tone.

"I was thinking it," I explain. "Anyway, since then she vowed that I would be her husband, and last night, somewhere between her attempt to give me a lap dance and her request to search for cupcakes with sprinkles, I gave in. I mean, what's better than having a wife who can bend and smells of cupcakes, am I right?"

Briggs scoffs a laugh. "You better come up with a better story when your parents find out."

"I would kill to have a front-row seat at that family dinner." Isla nudges Hadley's arm.

"But seriously, you two are going to end this thing, right?" Briggs hands me a bottle of water.

"Nope," I state proudly.

Hadley throws him a sweet overdone smile. "I'm moving into Connor's house that he bought a while back. It's the off-season, so I'm sure I can keep him occupied and make him feel so incredibly lucky to be my husband that it may feel like irritation, so much so that he will be begging to leave our happy house."

I grin at her humor. Two can play our game, and I'm ready.

"*Right*, I guess we need to… celebrate?" Briggs isn't sure.

"Yeah, we should get a few photos for the happy day. I guess you don't have any wedding photos?" Isla's voice raises an octave.

I reach for my cell phone in my pocket. "Funny you

should mention that. I was scrolling through my phone, piecing together what happened last night—I have the receipt for the ring, by the way. Tiffany's in the hotel, not bad taste if I may say. Anyhow, I came across this gem of a photo." I unlock my screen, swipe, and show Hadley and Isla my phone.

Hadley's eyes bug out as she examines the evidence from our night. We are in a Vegas chapel, and if it weren't for the fact that our eyes are clearly in a haze of alcohol, then it would be kind of believable. Because I'm looking down at her with affection while she peers up with admiration and an arm wrapped around my neck, with cheap plastic flowers in her hand.

"Oh boy," Isla mumbles.

My wife's breath catches as I take the phone back, and the fact that I'm calling her my wife hits me for a second. *What the hell am I doing?* This woman annoys me, and she can never know the things in my head, but I guess I'm making her villain fantasy come true, because I'm tying her into marriage with me… and that just fuels my pleasure from this situation.

Arriving at the airfield, we park on the tarmac near the plane.

"I'll ask the staff for champagne," Isla offers and still seems uneasy about this situation as she gives me a death glare mixed with a smile. As she should, she's Hadley's best friend.

"We'll go first then let you two love birds make a grand entrance," Briggs suggests as the car door opens.

"Sure, make sure Shawn gets a front-row seat," I call out as Hadley and I continue to give one another an icy stare.

"Real mature," she mumbles.

"You bring out the best in me." I slide out and offer her my hand. "Come on, Wife, don't smile too hard. I would hate for your cheeks to strain; they're important for certain activities."

Yanking her up out of the car, she squeezes my hand. "Gag. Your dick is not going near my mouth. In fact, we didn't even establish rules for that aspect of our blessed union."

"There are none. Let's just put on a good show, and consider it practice for our family."

Hadley rumbles another sound because she knows I'm right and begins to step in front of me up the stairs. My head tilts slightly to check out her ass because it's worth a look, and I'm going to reap all my husbandly perks.

Up the stairs I go, and I come to stand by my wife who looks at everyone. Our moment of opportunity is here. I slide my arm around her middle, gently squeezing her ass in the process which causes her to yelp softly. I bring her close to me with a bright smile glued on my face.

"Is the champagne out, boys?" I ask the plane.

"What are we celebrating?" Shawn asks as he holds up an empty flute, waiting for an attendant to fill his glass.

I lean down to kiss the top of my wife's head because we have a part to play, and it may be years later, but fuck it, Hadley still smells like cupcakes. "You tell them," I encourage her.

She giggles awkwardly to herself before loosening her tight smile a smidgen. "We got married last night… I'm Mrs. Connor Spears." Hadley shows her ring finger, and everyone goes silent for a few seconds, until cheers erupt, and the sound of a cork follows after.

My hockey crowd may be easy, but Hadley and I can agree on one thing; our families will be, by no means, a breeze.

IT WAS a quick flight back to Lake Spark. Sure, people had questions, but Hadley and I stayed firm that we were married, with no plans to write this down as a drunk mistake. We had feelings bubbling over after years watching one another grow up. It may be a fairytale we spew, but there is some half-truth to it. I also know that we are running out of time before our news goes public, which is why I drove us straight to my Aunt Violet's floral shop, The Flower Jar.

I'm close with my aunt Violet; she was only eleven when I was born, and the age difference makes her more like a friend.

Hadley is grabbing some items from the general store or Jolly Joe's, the bakery nearby, that she mentioned were essential for dinner, and we agreed to meet back here. Walking into The Flower Jar, the bell instantly announces my arrival.

"Connor!" My aunt Violet is quick to greet me with a hug. Her dark hair is down today, and she never looks like a woman who only got two hours of sleep due to having a kid; she's a natural beauty.

I notice my uncle near the parrot's cage, holding my three-year-old cousin Willow, my goddaughter. He steps closer to us, and I feel like his face is stoic because he already knows. "Hey, Connor." He doesn't blink, which raises caution in me. I was hoping to speak with Aunt Violet alone, since she's my sounding board.

"Hey," is all I can offer him, and it's awkward, can't deny that.

"How was your trip?" my aunt asks as she signs off on an order form and hands it to the
assistant.

"Yes. Do tell." Crap. My Uncle Declan for sure knows. I can tell he is waiting for me to spill the beans.

I scratch the back of my neck. "It was… Vegas."

My aunt looks at her husband, as she seems thrown off by my answer. Her eyes swim back to me. "And? You had a big group going, right?" She tries to keep the conversation moving.

I swipe my hand across my jaw. "Something kind of happened."

My aunt grabs my wrist when she notices something, then examines my finger. "What the hell is this?"

"I kind of wanted to see you first before my parents find out," I begin. "I'm going to

need a lot of sunflowers." That's my flower of choice that I give my mom when I want to butter her up, and it works. Every. Single. Time.

She shakes my hand. "Why do you have a wedding ring on?"

I take a deep breath. "I kind of… got married."

Her jaw drops open as she releases my wrist like a hot potato. "You don't have a girlfriend. You have flings. Now you're telling me that you went to Vegas and got married?"

I can't answer. Instead, I notice that she quickly glances to my cousin, reminding us all that we need to keep our words appropriate. My cousin's three-year-old brain is like a little sponge, it's crazy.

"What the duck, Connor!"

"Duck it," the parrot volleys.

Nope. Still not sure what to say.

"And who might the lucky bride be?" my uncle asks, even though I can tell he is already brushed up on the info.

I take a deep inhale. "Hadley."

"What the duck!" my aunt repeats her earlier sentiment.

Uncle Declan, or Declan in this situation because I know he is in business mode, puts my cousin down then walks to me and places his hands on my shoulders. Shit, he is in super-serious mode.

"The team publicist called me just now. You have exactly three hours before this hits the media." He waves his long finger at me. "You tell your parents. *Now*."

"I am. Hence the need for a bouquet of flowers." I raise a brow at him.

"You're going to need the entire bucket of sunflowers. A bouquet isn't going to cut it." My aunt sounds panicked.

I flash her a grin. "You're right. I need a bouquet for my new mother-in-law too, so whatever April likes."

Declan blows out a breath. "What happened?"

I shrug out of his hold. "Don't worry. We're staying married, at least for the off-season. I'm sure this will be positive press."

Declan pauses for a second and seems to be thinking. "You're right. We can work this angle to our advantage. Maybe you two can have a photoshoot, make this somewhat believable. But you're right. Baseball royalty marries hockey royalty, throw in the Spinners a few times in the interview, and it could be good. You're settling down." He's trying to convince himself it's a grand idea, but really, that's the angle I was going for.

"See? The bachelor settles down." I grimace and turn all my attention to my aunt, because Declan can stew in his plans without me. "So, about those flowers. Let's just go all out, shall we?"

She points the stem of a sunflower at me. "Your dad and mom are going to lose it."

My lips quirk out as I think about it. "No, they won't. Or at least they'll get over it fast. They love Hadley, they've been shipping us for years. It's their dream come true."

She shakes her head at me. "No, not like this. They will be heartbroken that they missed your wedding, didn't get to do all of that traditional stuff." She growls to herself. "Duck it, Violet, do not speak like this is a real marriage." Scolding herself seems to bring her into a more focused mode. "Connor, don't be stupid. I don't know what you and Hadley are playing at, but don't break her heart."

"Trust me. It's cold as can be for me," I promise.

"Then how are you going to explain this to your parents? They won't be on board with a fake marriage," she adds softly.

I sigh. "You're right. That's why Hadley and I are kind of going all in on this. We have a story, can fake it for a few hours in their presence, so I'm going to need those flowers."

She turns sharply to her husband. "Do something," she instructs.

Declan raises his hands in surrender. "No can do. The last thing I want is a quickie wedding and divorce in the press for my star player. Besides..." He snorts a laugh. "These two kids will come to realize they have a good thing underneath those angsty jabs."

"I mean..." My aunt's face softens. "You have a point." Her eyes whip back in my direction. "Fine. I'll go along with this, but I mean it... don't break her heart," she warns again.

A little late for that. I already did long ago.

I swallow. "Sure."

My aunt begins to grab flowers. "Okay, so most expensive flowers, no family discount—"

"Whoa, why no family discount?" I protest.

She raises her brows at me. "You're in the doghouse. Now let's just get these flowers to impress gathered."

The bell to the shop rings, and I turn to see my wife walk in with a bag from the general store.

"I got supplies," Hadley announces.

"I'm getting the flowers," I explain.

Hadley gives me a glare. "At least one of us is smart. Flowers won't be enough." She turns to my aunt. "No offense, we need bigger guns." Her attention returns to me. "I got wine for the moms. Open it as soon as we arrive."

"Genius." I snap my fingers.

My aunt walks around her table and straight to Hadley to give her a hug. "Mazel tov. Welcome to the family." I shake my head since my family doesn't have a single Jewish relative.

Hadley nervously laughs once as she accepts the hug. "Thanks."

My aunt steps back and looks affectionately at Hadley. "I should have known if my nephew ever decided to elope that it would be with you, only you." Now she's just being dramatic.

"Uh," Hadley's voice cracks. "Okay."

Checking my watch, I know we have to get moving. The clock is rolling. "Flowers, Aunt Vi, please. Our parents were having dinner together anyway, so they will be blindsided when we show up together, and we have to knock this off the list."

"Wine, flowers, and a damn good story is what you two need," my uncle says with a cheeky grin. "Good luck walking into the lions' den."

WE STAND outside Hadley's home, since it's her parents hosting tonight's dinner. She's fanning a hand in her face to calm herself down while a bottle of wine hangs from her other hand. I'm holding an armful of flowers.

"Ugh, this is not the conversation to be having while hungover. Or am I still slightly drunk? I don't know, but here we are." Hadley groans again.

I scrub a hand across my face. "This day is almost done."

"Just, we ease them into this. When you pour the second glass of wine, then we break the news. Just keep topping up their glasses," she explains.

I have to laugh. "Our moms are easy. Remember your sweet sixteenth?"

She looks at me, and after a second, a smile cracks. "God, they were tipsy on cosmos, then did karaoke. It was so embarrassing."

"But they really belted out Taylor Swift to perfection," I add.

We take a moment to look at one another. Maybe it's the first time today that we really sink into the fact that we are husband and wife. For a second, I could swear her smile is for me or the fact that we share memories.

Hadley clears her throat. "Okay, in we go. I'll pack a bag to take to your house between dinner and dessert or something."

I whistle a breath. "I love the confidence that we'll make it to dessert."

She nods in acknowledgment before opening the door. Right away we hear our moms in the kitchen area. We slowly make our way to the kitchen where our moms are busy with a glass of wine in hand and nibbling on the cheese board.

Immediately, their eyes light up when they see us.

"Oh, you arrived… together." My mother's eyebrows knit close, but her smile remains bright as she comes to hug me, and I hand her the sunflowers. "And with flowers too."

"Of course," I state simply before walking to April to hand her pink dahlias.

April looks at me, skeptical. "Oh, thanks." Her eyes dart to my mother. "Why is your son handing me flowers? Connor and flowers are never a good sign."

My mother shrugs. "I don't know. Mysterious."

"For hosting dinner. Oh, wow, look at that melted brie," Hadley says in an attempt to divert their attention.

"We brought wine," I announce, and Hadley is quick to showcase the bottle in her hand right before she reaches for their glasses to fill, because we came prepared with a twist-top bottle and don't care about mixing wine at this point.

My mom plants a hand on her hip then walks to April to stand next to her. They both focus on Hadley and me.

"They're up to something," April states and studies the scene.

Hadley laughs nervously as she hands back their glasses. "Don't be silly. Just a normal night."

"What's going on?" My mother gladly takes the wine, and her smile doesn't fade.

Hadley arrives at my side and nudges my shoulder. "Abort plan, just spit it out," she mumbles.

I bring my hand to rest on her lower back to ease her concern. "Okay."

"You both were in Vegas, right? How was it?" April asks as she takes a sip from her glass.

"About that…" I wrap an arm around Hadley's shoulder for a side hug. "We have some news…"

6

HADLEY

My heart is pounding so loud. This feels more profound than waking up hitched to the guy next to me.

Why did Connor have to start by saying we have some news?

His mother's hands fly to her mouth before she takes a moment to gather her thoughts. "It's okay, we're here for you both. Your father and I, we were in your very shoes, and we were even younger."

I glance to Connor, confused, and then a lightbulb goes off in his head. "We're not pregnant," he clarifies.

His mom takes hold of the counter and sighs in relief. "Phew. It's not that."

"Why does your mind even go there? They're not together!" my mom squeaks at her friend.

Connor's mom, Brielle, chortles then smiles warmly. "Come on, they've had a thing for one another. It's not out of reach." I hate that everyone thinks we have a *thing*. "I mean, just the other day, I caught my son staring at her dancing in her studio."

My eyes snap to Connor because I realize that he is my mystery watcher. He avoids my gaze, but it doesn't matter. Something inside of me spurs warmth. I'm not surprised it's him. I should have known, and I'm not sure why.

"Okay, so maybe it wouldn't be so bad these two together. Kind of cute. The whole neighbor thing. I mean, I'm positive they kissed or something when they were younger. Caught him sneaking out of her room." My mom crosses her arms and seems to be relaxing.

"Mom!" I shriek. I had no idea that she knew about that, it was when he told me we were a mistake. Oh my God, she's a freaking detective when it comes to me. Dear Lord, I hope she hasn't pieced together that I lost my V-card to Connor. "You knew?"

"Whoa, knew what?" Brielle asks.

"Oh boy, we're going into the vault of memories," Connor reflects almost fondly while he scratches the back of his neck.

My mom waves us off. "Nothing. I know nothing. Or at least, I've never and will never mention it to Spencer. *So, what is the news, you two?*"

Connor and I look at one another, and I give him a nod to just rip this band-aid off.

"Perhaps we gather the dads?" he suggests, and even I hear the nerves in his voice.

"For what?" My father's voice startles me, and I turn to see him arrive at the kitchen island with a beer bottle in hand. His eyes land on Connor, and I can see he isn't thrilled that he's touching me.

"What's going on?" Ford arrives by his side with a smile.

I feel the warmth of a hand entwine with mine, and I peer down to see Connor's and my hands together. I attempt to ignore that it's an image that looks right, and instead take a deep breath to give me courage.

But before I get a chance to announce our news, my husband does something incredibly stupid.

"Aren't you going to welcome me to the family, *Dad*?" He directs his question to my father as he holds up my hand with a shiny diamond ring on it.

The gasps in the room come from the moms, while Ford freezes, and my dad? Shit. Spencer Crews is a man who was a star pitcher and handled pressure well. Curveballs were his expertise. This curveball? Not so much.

I've never seen him so angry in my life. His jaw ticks, his fist clenches. That beer bottle he was enjoying? Slammed down onto the counter.

"Why is my daughter wearing a wedding ring?" he grits out.

I speak before Connor can. "Because we eloped. Last night. In Vegas."

The room goes deathly silent, and my heart may just break from the look on my father's face. I can't read him. I hate that uncertainty. Disappointment is the last thing that I would ever want from him. It's why I agreed to stay married, as I thought a quick annulment would be worse, and I may have also stayed married for a little revenge, but mostly not to break my father's heart.

"We decided that we didn't want to be apart. We cemented our feelings," Connor explains and pulls me into a tight side hug.

"Are you kidding me right now?" Ford gives his son a hardened look. "What in the world would make you think that every parent in this room wouldn't want to be given a clue that you two were getting hitched?"

"Because then I would have stopped it." My dad glares at my husband.

"Maybe we should take a breather, have some wine," Brielle says. "I mean, Ford, we eloped… plus, everyone… we are all family now," she points out, attempting to bring some light to this conversation. She flashes me a reassuring smile. I guess she's on our team. Then again, she doesn't get mad about anything.

My mom steps forward. "I just don't get it. I mean, your whole life you've talked about how you want a big wedding, fancy dress, cupcakes, and flowers. Vegas, it isn't you."

I step out of Connor's hold, because somewhere inside of me I'm cracking. That *is* my dream wedding. Nothing about this situation is something I fantasized about. I don't even remember my wedding. I glance over my shoulder to Connor who has a shade of guilt in his eyes.

Licking my lips, I do my best to carry this situation forward. "We didn't want to wait. But we can still have a big wedding later."

"I didn't even get to throw you a bridal shower! You know, with cookies, tea, and lingerie," my mom cries.

The dads in the room groan. "Do not put lingerie, bridal showers, and Connor into the same scenario when it involves our daughter," my father implores my mom.

She shrugs, then the corner of her mouth hitches up. "At least she married her prince. She's dreamt of him since she was six."

Shaking my head, I don't need the reminder that I was a naïve girl with a silly crush.

"We're relatives." Brielle nudges my mom's shoulder before my mom wraps an arm around her for a hug.

"No warm feelings right now." My dad seems stressed. "I

warned you that your hockey-playing son should stay away from my little girl," he seethes to his friend.

Ford rolls his eyes. "Yeah, when they were teenagers! They are legal adults now who drink and know how to sign their name on a marriage certificate. We need to focus on the now. They're married."

"Yeah, and your son didn't have the respect to speak to me before he made my daughter his bride!" My father is furious.

"I would have. It's just… passion and love caught us in a moment," Connor explains.

My dad rubs his temples. "Do. Not. Speak of passion and my daughter to me. If it weren't for the fact that you are Ford's son, then I swear I would kill you right now."

"That's a little harsh. I'm great son-in-law material." Connor doesn't seem fazed by my dad, and inside of me I want to laugh, because that's just Connor, always wanting a good time. And in this moment, as dreadful as it is, he's a beacon of humor that we all need.

"Let's calm down." Ford gestures his hands out to my dad and Connor, who look like they are ready to square off.

In that moment, my brother Ashton, along with Connor's brothers Wyatt and Alex, walk into the house from out back, where they must have been playing basketball.

"Mom, I'm hungry. Is dinner ready?" My brother walks to me to give me a hug—we're a hugging family.

"Uh, in a little bit, kiddo," my mom says uneasily.

"Why is everyone looking at Connor? What did he do now?" Wyatt asks as he grabs crackers from the counter.

Alex is only seven and shy when adults are around, so he only gives Connor a hug then runs to his mom.

"I think all the kids under the age of eighteen need to go

to the other room. Go play on the game console or something," Ford suggests.

Wyatt snorts a laugh. "You never let us game around dinner time. What's with the ring?" he asks, indicating with his head to Connor's hand.

My brother Ashton looks at me, and his eyes pop down to my hand that I attempt to cover. "You have one too."

Wyatt begins to laugh. "No way, you two. Classic."

My brother tucks his fist and brings it to his chest. "Yes! The downfall of the princess. Finally, Hadley does something to upset the parents."

I look at him, a little surprised that's how he views me, but then roll a shoulder as well. Daddy's princess isn't just a phrase.

"Boys. Out. Now," Ford repeats himself.

Our brothers stumble out of the room, which doesn't do much for breaking the tension in the air.

Connor wraps his arm around me from the side again, and my body seems to be growing accustomed to this. I might even find it comforting. *Oh no.*

"If you want to end this marriage then say the word, blink, give me a secret code, I don't know, anything, and I'll have my lawyers on it so fast," my father offers.

My mom walks to him and places her hand lovingly on his shoulder. "Stop it. Relax and accept this is what it is, and we are here to support them."

"She's too young to be married." His eyes seem sad as he connects his gaze with my mom.

My mom touches his cheek. "But old enough to make decisions for herself."

Ugh, there is a breach in my heart. I should just scream that I'm making a stupid mistake, but when I catch Connor in my side view, with remorse and tenderness on his face, then I pause because the words can't escape me, and I can't even question why.

"Don't worry, I'll take care of her. It's all I will do." Connor doesn't sound like he's acting; why doesn't he sound less convincing?

My father's eyes catch with Connor's, and the room goes eerily quiet.

"You. Me. You best believe that we're talking one on one this week." My father's voice is full of an edginess I've never heard before. It's only when his gaze transfers to me that his face grows delicate. "If he doesn't make you happy then I'll kill him," he announces before he storms out of the room.

I open my mouth to call out something, but my mom indicates for me to stay quiet. "Give him a little space. A day. Maybe three. I don't know, eternity seems a stretch. Just give him a little breathing room to digest this news."

"News that I'm still undecided about." Ford stretches with his hands behind his head. "I mean, love to have you in the family, Hadley. I knew you two little rascals' constant jabbing was a sign of something. It's just… wow." He breathes out and swipes a hand through his hair. "This came out of nowhere. Marriage is big. My son and I will be having a talk about responsibilities very soon."

"A lot of talks. Thrilling," Connor mumbles.

Brielle brings her hands together. "I think we can declare dinner… postponed." She grabs the entire bottle of wine. "We'll reschedule for a day when hunting my son doesn't seem to be on the agenda."

"I second that. Oh my, I guess this means you're going to live with your husband." My mom looks at me blankly then seems to shake it off. "Now I need to figure out a wedding gift." My mom deflates and sits on a chair at the kitchen island. She then enthusiastically waves to Brielle. "We should book them the honeymoon suite at the Dizzy Duck in town."

"I love that idea!" Brielle grins.

I lean gently into Connor's space. "If they mention consummating the marriage, run," I mumble under my breath.

"No shit," he responds, with his face concerned as he stares at our moms' excitement.

"I think you both should head out and enjoy your wedding week... Gosh, I did not just say that." Ford blows out a breath.

I turn to face Connor, and he must see my exhaustion and somber mood. I've just experienced whiplash several times over. He does something that surprises me; he leans in to kiss my forehead. Softly, sweetly, and I don't feel a shade of falseness.

"Come on, Sprinkles," he whispers and takes my hand.

I do my best to suppress the light feeling I feel when our palms touch.

LUCKILY, I followed Connor in my car, so we were saved from awkward conversation. Connor has a house in a subdivision in the hills, overlooking the lake, heavily wooded but with barely any neighbors. Mostly, it's sports guys who train here or vacation homes that are only filled in peak summer season. By no means are these houses cookie cutter; they all sell for a solid seven figures.

I've been here once when he had a party, and Isla dragged me along. It's a modern place, which I know his mom had a hand in decorating.

It doesn't matter. I can barely see straight from exhaustion.

Arriving at the front door, Connor looks at me, and his lips twitch right before he steps forward and is quick to throw me over the shoulder before I can protest. "Carrying the bride over the threshold, right?"

I can't help but let a giggle escape. My traitorous body seems to enjoy his effort, even if it is to tease me. "Put me down," I tell him. I don't think I mean it, but I can't let him know my enjoyment from this.

He twirls me around before setting me at the bottom of the stairs. "Welcome home."

"Home," I scoff before I walk straight up the stairs with Connor in tow.

"The guest room doesn't have any sheets on the bed," he states.

I turn at the top of the stairs to face him, stopping him from taking the final step as my body acts as a gate to the upstairs hall. "Where are the sheets?" I sound only slightly agitated.

"Hell if I know. The housekeeper that comes once a week takes care of that stuff." Of course, he wouldn't be capable of living independently. His whole life he's been doted on by his mother and most women within a fifty-mile radius.

I huff out a breath, and I'm past the point of caring. I march down the hall directly to his room, and yeah, I know it's his room because my radar just sends me on roads that lead to Connor Spears.

Ignoring him, I slide up my dress and swing it to the side where it lands on the floor. I walk straight to the dresser, taking my bra off in the process before I open the drawer, not afraid about what I might find, grab one of his t-shirts, and throw it on.

He doesn't say anything, just watches me from where he

stands in the doorway, enthralled, even though I ensured that he could only see my back in the process.

I flop onto the soft bed, landing on my stomach, already feeling like heaven hit my head. "I just don't care anymore. I've slept two hours in a forty-eight-hour period, got married by mistake, broke my father's heart, and have you as my husband. I'm tired and want to sleep. It's a dire situation that I'm sleeping in your bed, even though make no mistake, I'm not a puck bunny that you bring home, so burn this damn mattress tomorrow."

He snickers, and I get a glimpse of him peeling his shirt up and over his head as he walks toward the bed. "It's a new mattress, Sprinkles. Get a new one every year due to wear n' tear."

I may be drowsy on tiredness but even I hear the humor in his tone.

"Good. A new mattress is one less thing we need to worry about." I begin to close my eyes on the indulgent pillow that my cheek rests against.

His chuckle is low and in the back of his throat as I feel his body cause the mattress to dip. "Sharing a bed was in your plan. That's good. I wouldn't have it any other way."

He places his phone to the side, and I vaguely hear him mention he got an email about a photoshoot tomorrow, but my eyes give out and sleep takes over, as I lie in Connor Spears's bed, my doting husband.

7
HADLEY

I sit in the booth at Jolly Joe's, the old soda shop in town that decided jellybeans in coffee for luck and surprise would be what people remember about the hotspot. Well, that, and the amazing ice cream, cinnamon buns, and every carb imaginable.

Overlooking Main Street, I lean my head against the window while I hold my mug of coffee. Admittedly, I sneaked out before Connor woke. I may have crooked my head a few times to study the way he sleeps on his stomach, yet his muscles still stayed flexed with pure shoulder perfection. He smirks in his sleep too; must have been imaging ways to kill me, except I now know his secret.

"Earth to Hadley." A voice breaks my thought. Looking up, I see Isla waving a hand in front of me. "Shouldn't you be cooking a warm breakfast for your *husband* who you are currently dreaming about?" she says, enjoying teasing me.

I roll my eyes and take a sip of coffee. "He'll survive. I am sure he has his mom on speed dial if his housekeeper can't solve his cooking and cleaning needs. Besides, I had a class of toddlers to teach first thing this morning. Also, I wanted to catch up with you before I get roped into this photoshoot. Leave it to Connor's uncle and dad to turn this around real fast. I woke this morning to about a gazillion emails about an interview with my husband about our blessed union."

"Oh yeah? How is that going to go?"

"Fake it till we make it, right?" I shrug.

Isla squints her eyes at me. "You know, alcohol… it tends to bring out our inner inhibitions…"

My palm flies up to stop her. "Do not lecture me. Besides, after the shock when we told our parents wore off, our moms are in a glow of happiness. I'm not going to ruin that in less than a day by saying I'm getting a divorce."

"Your dad?"

A long exhale escapes me. "He… isn't pleased."

"So then why didn't you tell him it was a mistake?"

"I was going to, but then I figured an accidental marriage is even worse."

Isla looks at me, not believing my words. "What's the game plan? You married my boss's son and brother's teammate. Classic move, Hadley." Her sly grin plays on her lips.

I cross my arms. "Turns out Connor is my mystery watcher at my dance studio. His mom let it slip. Either he still harbors a little crush, finds me attractive, or has some twisted perverted thought in his head. My vote is on the latter. All of those options are excellent for using to my advantage to bring him to his downfall. Then, before hockey season starts again, kaboom, our marriage ends with his little feelings in pieces." My hands accompany with gestures.

Isla laughs, almost hysterically. "Kaboom could also be that you two want to stay married because you both enjoy it."

I'm about to protest, but my phone vibrates on the table. Flipping the phone to check the screen, I see Connor texted.

CONNOR

> SOS. Where are you?

My eyes bug out from instinct, and I quickly type back.

ME

> Oh dear, did you miss me when you woke up? I had to teach a class. I'm surprised you weren't lurking outside, since we know that's your favorite pastime.

> Says the woman who threw on my shirt with no bra on in front of me. Easy as a breeze. I think someone enjoys being watched.

> Shove it.

> Mouth or pussy?

I choose to ignore his crass comment.

> I'll see you at the photoshoot thing.

> I'm already at my parents' house. Need you here now. We have a situation.

> What kind of situation?

> The moms...

I growl in frustration and choose to ignore my phone for a second. He's being overdramatic.

"Apparently there is an emergency for the photoshoot, and someone can't put his big boy pants on and handle it himself," I tell Isla.

My phone pings and a photo pops up. Studying the image, I shake my head. Clearly someone didn't get the memo that the photo session was going for casual, as the patio table at

Connor's parents' house, my neighbors, is covered in flowers, cupcakes, and I'm positive the balloons are filled with confetti.

Growling, I know I need to head there sooner than later.

> On my way.

> Cooperative.

"Looks like I need to head there now. I'll let you know how it goes," I say as I gather my purse.

"Enjoy the honeymoon phase. Have an O or two for me." Isla smirks as she sips on her coffee.

I give her a warning glare. "Don't… I learned my lesson once… but maybe I need to sacrifice an orgasm to make him pay. I'll do it if makes him weak." It causes Isla to laugh again as I leave.

Inside me, something tingles from the thought of Connor having his wicked way with me, and I hate that the image flashes in my head. I should be stronger when he's involved.

———

Looking in the mirror, I try to suppress the smile that wants to spread. My palms rest against my belly as I study myself from different angles.

Arriving at Connor's parents', my mother quickly ushered me to the guest room to get dressed, as the hair and makeup lady was waiting for me. I didn't realize we were going all out. I don't even want to know how this dress was chosen or by who. It fits me to a T, and although not a wedding dress, it could be if you were going for dressy casual in white. It dips down my back, cuts off just below my knee, and I feel beautiful.

"I can't wait to see the photos. You're so stunning." My mom arrives by my side, holding up a necklace. "Here," she says as she brings the jewelry around my neck. "Your dad gave this to me on our first anniversary. I was saving it for your wedding… which I missed." Her happy tone dips to disapproval before her smile returns. "So, I will give it to you now and be sure to steal some photos."

I touch the pendant with a small diamond and smile tenderly at her. "Thank you, I love it." And I feel kind of guilty too. She wanted to save it for a special occasion, but I guess to her, this is. "How early were you up this morning?"

"Oh, it's nothing." She waves me off.

I throw her a funny look. "There is a cupcake tower downstairs." And she made it because she's an excellent cook and baker, even works in nutrition.

"I'm up early anyhow. Besides, you used to go on and on about cupcake towers for weddings."

"This is a photoshoot… one that you and Brielle invited yourselves to." I laugh.

She brings her fingers together to show size. "We are a little excited for you and Connor."

"Clearly," I deadpan.

My mother touches my curled hair that is mostly down. "You know, love hides under the surface. We don't always embrace it in the right way first, but once you uncover it, then it can be amazing and long-lasting."

"Is this our marriage talk?"

She nods once with a closed-mouth smile. "It is. Also, remember your father and I couldn't stand one another until we realized it was because we were completely right for each other. Soulmates."

"So you've mentioned at every opportunity that arises."

My mom gives me a loving knowing look. "I'm not sure

what you two are up to, but I see it. The potential, I mean, and I'm here for it."

She is dead serious, and I'm taken aback slightly by her conviction. There's experience behind her words, which means her advice isn't to be ignored. That unnerves me slightly, as it means there may be truth to what she says.

Clearing my throat, I decide that we should probably get on with this day. "I guess there is a fancy journalist and photographer downstairs that I should get to."

She nods, and we leave the room to walk down the stairs and head outside into the beautiful day. The Spears home is much like my own childhood home. On the lake, with a dock, but they have an outside swimming pool, whereas we have an inside one. Connor and I both grew up in a life of love from our parents who did their best to give us more than most but keep us humble.

Our parents, two photographers, a journalist, and Declan is here, probably under the ruse of uncle duty. They are all huddled around the table full of refreshments.

But in the corner of my eye, I spot Connor and my dad deep in conversation near the willow tree and away from everyone. It strikes me that they seem serious yet they're speaking in hushed tones, and I wonder what they are discussing.

My father peers up, and he seems to pause instantly in his sentence, with fondness flooding his face.

Connor is wearing a linen dress shirt and khaki pants. His back is to me, but when he notices my father hypnotized, Connor glances over his shoulder. He does a double take before he slowly turns to face me. His eyes draw a line up and down my body, and his lips tug from a smile he can't commit to. But when he steps forward, abandoning my father, his eyes lighten before he gets to me, stops, and touches my elbows with his fingertips, sending a current through my blood.

"You look beautiful." His voice dips low, ensuring nobody can hear. "Then again, I wouldn't marry anything less."

I give him an unimpressed look. Maybe because for a moment, I thought he was being sincere, or he was then ruined it. Both options enrage me somewhere deep within.

Glancing around, I realize we have an audience. I chuckle softly. "Wow, what a spread."

My eyes nearly bug out at the abundance of fresh flowers, and Connor notices. "They roped my aunt Violet into this event; she dropped them off this morning. Peach-colored roses for Sprinkles, apparently that was in your wedding dream diary."

"Oh God, I guess my mom really did dig that up. I made that when I was like seven, by the way."

"Don't worry, my mom went off the rails too. See the dog?" He tips his head to Puck, their family's yellow Labrador, who is sporting a little bandana around his neck. "Dressed up for the occasion."

I snort a laugh before I fix my gaze on my father who walks to us. "Hi, Daddy."

"You look so pretty," he notes.

I blush because the two men in my life are staring at me as if I'm something special. "It's just a dress. Not a wedding dress or anything," I say, trying to downplay it.

"Still." He shrugs.

Lifting my shoulders, I look between them. "Everything okay? You two seemed to be in quite a discussion."

My father plants a hand on Connor's shoulder, causing Con to tense slightly. "Peachy. Just reminding my son-in-law what I expect. You are precious goods and deserve the best.

I'm confident he won't do anything I wouldn't do. Warned him I'm too young to be a grandpa. The usual talk."

I don't believe a single word he says. Spencer Crews doesn't say peachy unless sarcasm is the root. I smile anyway because he clearly doesn't want to clue me in.

"Don't worry, she's in excellent hands." Connor's death glare lands on my father.

Lines crease my forehead. "Okay, you two are acting weird."

Connor smiles at me and then playfully pinches my cheek. "All is fine. Your dad and I were debating if the batting cages or ice rink should be our next bonding session."

My father touches my shoulder. "Had to be a hockey player that you married, huh," he states warmly.

"Okay, kids, they want to get started with this. Ready?" Ford calls out.

My father gives me a nod before leaving to give Connor and me a moment.

It takes a few seconds for Connor to refocus, as his eyes are locked on me, and he seems to be pondering something.

"Pretend. You're good at that," I remind him of our day ahead.

A sincere grin spreads on his face, and it unnerves me. "We just go with it?"

"Well, we have no other choice. We sure as hell didn't rehearse this for weeks on end, considering two days ago neither one of us had marriage on the mind."

He leans in to kiss my forehead, and it catches me off guard until he mumbles against my skin, making it clear that it's all part of the act. "Showtime."

Ford, Connor's uncle, and a journalist arrive before us.

"Hi, Hadley, I'm Julia, the reporter and old friend of Declan's. He called, giving me the first chance to jump on this wonderful news. Sam, over there, is my photographer, and Rupert is his assistant. Congratulations on the marriage." Julia seems sweet, but growing up with a famous dad, I'm wary of reporters. Julia looks to be a few years older than me. I'm sure if my husband wasn't tied down to me, she would be his type.

I smile politely. "Hi, nice to meet you."

"Why don't we sit down, chat for the article, and then we'll have a photo session after. Pretend the camera isn't there." Her overdone smile doesn't do it for me, but I play along.

"Of course," I reply.

We begin to follow her to the seating area on the other side of the deck, but Ford and Declan gently touch Connor's arm to stop us.

"Marriage equals better focus for you, which equates to a better team, and the Spinners are going to be a winning team next season," his uncle Declan mutters, a reminder to Connor. It seems they have an agenda. But then Declan relaxes and gently slaps Connor's shoulder. "Hot damn, you two kids look great together."

"We'll be by the refreshment table reining in your mothers. Just holler if you need anything. A balloon, a cute Labrador, a rose, maybe champagne. It will be a great hour that makes up for the lack of wedding festivities that you denied your mother who labored for hours to bring you into the world, only to have her son elope." Ford smiles tightly.

"This right here is exhibit A of why we did." Connor throws a smirk to his father.

I have to laugh. Apparently, our marriage has made our parents a little crazy, but a good warm-hug kind of crazy.

Connor and I take a seat in front of Julia, and Connor instantly interlinks our hands. He's going all in.

"Thank you both for meeting with me. I love that we are doing this at your childhood home, Connor. Considering you both grew up together as neighbors and your parents are close friends. Did you two ever feel like your relationship was a sort of arrangement or pushed from them?" Julia begins in the deep end.

Connor laughs. "*Oh yeah*, every BBQ was a discussion about our future." He is completely joking.

I unlink our hands and place my palm on his thigh. "Isn't he a funny one? No, I don't think they did. Of course, it might be a dream come true for them slightly, but we are the product of our own feelings and attraction."

"Considering Connor was living quite a big bachelor life last season and now he has a wife, many might say this is sudden."

Connor reconnects our hands, almost to counter my every move. "Everyone loves a second chance, right?"

"Oh, so you two are a second-chance story? You dated before?" Julia asks.

I laugh nervously. "You can say something like that. How could I live next to this hockey god growing up and not have had a thing for him? And since he has a thing for dancers, preferably the kind who keep their clothes on, then I think we can let the cat out of the bag and admit that we acted on it before. It's not like we went to Vegas and acted careless." My smile is far too easy for these half-lies.

Connor seems to enjoy my explanation. "She keeps me focused, this one. We were celebrating my good season and talking about how next season will be even better, then I realized that I can't do this whole 'will she or won't she finally commit to my charm' thing. I told her how I felt, and she said that I was right like always, and she wanted all in. We've known one another since she was in elementary school, we don't need to go slow."

"That really sounds like a whirlwind, but we also can't deny the obvious. Connor, you come from a family of hockey professionals, a star player yourself, and Hadley is the daughter of a baseball legend. Surely, a grand wedding would have been in order. This is sports royalty at its best," Julia comments, and I'm sure Connor's uncle fed her that line.

I retreat my hand from Connor's and return to his thigh that I clench, and he nearly yelps but keeps his smile. "Sometimes romance is better when it's between two people," I tell the reporter. "Besides, we're here today at the spot where we grew up. Where Connor here would throw his teenage parties and walk me home. Always the perfect gentleman."

"I would always be in the pool, and she would stop by with cupcakes decorated with sprinkles, throwing in indecent proposals that I just couldn't deny," he adds with that grin that could make a woman faint. Instantly, I squeeze his thigh with a bit of aggression.

"This is so cute. You're both young; what plans do you have for newlywed life?" Julia asks as she adjusts her sunglasses on top of her head.

Connor nuzzles his nose into my cheek for show. "Practice for family expansion, of course."

I nearly choke, and I'm positive my father over by the iced-tea pitcher just stretched his neck in agitation.

I nuzzle Connor back with my nose. "Con, I'm sure that's a given. But I think what she meant was honeymoon or not." I turn to Julia. "Probably down to the Florida Keys for some beach time. Nothing like a string bikini and a hockey player on your arm, right?"

"I think most women will be jealous of you, Hadley. Considering the Spinners are stars on and off the ice with those fun videos on social media. Connor is somewhat of a sex symbol, especially amongst romance readers who peg him for hockey boyfriend material in a book."

Connor smirks proudly and relaxes his shoulders. "Am I? Nice." I gently elbow him. "I mean, they better get in line. My wife is my one and only. Connor Spears is committed and tied down."

"He loves being tied down," I deadpan.

Julia's eyes have curiosity in them, as if she is investigating the dynamic between Connor and me. Good for her, she might actually be good at her job.

Or we may just have calmed her skepticism when the photo session goes into full swing, and I find myself sitting at the end of the dock with Connor next to me and a request that we kiss for the camera…

8

CONNOR

With our feet hanging over the edge of the dock while we sit, my arm is firmly wrapped around my wife while we look out at Lake Spark. Hadley's head leans against my shoulder, and I can't help but kiss the top of her hair. It's not my fault that she's in prime position for a chaste kiss.

"Could we have a photo of you both kissing?" The photographer raises his request from where he stands at the start of the dock.

"I'm sure my wife can handle a little public affection," I call out since they're not close enough to hear.

Hadley grumbles a sound only I can hear. "Of course, our first kiss as husband and wife would be with our parents spectating."

"Except they don't know that, *and* it's not really our first kiss in general," I give her in recap, "but enough going down memory lane."

"Don't remind me of my naïve self and your douchebag tendencies. Careful, the lake is deep here, I would hate for you to fall in. Then again, I didn't sign a prenup, so that's your bad if something should happen."

My finger curls, and I capture her chin to tip up and guide her gaze to me. "I would take you with me. You enjoy getting wet around me." I give her a contrite grin.

"Wishful thinking, Con."

"Let's deliver the fairytale, shall we? Committed, loving, insanely handsy." My fingers land on her thigh, dragging the fabric of her dress up slightly to touch her silky skin right above her knee, feeling her body flinch, then seeing her mouth thin into a line as she tries to hold a breath because she enjoys this but will never admit it.

"Just kiss me," she grits out, but it feels like an act.

Gladly.

Dipping my head down, I press my lips softly against her bottom lip, taking a moment to feel the connection that I remember from years ago. I take more, kissing her top lip, feeling her kiss back, letting go of her tightly wound rope and giving me something that makes me feral inside, needy for more. I make no mistake that she kisses me back, and when I dip my tongue inside her mouth to meet hers, I feel no protest. A little moan vibrates in the back of her throat, and damn, that's a sound I like. I tilt my mouth to cover hers in a different angle, only to feel a new jolt of electricity that makes me go slightly blank.

This isn't a hard kiss, but the damage is the same. Kissing her gently, I brush her lips with mine as I pull away very slowly, wishing I could prolong this.

I like her quiet this way, with my mouth on hers. She's more receptive, slightly bewitching, but also mine to kiss.

My eyes skim down to see her plump lips, and I smirk to myself from accomplishment, especially when her breath grows shallow. Taking my thumb, I rub a circle on her bottom lip to touch where I kissed her.

"Not bad," I rasp.

I don't let her chin go and keep her face in my hold while her tongue darts out to lick the corner of her mouth.

"Somewhat decent," she lies and avoids looking at me, but her flushed cheeks inform me that she may have felt the buzz flowing between us. Dislike sometimes makes passion more attuned.

"You know, we haven't discussed certain needs we might have during our marriage." I throw that out there because I love riling this woman.

Hadley places her hands on both of my shoulders and digs her nails into the fabric of my shirt. Any bystander watching would assume we are being a cute couple who can't keep our hands off one another, but that's not the reality I'm facing.

"Oh, trust me, you're going to need to work a little harder than *oh by the way, honey, I need to release one out*," she mocks me.

"Don't worry, I assumed you wouldn't be so easy. But just so you know, if you need to unwind, I'm able and willing since we *are* sharing a bed. I'm loving my shirt-and-thong look you have going at night," I compliment.

"Can we end this conversation considering who is in earshot?" she suggests.

I glance over at our parents. We should have known that our parents, oh so wise, saw this coming; Hadley and me together in any form. They've patiently been waiting, well, except Spencer, but you can't win them all.

I release her chin and move to stand, offering Hadley my hand. She accepts, willingly, and I yank her up. I can't help it and give her the once-over for the hundredth time, but she's absolutely gorgeous; it's natural too.

She seems to notice I'm a man who observes. "You okay there?"

"Yeah, you just really… look beautiful." I can't even turn it into a jab because it's the honest truth.

Hadley blinks a few times, and when I don't add on a retort, she seems to understand that I'm being sincere. "Thanks. You're not bad yourself." I nod once, not sure what to say. "This is kind of crazy, right? All of this." It sounds like she's letting down her defenses for a moment.

"A little crazy," I admit.

She scans the area and then lands her sight back on me. "Part of me hates that this is pretend. The other part wonders how deep into the fantasy I should go. You're trouble, Connor Spears, and you know it." She has some serious conviction in that statement, but I like the way her eyes have a sparkly glint and the line on her mouth stays stretched when she says that.

"And you're insufferable most of the time, lucky me," I answer softly.

Hadley is right, though. She should have run when she had the chance, but now everyone can get off my back, except her, and I don't mind that. Our game of rivals is just that, and I'd play it forever if it means that I at least get to have her words and sight directed at me. She just doesn't realize, and that's my doing.

In the corner of my eye, I see the photographer approaching us again for closeups. I encircle my arm around Hadley's waist and pull her close and tight to my body, enjoying the way she molds to me. She'll always have to look up because of our height difference, I just hope the marvel in her eyes will always remain.

By the time we wrapped up the photoshoot, ate cupcakes, and avoided champagne toasts with our parents who are planning joint family holidays, we were tired. Hadley took a few more items from her house to bring to mine, which just means she'll get more established at my place, harder for her to escape too.

I helped take a few bags from her car inside, refusing to give up the location of spare sheets for the guest room because I might have an inkling where they actually are. I led her to my room and cleared out some space in my closet instead.

She may hate me, but last night when she slept and unknowingly rolled into my arms, I couldn't help picture what it would be like to have her naked and under me… again.

I have every intention of driving her wild. She can get under my skin, then I will get under hers. That's marriage, right? Two-sided bliss.

After a shower and a check of my schedule for the week, I enter my kitchen to find Hadley in shorts, a t-shirt, and sitting at the kitchen island with a sewing needle and thread.

"Already getting domesticated on me?" I inquire as I open the fridge for a beer.

She snorts a laugh. "Never for you." Closing the door to the fridge and grabbing the bottle opener, I study her while she seems focused on cutting thread. Hadley must notice, as she pulls her eyes up. "Yes?" There's a little attitude in her tone.

"What are you doing?" I throw the bottle cap to the side.

"I need to sew the ribbons on my new pointe shoes."

Sipping my beer, I picture her in my head on her toes, spinning around for me until she lands on my lap. She's a great ballerina. Even though she dances a lot of styles, ballet is where she's kind of extra hot, and she dances flawlessly but adds her own alternative flare to her song choices and choreography.

She raises a brow at me. "Why did you watch me the other day?"

Ah, I knew this was coming. My mother gave away my secret, that she caught me surveying Hadley when I ran into my mom on the street, the reason I was delayed meeting my dad and uncle.

"I might not enjoy your presence, but you have talent."

She seems to be debating if my answer is worthy of her approval. "It's strange."

I slant my shoulder up in doubt. "You shouldn't dance with the door open; anybody can watch." I set my beer bottle down.

"It gets warm in the studio. I wanted some air."

I begin to walk slowly to her, determined to try something. "I'll buy you an air conditioner, consider it a present for *my wife*. But what I meant was, any guy could watch."

A sly smirk forms on her mouth that I want to devour. "Ah, can't have that now, can we? Connor throws a fit at the idea of another man watching." Her tone is taunting me, and I don't like that one bit.

I circle around the island, getting closer to my target. "Hadley, while we're married, no man will look at you." I slide the pink satin ribbons off the counter. My eyes stay connected with hers while I tie the ribbons together.

Her eyes slide down, but then quickly back up. "What are you doing? I need those."

A sinister scoff leaves my mouth. "I'll buy you a new pair, twenty if you want. We need these for something else right now."

My hands land on either side of her legs, then I slide the chair so she is squared off with me.

She isn't protesting, and that's a positive sign.

"Do you know what I think?" she husks.

"Humor me." I pull the knot on the ribbons ceremoniously.

Her head lolls slightly to the side. "You enjoy watching me because it makes you hard, doesn't it, even though you're supposed to despise me." Her sultry voice should be a crime.

Ignoring her valid observation, I get to work. "Hands, Hadley," I demand.

To my utter amazement, she lifts her hands together, wrists tight, offering herself as the prize.

I whistle in approval. "Well, well, well, someone is a good girl and listens to her husband." I begin to wrap the ribbon around her wrists.

"Or you just followed instructions and are working a little harder than saying you need to tug one out." Her reminder of what she said earlier causes me to smirk. "Plus, I have a weakness for curiosity," she states blandly.

Scoffing a sound, I decide to call her out. "Or you're just as twisted as me. I know you found the sheets for the guest room, so you could make yourself cozy in one of those rooms, yet the sheets haven't been touched." I flash her knowing eyes, but she doesn't break. I tighten the ribbon around her wrists. "You want to know why I really observed you dancing the other day?"

Her tongue swirls across her bottom lip as she nods.

I cup her jaw in my palm, with my thumb sliding along the curve of her face. "Because we may irritate one another, but I was your first, and your disdain for me, mixed with your legs wide open, is an image any man would think about. Now, spread," I nearly growl.

Hadley's jaw hangs low, but our eyes stay locked. Her tied wrists rest against her chest. I can't read her right now. Maybe I've pushed too soon.

"You didn't say please," she scolds.

No hesitation from me. "Please."

Her knees part open, and I glance down, figuring out how to strip her. One button and a zip. Should be easy. This stool at the island? Not so much. In a swift move, I lift her into my arms and plant her on the counter where her back rests against the marble while I spread her wide again.

With no elegance, I begin to work the button and zipper. "Arms above your head," I order.

She willingly complies, and I slide down her shorts. My fingers skirt the fabric of her panties, feeling her warmth and arousal radiating through the cotton while a soft moan escapes her lips, which causes me to focus my attention on her mouth.

Gosh, I want to kiss her again, but this isn't that kind of release. This is about power and testing how easily she succumbs to me.

She's crumbling, and I love that I have that effect on her.

I hiss a sound as I watch her eyes hood closed. "For someone who doesn't like me, you sure seem eager." My finger slips under the fabric to slide along her pussy, and the touch instantly shoots desire straight to my groin. She's soaking, and I'm already satisfied that I'm the reason. "My oh my, my wife wants this." I circle her clit, and her hips buck from the contact. "I wonder if you still taste like cupcakes. Is that what you want? My tongue on you?"

"Connor," she gasps. "I swear the only reason I'm here is because orgasms are essential for living and tequila made you my husband."

I chuckle because I love when she's feisty. "But babe, I'm

a giver. Don't worry, I'm going to be a good husband tonight," I promise.

She can't protest because I lean down and swipe my tongue up her heat, tasting my confirmation. Her hips bolt up from the contact, and her lips gasp a breath. She's sweet and at my surrender, everything I was hoping for. I dip my tongue inside then swirl back up, her little moans encouraging me. I feast on her, nip on her clit, then circle again until I find a rhythm that leaves her jolting underneath my tongue.

I hook my arms under her legs and bring her forward to the edge of the counter. "You taste good," I murmur against her inner thigh.

Her body writhes and attempts to arch up to encourage me to use my tongue some more. I want to make her come, and I will, but not yet.

"Then don't stop," she breathes.

It causes me to widen my eyes due to her insistence. Hovering over her body, I fist some of her hair around my hand and carefully guide her up to sitting. "I won't. But you need to work for it a little."

She raises her brows. "You tied me up. Whatever would you like me to do?" Sass. That's my girl.

I plant my hands on her hips and hoist her off the counter. "Knees," I demand. She sighs but yet again complies, while I lower my basketball shorts and boxer briefs. "Mouth."

Her eyes blaze with a hint of surprise, but she only licks her lips before she parts them to welcome my cock into her mouth. I bring my tip to her lips and the edge of her tongue greets my head.

"Damn. You're a sight. My little dancer, wrapped up and willing." But I step back and instead weave my fingers into her hair. "Would you like that? Having my cock inside your mouth? Your lips wrapped around me? Because you would look good with your mouth full and getting destroyed." My words cause her to moan sharply, and I raise a brow. "Bet you wish you could touch your pussy now. Tell me that you need my tongue on you." Words don't escape her lips, as she seems lost in a daze. "It's okay, I'll check for you."

She smirks with pleasure. "How giving." I still sense some sarcasm, but she's an equal partner in this scene. A far cry from her first time with me, definitely not innocent.

I lift her back onto the edge of the counter, taking my cock in my hand to give it a stroke, while she spreads her legs, and my tongue finds a home on her clit.

"Connor, right there, please."

Her moaning my name, pleading, is music to my dick. A perfect melody that I plan on putting on repeat.

I work toward my own release while I take care of her until she's shaking against my tongue, cursing out my name, with her head fallen back as she convulses on the kitchen counter. I keep my tongue on her, and my balls tighten before I still and unload onto her inner thigh.

Rising and then leaning over her, I'm panting as my forehead falls against hers, using one another for support, as she has no use of her hands. We both have labored breathing and say nothing, instead melting into a pile of orgasmic bliss. It takes about thirty seconds for me to adjust that this actually happened, then I reach for a kitchen towel to wipe her thigh, with the flicker of a memory of the last time I did this with her. She was shy and innocent, and I made her mine. For that night at least. Before untying her ribbon, noting that I really do owe her new ones.

We don't say anything, even when she hops off the counter and swoops up her shorts, and I pull up my own.

She walks away, and I rub my face as I try to find my feet, as I'm trapped between endorphins and unsure of what to say to her. It doesn't matter, as she is already halfway upstairs.

I decide to give her a little space while she takes a shower, then when she emerges from the bathroom in another one of my shirts, I relax a little more and lie back against the headboard, watching her approach the bed.

"You okay?" I check.

She laughs once. "More than." She hops onto the bed then does something that surprises me; she straddles my hips, and my dick is instantly intrigued. Her finger pokes out and jabs my chest. "Downstairs was appreciated because now I know that you *do* want me." She swivels her covered pussy on top of my cock, and my breathing grows labored. "I fully intend to drive you insane, so thank you for the intel, Con." Hadley dry humps the fuck out of me in one sensual move, a wave of her hips churning as she tosses her hair behind her back, causing her chest to perk out. "Mmm, someone is hard. A shame he's not getting anything." She gently pats my cheek. "Night-night, Husband."

Then she's off me, rolls to her side of the bed, and turns away from me. Leaving me with a massive hard-on that I'm going to have to rub out in the shower.

Great, my determination paid off only partly tonight. But what the hell happens tomorrow? She's up to something, and I will bring her to her knees again, that I'm sure of.

9
HADLEY

Banging my pointe shoe against the counter in one hand, I press the button on the blender for my breakfast smoothie using my other hand. I have no qualms that this will ruin any sleep-in plans that my dear husband may have envisioned.

A proud smirk takes over me when I notice him walk down the stairs, though shirtless, and scratching the back of his scruffy morning hair. He seems rather grumbly, and I don't mind. The man is the king of mixed signals, because what in the world was last night? I'll never look at ribbon the same way.

The drilling of the blender sounds like my agonizing heart. I'm slightly disappointed that I caved so easily yesterday. Then again, Connor is the one who faltered first, right? Yet, I gave him the power…

"Uh, what in the world is going on? It's not even nine," he groggily calls out over the noise and walks to the cupboard to take out his protein powder.

I stop my noise for a second. "Some of us work all year round. I need to teach old ladies tap dance this morning."

"Fine, but must you do it making all this commotion?"

I offer him a pointed look. "I always have a smoothie for breakfast when I can. Vitamins are important, just like staying hydrated. And my shoes? I need to break them in."

He smiles to himself as if he is reflecting, and his gaze falls low to my waist. "Ah yes, your shoes." He clucks his tongue. Not even two minutes in and he is reminding me of last night.

I hold up the blender cylinder. "Shake? It's banana, avocado, oat milk, spinach, mint extract, some Brazilian herb, and a hell of a lot of contempt for you."

Connor walks my way with a swagger in his step, then purposely brushes his arm across my body, sending a tingle to my nipples as he reaches for a glass behind me, our eyes in a deadlock. "Aww, you're the sweetest. Both figuratively and literally." Oh crap, he has a saccharine tone, and his grin is too charming for this early in the day. My defenses are too weak before lunchtime.

But I will stand firm. "Let me state the obvious. So what? We had an orgasm. It might happen while we are husband and wife. It is what it is. But make no mistake, it's not me weakening my resolve, because I didn't magically forget what an asshole you were the first time around." His grin disappears and his jaw moves side to side. He hates when I remind him of that, I've learned that pretty quickly.

Stepping away from the joint bubble of space that we created, I walk to the other side of the kitchen to grab a massive water bottle and my to-go cup to pour my shake into. Twisting the cap, I ignore Connor who is like a lost puppy right now, unsure of what to do.

But then I freeze mid-twist when he pipes up.

"Let me put in the effort."

I slowly turn, with fear running down my spine. "What do

you mean effort?" My eyes land on Connor leaning against the counter, ankles and arms crossed, and that cunning look is back.

"Let's call a truce. If we are going to be married for a bit, then let me show you that I can be a *good husband*," he casually mentions, and my mind flashes to his use of the label last night and hate that my body responds positively.

Shaking my head, I huff out a breath. "I don't have time for this. Whatever game you want to play today, have fun. I need to get to my studio," I declare and grab my shoes and drink in a hurry.

I vaguely hear him mention that he will see me at noon.

THE OLD LADIES WERE HYSTERICAL. They always are. Tap dancing isn't my go-to choice of style, and I'm counting on one of the teenagers from my dance company to start teaching in the summer. But something about teaching a classic dance number à la "Singing in the Rain" always puts a smile on everyone's face. After their morning class, I worked on invoices. It's a weekday, so other than adults and toddlers in the morning, my days are fairly free, as it's summer, so I have a lighter schedule.

I threw Radiohead on my Bluetooth, put on my new shoes, and ignored the fact that the new ribbons are a little stretched. It doesn't matter, I get lost in my movement with nobody around. Swaying to the music and seeing where my body flows. I do this for a solid twenty minutes.

I'm landing from my pirouette when I get startled. "What the hell?"

Connor is leaning against the doorframe to the back door with his hands in his pockets, a man confident and eager to show power. Connor's eyes are filled with… sizzling heat, darker than normal. "You look good twirling around with my wedding ring on your finger." I tip my head to the side slightly, waiting for him to explain why he's here. "I guess being your husband gave me the privilege to watch you."

"Without lurking, oh gee, lucky me," I retort and turn the music off. I walk to a chair in the corner to unwrap my shoes. "Why are you here?"

"I'm taking you to lunch, of course."

I glance up as I slip one slipper off then massage the pads on my toes, a soft whimper escaping me as I notice a blister forming. "You're not taking me to lunch." I continue to my other foot.

"Truce and effort, remember?" He steps in my direction, examining my foot. "You okay?"

I look at him like he's crazy. "It's a blister. I'll survive," I answer rather dryly. In truth, I'm far too curious what "good husband" Connor is like.

"Come on, Jolly Joe's? Catch 22? Dizzy Duck? What do you want to eat? You need to eat, you've worked up an appetite."

My eyes bug out at his insistence, but my heart also flutters at his concern. "You sound like my mother. Next thing I know you're chasing me to go see a doctor about my allergies."

"You have allergies?"

I shrug as I grab my sandals. "I don't know, still need to test. It's probably just hay fever or something. Again, not going to die, to your dismay."

He offers me his arm, and his demeanor in the last five minutes is unnerving me. I don't like when he's unapologetically sweet or even appears to be. Still, my traitor of a subconscious disagrees with my thought, and I offer Connor my hand to pull me up. His strength causes me to shoot up like a rocket, and I stumble forward. His arms instantly balance me while my face buries into his chest. Inhaling, I make a note to figure out his laundry detergent; it's a delicious fresh smell, not too masculine.

We cling to one another a second more than we should. Oh, how I hate the way every fiber inside of me clings to him like a magnet.

"Lock up and let's go," he requests softly.

Stepping back, I feign a frown. "If I must."

A minute later, we are walking down Main Street, with the spring air fresh and the sun shining down, arm in arm because Connor believes I hate it, but I know he, and even I, might enjoy it. I notice a few spectators surveying us as we stroll down the sidewalk.

"Do you feel like everyone is watching us?" I whisper to Connor.

"I'm me. Of course they are."

I snort a laugh because he's serious, yet he means it lightheartedly. Connor enjoys being popular, but he also tries to use it to his advantage, both on the ice and when he helps out with charities. Ford and Brielle raised a man of character, just not when it comes to me.

"Relax," he assures me. "We just hit the news, so give it a few days."

I pull out my phone from my side pocket to look at the few headlines that I noticed after tap class.

"It's positive, I guess." I begin to read the headlines.

Hockey MVP Marries Baseball Princess in Shocking Vegas Wedding!

Curveball! Connor Spears Elopes with Former Baseball Star's Daughter.

Hockey's Favorite Bachelor Marries in Secret.

Connor Spears is Officially a Husband.

Two Famous Sports Families are Now United by Marriage.

"Oh, here is the article from Julia."

Like a sheet of black ice, the public never saw the nuptials between Connor Spears and Hadley Crews coming. The reality is that these two are a match made in heaven. Connor, the son of former hockey player Ford Spears and his wife Brielle, plus nephew of The Spinners owner Declan Dash, has always proven he is worthy to be on the road to becoming the future captain of The Spinners. His off-ice antics gave him a notorious track record for enjoying life, but he's now even more determined and committed both on and off the ice thanks to the love of his life. Hadley, daughter of former baseball star Spencer Crews and his wife April, is not only accustomed to pro-athlete life, but grew up with Connor as neighbors. Some may call it Vegas magic, but those close to them have always known about the soft spot these two share and are not surprised by this romantic elopement. The couple plan on making their home in Lake Spark where The Spinners train and to be close to their families. The female population may be sad that Connor's off the market, but we look forward to watching sports' newest hot couple appear at future events together.

"Who writes this fluff?" I comment.

"Julia," he answers dryly.

"Yeah, no shit. But this sounds so…" I stare down at the accompanying photo, and I don't even remember anyone taking this. It's Connor kissing my forehead and a smile that even I know isn't fake is hinted on my lips. Our hands are connected and hanging between us as I lean my head against his shoulder. If it wasn't for the fact that this article has me boiling, then I might just admit that, gosh, we look good together… I mean, we are a photogenic couple, which tends to happen when two people are good-looking. And it looks like a stolen moment between husband and wife, so kudos to the photographer for doing his damn job.

"It's a little sappy, but it does the trick. It's a good article. I'm sure our moms are framing it as we speak." Connor isn't fazed by this.

I grumble a sound and stomp a few steps as we continue to walk. "I guess it's… what we needed."

"It will blow over in a few days when Shawn Cann does something stupid to land in the media." He leads us and motions up ahead to Jolly Joe's. "Grilled cheese?"

"Sounds good, actually."

A few minutes later, we are sitting in a booth by the jukebox that's barely used in Jolly Joe's.

"Is this going to become a frequent occurrence? Lunch?" I ask one-toned and drop my straw into my iced tea.

"I do think humans eat lunch, so yes." He's being coy.

"I mean you, me, lunch."

Connor crosses his arms on the table. "Get used to it, Sprinkles. I'm going all in on this. I know you hate it, which is why I love it."

"Wonderful." I'm not at all serious.

He bows his head and an almost shy half-smile forms. "Can I ask you something?"

"Might as well or it may be a long lunch."

"Are you 100% certain that we didn't… in Vegas…" His face strains before his eyes draw a line up to mine. "I mean, we probably didn't use birth control."

I'm amused by this. "You mean, am I sure that we didn't have sex in our drunken haze? Or am I sure that I'm not miraculously pregnant?"

He isn't entertained by my statement, and he rolls his eyes to the side.

I snort a laugh. "Connor, your dick isn't that magical. No immaculate conception happened, so yeah, I'm sure. Why do you even ask?"

His head bobs side to side. "I think we can both agree that we share a similar history in that department."

I think about it for a second then realize. "Ah, you mean that you're the product of an accidental pregnancy and so am I?"

"Exactly that. Don't get me wrong, I love my parents and they love me. But I know I wasn't planned and ruined their life only slightly." He's only partly joking. "And you, well…"

"Also a surprise. Although my dad was in his mid-twenties, not eighteen like your mom."

"Do you ever wonder about, well, I know April is your mom, but…" He treads delicately with his words.

I stir my drink. "April is my mom, I don't need biology for that. My birth mom is purely someone who birthed me. She never wanted me, so I will never give her a second thought, and I'm completely at peace with it. She had options when she got pregnant but chose my dad, who gave me the best life, so in a way I appreciate it."

Connor swipes a hand across his jaw, and I notice that he's growing out a little stubble, and it's kind of sexy. I felt his five-o clock shadow against my thighs last night, and I cross my legs from the thought.

"That's a good way to evaluate it. You are such a daddy's girl too."

I laugh, appreciating how easy our conversation is going, how open we can be. "I am," I admit proudly.

"I have to go the rink at the training center this afternoon.

I promised Wyatt some ice time, plus I want to talk to my dad about summer camp this year."

A sincere smile beams on my face. Connor's good with his brothers. Like me, we pack an age difference with our young siblings, but that makes it more fun. "You're volunteering this year at summer camp?"

"Always. My dad has been running it for years, and I have to give back. We have a few extra weeks this year because we have more inner-city kids coming out, it'll be good." There hasn't been an ounce of fakeness in him in the last ten minutes. I dare say that he's being endearing right now.

I recall something in my head and bite my lip. "Weren't you a camp counselor once for the summer camp?"

Connor leans back and brings his hands behind his head with a glimmering smile. "Yeah, when I was sixteen. The summer my aunt and uncle were sneaking around, and my dad had no clue. It was awesome," he reflects fondly.

I have to laugh, because of course he loves mischief, and that summer he caused a lot.

And that's just how our conversation goes for the next hour. A memory, a laugh, one topic blending into another, everything easy.

By the time he's paid the bill and we are walking back to my studio, I almost forgot that I find the guy insufferable on the edges. Instead, I'm conflicted inside.

Our arms brush as we move in a leisurely stroll down the sidewalk, appearing like a perfect couple. When the man up ahead locks his car, he gives me a nod, and I return the gesture.

"Care to explain why Harry, the sheriff's brother, greeted you with a nod?" my broody husband requests.

I smirk to myself before I pull his arm to stop walking, because I want to see his face. "We used to date."

There we go, the territorial glare begins to brew on Connor's face. "As in…"

I cross my arms over my chest and stand tall. "As in did I sleep with him? Believe it or not but you may have been my first but not my last. It was like one month of dating, and he's now with someone he met in college."

"He doesn't seem like your type. He looks like an ass. Then again, you had a phase. I remember when you dated O'Keefe who didn't even bother getting you roses."

My eyes turn surprised. "That was when I was like seventeen, and he brought me flowers for my dance recital. How the hell do you remember that?"

Connor rubs his shoulder. "I don't know."

Rolling my eyes, I get us moving again because maybe I'm reading too much into it. "I don't really care about your opinions on my dating history, since I know I've kissed a lot of frogs, including you." I flash him a pointed look that he appreciates because he enjoys when I offer him snipes on a continuous basis.

It's a silent block that we walk, but I don't mind. It's kind of peaceful. I hate to say that we are more comfortable with one another as the hours since our time in Vegas pass. Then again, comfort isn't our issue, because even when arguing we're comfortable.

After I enter the security code, he holds the door to the studio open for me. "I can stop by the grocery store on my way home from the rink. What do you want for dinner?"

I'm melting into a pile of goo. Who is this guy? Oh yeah, the man who thinks being a good husband is the way to break me. Except, he looks far too convincing right now, and I've actually lost what's happening. I need to take a breather, create some space.

"Oh, don't worry, I'll grab a salad from the store. Weekdays are pretty busy for me. Four to nine pm are primal dance class times, so don't expect me back until later," I explain, even though it's kind of a lie, as I'm on my summer schedule.

A wave of disappointment glazes in his eyes. "That makes sense. I'll leave you something in the fridge."

I nod once. He leans in, and I pray to myself he doesn't do what I think he's going to do.

Don't. Please don't. No. Yes. I mean, really don't.

He places a small kiss on my cheek as a parting.

It's the type of affection that is concerning to a woman like me. Because it's effective and sends a whisper inside me, awakening a small beacon of hope that maybe we could be everything.

10

CONNOR

Gently pulling the back of my brother's shirt as he leaves the ice, a proud smile takes over my face. "You're getting good, kid."

Wyatt glances over his shoulder with excitement in his eyes. "Oh yeah?" He's only ten, so I'm not going to tell him he could work on his swiping of the stick from the left during a pass.

"Might even be half as good as me one day," I tease him as we flop onto the bench and begin to untie the laces of our skates.

"Ha. Wishful thinking. You don't want me to steal your light." Wyatt pulls a skate off.

This guy is 100% me when I was his age. Now that it's the off-season, it will be good to hit the ice with him a little more. It's not like I can take him to a bar with me.

"You are completely in the doghouse, by the way. Mom and Dad can't stop talking about you and Hadley."

"Oh yeah?" A sheepish smirk hits me before I take a sip from my water bottle. I figured as much. I would question it if they didn't get thrown off their axis a bit.

He nods. "I even escaped my chores because they didn't notice. In fact, Mom even fed Puck and crossed it off my chore chart, not even realizing she did it for me. Same with putting my laundry away."

"You should be thanking me then."

Wyatt scoffs a sound at me. "Dude, you married my babysitter."

I muss his hair. "Hadley *was* your babysitter when you were younger. Now she watches Alex occasionally with you reading a book in your room since you feel you're too mature for a babysitter."

"Whatever, if she wants to marry you, then good luck to her. Anyhow, Mom and Dad can't stop talking about you. Even when they think I'm not listening."

A curious grin takes over me. "Good or bad?"

Wyatt scoffs. "Well, Dad had to calm Mom down when she wanted to buy a toaster for your new bride. Something about it being a traditional wedding gift. Dad stopped her, and then she said he was right, she needs to go bigger, so she started looking at honeymoon destinations. She's completely hyped up on your news."

I scratch my stubbled jaw and can totally picture my mom doing that.

"*Dad* needs to talk with your brother," our father's voice breaks the conversation. We both look up to see our dad towering over us. He gives a pointed look to my little brother. "Go to my office, have a snack, and we'll leave in a little bit so we're back in time for dinner with your mom and little brother."

Wyatt hops up and throws on a beaming smile. "Someone is getting a talk," he taunts me and nearly skips away happy.

It only makes me entertained, and I look at my father. "I was going to find you, figured you would be in your office."

He hums a sound and comes to sit next to me, scanning the area to ensure nobody else is in earshot. "Let's have a chat, *Son*."

I roll my eyes to the side but my grin stays. "Oh boy, here we go."

"Now that the shock has worn off and I realize that you and Hadley weren't joking with us, then I think we should talk."

I hold up my hand to show him my ring. "You mean about this? My marriage." It still astonishes me how easy it is to say that.

He gives me an unimpressed look. "Connor, I don't care how you two kids ended up married." Drunk, that's how, but I'm not going to highlight that. "What I care about is that you put in the effort to *stay* in a lasting marriage."

My grin fades as his words hit me a little more than I was expecting. "Go on," I say softly because I owe him this. Even more, I owe it to myself. I've been living in the moment the past few days, but maybe someone needs to pour a dash of reality on me.

"You play hockey, and that's a team sport. But the greatest team that you will ever be on is the one with your wife." He's serious, but I can't help it because it's so cheesy that I burst out laughing. "Connor Spears, I'm serious. Communication, practice, and determination to make it forever are the qualities you want in a marriage."

I hold my hand for him to stop. "Come on, Dad, even you can admit this is a stretch on the ridiculous side? Didn't you rehearse this? Come up with a different angle?"

His lips purse out then he pauses before he too has a line stretching on the corner of his mouth. "You get my point, though, right?"

"I hear you."

He affectionately touches my shoulder. "Do you? Because you have a bonus in this situation. You've known your new bride since she was a little girl, and you were the boy who would pull her pigtails. Spencer and April are not only neighbors and friends, but they also care for you as if you were family, and we feel the same for Hadley. You've watched Hadley flourish into a woman, and she watched you turn into a man. Not many spouses can say that."

As touching as his speech is, he's killing me here. "You lost me at Hadley flourished into a woman. Seriously, you have a few years before Wyatt starts to date. Work on this." I gently nudge his shoulder. But when all is said and done, he is right.

My father laughs. "Fine. Let me keep it basic. You be there for Hadley, you treat her like a queen and with the outmost respect. I don't care if in your head you did this because of the talk we had the other week. You will stay married, not because I don't want my son divorced before he's twenty-five. No, you will stay married because you've both been blind. She cares for you, more than she wants to admit, but I bet my life that if she thought today would be your last then she would be honest, and you would do the same."

I begin to protest, but my words are trapped at the bottom of my throat.

He continues our heart-to-heart. "She's wrapped you so tightly around her finger that you don't even realize."

My bitter laugh interrupts him. "What if I have always realized?" I'm sincere in my answer. My father's words only scrape the surface of the obvious that my consciousness decided to hide away.

He smiles gently. "I've seen the way you get, and it's only

with her. You get one soulmate in your life; don't be stupid and ruin your chance to keep her."

He might be disappointed in a few months when Hadley and I call it quits, except nowhere in the last forty-eight hours, other than saying we would be temporary, have I actually *believed* we would be temporary.

"Uh-oh, my first born is pondering. I can tell by the troubled scowl appearing on his face." He stands and grins in accomplishment. "There. Talk done." He points at me. "Don't forget, charity hockey game next weekend to raise money for puppies." He walks away, knowing damn well my brain is now working in overtime.

The truth is it doesn't take much to think about. I know his points are valid. The only problem is that Hadley and I are so far gone on our game of cat and mouse that I don't know where to begin to unravel what we're doing.

———

IT FEELS like a long car ride before I stop at my aunt Violet's flower shop. She normally has an answer when I need one.

Entering The Flower Jar, she smirks as she arranges a bouquet of mostly purple blooms in a vase, her eyes staying focused on adjusting the height of the flowers. "What brings my newly married nephew to me today?" she asks.

"Duck it," the parrot in the cage chirps. He doesn't know many words, but the ones he does are very questionable. My aunt had to keep the bird when she took over the building from the landlady, and despite telling everyone she hated the parrot, when Uncle Declan bought the building from the landlady and promised to get rid of the bird, Aunt Violet said Nugget could stay.

I walk to Nugget's cage and cluck my tongue on the roof

of my mouth to grab his attention before I answer my aunt Violet. "Flowers."

"Again? Did your old schmooze-your-mom trick fail?"

I throw her a glance over my shoulder. "Nah, that worked well. I need flowers for my wife." I walk over to my aunt's workstation; this is probably her last order since she should be closed now.

She stills mid flower tuck and raises a brow at me. "Flowers because you enjoy teasing her or flowers because you actually want to make her smile?"

My jaw goes slack because my aunt is going to break me down too. "The latter," I admit. Instantly, our eyes hold, and I know she's studying me.

Her hip tips out, and she gives me a closed-mouth smile. "Ah, that's right. Hadley is your wife now, which means she's madly in love with you and won't throw them at you?" She taps a purple flower.

"Have your theories, but I don't know, I feel like… I need to change the playbook a bit. Shake it up." I'm supposed to be a good husband to annoy her, but now I know it's because I want to convince her, I'm not entirely sure of what because we shouldn't be the end game, even if we're meant to be.

"Sometimes we realize it's true love a little later." She indicates her head to a bouquet behind me. "Pick one. She likes roses, especially single roses because it's simple and more fitting for a dancer, she says. Hadley orders one for each of her dancers at the year-end recital."

That sounds like something she would do, she's thoughtful like that.

"Then the red one it is, but make it six."

"Classic." My aunt walks to the bucket on the ground. "Remember when you helped me out here one summer?"

I snort a laugh. "You mean when I was grounded for

throwing a party when you were watching us and had to volunteer my services? Yeah, I remember."

"I made you study the meanings of flowers, especially the significance of numbers and roses. Funny that you pick six."

Damn, she's good.

I awkwardly rub the back of my neck. "Is it so wrong that a husband asks for six roses?"

She ceremoniously snips her scissors for the wrapping paper. "Not at all. I'm just happy that your inner emotions chose the number six, which I know you know means 'I want to be yours.' Someone is hopelessly romantic for their new wife, I'd say."

So what? I'm using other methods to state the obvious. It's far easier than saying it.

"Maybe," I play coy.

My aunt laughs wickedly. "If your new playbook is to woo your wife into staying your wife, then you are off to the right start. Do you know what I think?" She adjusts her stance. "You're going to hear it anyhow. You woke up married by accident and now you're trying to decide the path to convince her to stay."

I heave a long sigh. "Have you ever been in a situation where something feels too right but you know it won't work?" Not after what happened.

She laughs as she tapes the paper. "You mean, did my now husband feel he wasn't relationship material, even though we were explosive together? Yeah, I've been in

that situation, but eventually you can't ignore that plans and feelings change, and you might just be inseparable."

I tap the counter and stare down at the roses. I feel like I'm crawling in my skin. I'm beginning to think that I've done something so wrong, that it's too late and the damage has been done, that I can't make Hadley fall for me. But I think I should try, really try. It's what I would have done all those years ago. It would have been easier, as she was already mine then.

"I hope you're right," I nearly whisper.

Maybe it's time to fix a mistake.

I'M BURIED amongst a pile of deliveries and presents when Hadley returns home.

"What in the world?" She drops her keys on the counter and surveys the breakfast-nook area.

"Wedding gifts. News spreads fast, and now we have sponsors and anyone who is anyone in hockey sending us stuff," I explain as I open another package and pull out his-and-hers t-shirts and drop them like a hot potato.

Hadley studies the contents on the chairs and tables. "We have to donate some of this stuff. What would we do with a basket of a hundred candy bars? And do we really need *another* blender?"

I play with the card for the next gift. "You could always hoard this stuff and save it for when we decide to part ways." I'm testing the waters.

She clears her throat and chooses to ignore my comment and instead opens a neatly wrapped box. "This is from Piper and Hudson." Our parents' neighbors and April's uncle and aunt. "I can tell it's from Piper's boutique."

"Oh yeah?" I'm invested because Piper owns a...

"Of course, she sends this." Hadley holds up a black mesh nightie that leaves little to the imagination, since Piper owns a lingerie boutique.

I nod once. "Not bad, someone understood the assignment."

Hadley looks at me, horrified. "They are our neighbors! They're family to me."

I lean forward to swipe the card. "'To Hadley and Connor, enjoy the honeymoon phase. We are so delighted with the news. You two were always adorable. Hugs, Piper (and Hudson).'"

"Didn't someone send us matching flannel pajamas that cover every inch or something?" She searches the pile of presents.

"Actually, yes, over there by the chair." I point.

She gets sidetracked by looking at the matching champagne flutes with our names engraved on them, and then examines the fruit basket. "Seriously, what do we do with this stuff?"

I shrug a shoulder. "Let me call someone tomorrow. Some of this stuff is from sponsors. I'm sure they want us to post a selfie in our pajamas on a Sunday morning with some ridiculous scented candle lit and mug in hand."

Hadley laughs, then her eyes land on the roses and her face scrunches in confusion. "Your aunt sent more flowers?"

I lean back in my chair and watch her gently pick up the stems to smell the flowers.

"Nah, I was at her shop and thought I should get something for my wife since I'm a good husband."

Her eyes flick in my direction, and she smirks to herself as she taps the petals against her cheek. "Going all in on that, huh?"

"You love it." I don't blink.

Hadley tips her nose up, and she seems to be in contemplation. "Excuse me." She drops the roses then slides something off the table before leaving me alone amongst the mountain of congratulations.

But I'm not done with this conversation, which is why I

follow her. She's already in the bathroom when I make it to our bedroom, and even I know not to interrupt a woman when she's in the bathroom with the door locked.

Instead, I hop onto the bed and kick up my feet to get comfortable. I'll just wait, and luckily, it isn't long, because precisely a minute later, the lock clicks, then the door opens to reveal Hadley in black make-me-instantly-hard lingerie as she leans against the doorframe.

This design should be a crime. It's a little dress that ends just barely below her ass, and those straps appear easy to slide down. I don't get a chance to debate that, as my eyes are drawn to the plunging line between her breasts that are pert from the fabric pushing her tits together.

"You want to be a good husband, then I'll play that game and be your good wife, even dress the part, when I go to bed *to sleep*." Her sexy-as-fuck smirk causes me to propel off the bed.

Don't falter… yet.

"You know what I think, Sprinkles?"

"Your ploy to take me to lunch and charm me with roses has backfired? And yeah, I know what six roses means. I worked one summer for your aunt, and she made me study that chart like it was the exam of my life."

I chuckle under my breath as I stride my way to her. "I don't think my plan has backfired. Because I'm kind of confident that the walls you and I built around one another, you actually want to burn them down."

I stand right in front of her and plant my hands firmly on her hips then pull her forward, which causes her breath to catch, but it does the job because her mouth is now in a kissable distance, and I feel her breath spread along the line of my neck.

Her eyes sparkle with intrigue, and when her mouth parts

open, I can't help but trace her jawline with the pad of my thumb. It feels as though she's entranced by me, and by all means, I get a kick out of being the one to possess her, but ultimately, it's the fact she trusts to let me lead.

"Hmm? Isn't that what you want? For me to break down that wall you have when it concerns me? Even for a night?" My voice is heavily laced with lust as I set my sight on her mouth.

"Sometimes my head spins around you. Unlike dance where I can control it and land perfectly, with you I don't know how," she admits in a whisper.

I step closer to bring our bodies flush. "I can show you how," I husk.

She shakes her head, but a smirk appears before she meets me halfway because she stands on the balls of her feet as she offers me her mouth, the mouth that I cover with my own.

Because I have every intention of grounding her through a kiss, followed by laying her on the bed.

11

HADLEY

Why am I doing this again?

I am voluntarily surrendering to him because this man knows how to curse me with a stare, and it's not even a vile curse. Instead, he is shaking me and waking up every dormant feeling that I have for him.

I changed into expensive lingerie because I like teasing him. I wanted him to suffer, look but not touch. We all have a weakness, and mine is the way his eyes fill with a warm possession when I'm the object he stares at.

Which is why I am standing right here locked in a lip tango with my husband.

Connor's lips firmly kiss mine, with his tongue requesting entry, and I eagerly give. We always want what we probably shouldn't have. Except, I never say no to ice cream, so the same rule can apply to the only man who kisses me with electricity.

Because Connor's kisses seep through my veins and sink me down, and my body comes alive when his lips are on mine, something I hate to admit.

My body curves into his as his arm tightens around my

waist and his kiss deepens. We sizzle together, and maybe through the years, we've both feared that.

We kissed for the camera, we made one another come, but an intimate kiss like this? It's our first in this chapter of our lives, and it's from our own initiative.

I murmur a sound of enjoyment as my eyes remain closed so I can drown in this kiss and in his arms, ignoring any warning flare looming in the back of my head. If I'm giving into this moment, then I'm going all in.

Even when he begins to walk us back toward the bed, I'm lost in a spellbinding moment. That is until his mouth leaves my lips and skims down my throat, and his free hand spreads along the back of my neck like I'm his to claim.

"You drive me crazy," he hums as he nuzzles into my neck, creating a sensitive wave that cascades down to my nipples.

"My life's mission," I whisper in retort, but really, I should scream ditto.

He growls and hoists me up, my legs naturally wrapping around his waist, and a sound escapes me because I feel he's more than ready.

A flimsy strap falls off my shoulder, and it only encourages Connor to trail his mouth along my collarbone, causing my head to fall back and my thighs to bind tighter around him.

It's a worthless move on my part, because a few seconds later, he plops me onto the bed and hovers over me with his eyes hungry and my heart growing heavy—the good kind.

I watch as Connor peels his t-shirt up, and I bite my lip from the show. There is a reason why women peg him as the hockey player with looks. I can't decide if I should focus on his arms or chest; it's a hard choice, so I choose the dangerous one and lock my gaze with his smoldering eyes.

The corner of his mouth tugs when he combs a few

strands of hair behind my ear. I hate when he's sweet like that—no, I don't, but I should. I'm a woman who has self-respect, I remember what he did, but I can't seem to shake that there is a reason, and we're no longer as young and foolish. Maybe he was meant for a second…

I shake my head. "This is just sex," I lie.

He smirks. "Sure, whatever you need to tell yourself."

"Can you just, I don't know, step up your cocky ego factor? You seem to have left it at the door, and it's confusing, distracting, kind of infuriating," I begin to mumble and pout.

He pauses as he holds his weight over me. His head falls forward when he laughs, then he glances up to study my face. "You want me to be an asshole during sex?"

"No," I stutter. "Just… you're sending mixed messages. I don't know if this…"

Something sparks inside of him, and in a swift move, he grabs my wrists and pins them above my head. "This is me about to take you with a ring on your finger that confirms you are my wife, so I intend to fuck you the way a wife deserves to be fucked. Is that clear enough for you?"

I'm speechless because he has determination in his tone to prove me wrong from whatever doubt is floating in my head.

Gathering my bearings, I remain firm. "It's just sex."

He lets go of my wrists and sighs. "Fine. The choice is yours; you lead, or you let me prove you wrong."

My pussy squeezes from the thought of what that could entail, but emotionally, I'm not sure I'm ready. "On your back," I demand. The safer option, that's what I choose.

He tips his head slightly to the side. "This could be fun." He complies by standing, removing his jeans, then lying on the bed.

I quickly swing my legs to straddle him, and from instinct, my hips roll to ride his boxers. The matching panties to this baby doll are barely a layer, and I feel everything against my heat. My senses are heightened, and I should beg for him to touch my bundle of nerves to get some form of release.

I assess my fingers as I walk them up his stomach then stop at his chest. Leaning down, I place a kiss next to my hand. His skin is warm, and my hair falls along his body, tickling his skin, but it's his hand that is stroking my behind and drawing up to my lower back in mollifying circles that drives me wild.

He's boosting me through touch.

Lifting my shoulders back up, I hold his gaze as I slide the straps off my arms and inch down the lingerie. He sits up to kiss my breast, and I hiss a breath when his lips latch onto a nipple, and he sneaks his fingers between us to stroke my pussy.

He groans but keeps his mouth on me. "You're so wet for me," he murmurs between switching breasts.

I breathe out to pace myself. I'm aching for a release to come quickly.

"Mmhmm." It's a cop-out answer, but I'm too lost on his fingertips that circle my clit. Then he dips one finger inside of me and my head falls onto his shoulder from the intense feeling.

"I think you're desperate for my cock. Always have been."

I want to hate his sweltering words, but I'm already half gone.

I reach between us and sneak into the waistband of his boxer briefs, setting his cock free and wrapping my fingers around him. His throaty moan appeases me, and I'm desperate to do more to him.

One stroke then two.

We're touching each other and working ourselves into a frenzy.

"We have too much on," I whisper.

"I agree."

Quickly, we both discard any remaining scraps of cloth, then I'm back on him, sitting together face to face and his cock sliding between my center, getting soaked in my arousal. The tip of his cock is dangerously close to my entrance and our foreheads touch while we take a moment to digest that we're about to do this.

"We're good?" he asks gently. "I've never…"

My heart is palpitating, and my breath runs wild. Fuck, why does he have to make me feel like this is special. I'm his first for something, wife and no condom.

"Considering you think I can get pregnant from immaculate conception, then I think you're a little late to ask, but yeah, we're fine."

Mischief twinkles in his eyes. "Then ride me."

A short laugh escapes me. Half of him just said that because he is goofy that way, while the other part is because he means it.

Positioning myself over him, I slowly press down, and everything inside of me coils from the instant gratification of having him inside me. I move and move until he's filled me up, with my inner walls clenched around him.

"You feel so fucking good," he grits out, and his hands grip my hips to hold me in place.

I'm nearly stuck on top of him as I adjust to his size, but then I move an inch, then a little more, until I lift myself back up to his tip and root myself back down on him.

I do this a few times until I find a rhythm that feels right.

He gently slaps my ass and then palms a soothing circle.

"Use me. Take what you want. It's all yours," he whispers.

That sensitive demeanor is back, but I don't argue.

I meet him on thrusts, when I'm halfway down and he tips up, with the angle hitting the right buttons inside me, and I moan while he groans. I'm not sure I can feel my legs anymore, everything is barreling to my pussy, and I'm on fire in the best possible way.

Maybe he notices, or maybe he's just being dominant, but he grips my hips with vigor then pulls me close and flips us so he's on top, all without ever leaving me.

"I lied. I'm taking over."

A drowsy sound escapes me. "Surprise, surprise, you lied," I tease with an underlying truth.

"Hadley," he warns.

My response is to reach up and frame his face affectionately while he picks up our speed. My toes dip into the muscle of his ass, widening my legs, and my clit enjoys the friction of his body rubbing against me.

"Eyes on me," he demands.

Our eyes meet and lock, and my heart reminds me that it's still beating and all of my energy hasn't, in fact, flowed to my pussy. This feels like entrapment; I'm under him with no escape and his eyes are a shackle. But there is nowhere else that I would rather be.

We stay in this trance until our rhythm is uncontrollable, and I know I'm near the end. I use my fingers to play with myself to help me reach the destination at the same time.

"I'm coming inside of you. Need to mark you, and I fully intend to use those ribbons again if it means you won't be showering tonight. All night, you will have to feel me." Ah, there is his cocky comment that I needed to hear, except it's hopelessly hot.

"Figured you would go barbarian on me." I smirk and moan.

He leans down and kisses my mouth, gently biting the corner. "Call it perks of being your husband."

"Then do it. Leave. Me. Dripping," I gravel out, wildly eager for his words to come to fruition.

"Good wife." He places a kiss on my cheek before focusing on taking us to the finish line.

I close my eyes and see stars, with my body exploding.

When all is said and done, he stays seated between my legs, as our connection doesn't break even when I feel his warmth trickling down my thigh. I lie there taking in the post-orgasm bliss. I can't help the faint smile that wants to form as I rake my fingers through Connor's hair where he rests his head against my chest, his ear near my heart.

Living the fantasy is completely okay if it's only for a little bit, right?

12

HADLEY

I let out a deep breath as I brace myself to walk down the stairs and into the kitchen where Connor is busy making a smoothie, I can hear the blender. Taking the plunge, I walk down a step and recall last night. After he rolled off me, we didn't say anything, and sleep took over. Sure, I may have noticed how his arm clung around me during the night while he slept and I pretended to sleep. Nor did I slip out of his hold.

As I walk into the kitchen, Connor pauses the button on the blender. He offers me a warm half-smile that makes me feel all light inside.

"Morning, I'm making you a shake," he mentions.

Instantly, I freeze then study the counter where I see my favorite ingredients, banana and peanut butter mostly. "Why?" I ask cautiously.

He flashes me a cunning grin as he grabs a clean glass from the counter and goes a little over the top when he pours the contents into the glass. "Being thoughtful, of course."

I smile tightly and take the drink he offers. "Let's not make a big deal about last night, okay?"

Connor chuckles as he grabs a glass for himself. "*Yeah…* you kind of mentioned last night." He crosses one ankle over the other as he leans against the counter. "Doesn't mean that I agree. So, here's the deal, Sprinkles." The rim of his shake hits his lips, and he takes a sip, even smacks his lips together for good measure. "I'm going all in on proving to you that we might as well admit this thing between us and knock down a wall or two. If you're going to be a little slower to step up and be a team player, then so be it."

Holy shit, he was serious.

"A ring, an orgasm, and flannel pajamas with our names on it doesn't change the fact that I should probably be a little wary of the sudden change of mood, considering our past." I drink from my smoothie and hum out a sound. Damn, that's good.

Connor sets his drink down and strolls my way. He lifts my glass from my hold and sets it down on the counter next to me. "Sprinkles, you're not a teenager anymore. I was an ass. Want me to get on my knees and admit it a hundred times?"

I tip my nose up. "Why were you?"

"Let it go. At some point you have to decide if holding a grudge or moving on for something better is more worth it." He raises his brows at me, waiting for an answer, one I don't give. "What's it going to be?"

I scoff. "It doesn't work like that. Not at the snap of your fingers. We're married, so I'll consider it, that's it." I give him a hardened look, but inside I'm melting, my defenses are breaking, and the dam holding everything in is on the verge of collapse, including my pussy that is eager this morning for Connor's touch.

The back of his palm glides along my cheek, and he smirks from accomplishment. "That's a start."

I shake my head gently, kind of exhausted that this is how my day is starting. Not energy-wise tired, more like my mind is muddled and I haven't even had coffee today yet.

"I'll take care of all of this." He indicates his head to the pile of gifts, some we haven't even opened yet.

I shrug a shoulder. "Maybe first we should see what everything is?" There could be some cute stuff, and I always need sweatshirts, plus it's not every day you get wedding presents to gawk at. "We won't keep all of this, and I don't have time to write thank-you notes."

"I'll have someone handle that. By the way, I have a charity game this weekend. You'll be there, right?"

"Oh." I'm taken aback. "I guess your wife should be there, uhm, sure. What's the charity?"

He grins. "A dog rescue shelter. Which is awesome since I know you can't be mad at me if I'm holding a puppy."

It causes me to grin and bob my head side to side. "You're kind of right. I wish my parents got a new dog after Pickles passed, but it just isn't the same."

Connor touches my shoulder. "He was the laziest dog ever."

I laugh. "Oh boy, he was. Then again, Puck is like a retriever on speed."

He laughs too. "My dad trained him for dog competitions. Biggest mistake, he's like addicted to chasing balls."

"Maybe we should have a joint calendar or something? Then we can plan events where we need to make an appearance as the perfect couple. My studio has a summer dance show at the summer festival, so you should probably be there. Oh, and family events."

He slides his arm around my shoulders. "Look at us, going all official with a shared calendar."

I chortle. "Uhm, I'm positive we can't get more official than a marriage certificate and rings."

"True. We're in the honeymoon phase, so may I make a suggestion?"

Skepticism takes over, yet I'm still enticed. "What?"

He begins to spin me slowly around. "We should be at it like rabbits. It's tradition."

Heat spreads through my body as he places my hands on the counter with my back to his front.

Yikes, I should be a little more resistant, but his breath caressing the back of my neck feels far too good, especially when his teeth scrape my earlobe.

"What the hell, why not," I sigh in defeat, and my body is already two steps ahead of my brain, and I press against his cock while he reaches for my front.

When I glance over my shoulder, Connor acts fast and captures my lips for a kiss, as if he knew he had a small window of opportunity.

Morning kisses, this is very new for us. He's a bit more sensual than I anticipated.

That is until my yoga pants are yanked lower, and he aligns himself with me.

"Hold on to the counter," he instructs.

I do as I'm told and look forward as I feel him plunge inside of me before he pumps. My entire body jolts on every move, my hands spread along the counter for more support, and as his robust movements intensify, I accidentally knock over my smoothie and neither of us seem to care.

"Connor." I'm not even sure if it's a beg or plea. We're moving fast, and I want it all. "Turn me around," I decide.

We quickly smack our lips together for a kiss before he retreats out and guides me over to the cabinet and traps me there. I lift my leg, and he enters me, stretching my leg farther.

He peeks down then at me with impressed eyes, and they grow bold when I lift my leg even higher.

"Benefits of having me as your wife. I'm flexible." My breath is heavy.

"Benefits of having me as your husband. I have stamina and can act fast when needed."

We both laugh for a second before we go at it with pure abandon until I'm shaking around his length, and he chases me not long after by unloading inside of me.

We stand there, draped around each other, completely spent and satisfied.

"You have the newlywed glow," Isla remarks as she leans against the ballet barre at my studio in workout gear, waiting for my ballet barre class for adults.

I attempt to avoid her gaze because I need to hide a ridiculous smile. "I don't," I deny. But I know the opposite is true. There was yesterday in the kitchen, then last night we might have gone another round after lights out in bed. This morning, I might have let him join me in the shower too.

It's bad. I'm addicted. But for an unexplained reason, I don't feel like I should run.

"I'm cautious," I reaffirm out loud.

"Sure, but you look like someone who can barely walk due to living her best life."

I have to laugh at her observation while I connect my phone to Bluetooth. "Maybe tone down the orgasm accusations, I have to deal with our moms in like two minutes."

"Oh please, knowing you and Connor can't keep your

hands off one another would fuel April and Brielle's souls. They already texted me asking when we can throw a late bridal shower."

"What?"

She gives me a knowing nod. "I'm responsible for inviting all the girlfriends and wives of the hockey team." I'm not surprised, they text Isla like she's a daughter on a normal week, which I love, since other than her brother, Isla doesn't have a lot of family.

"Well… I guess it could be fun." I can't decide.

Isla has a sheepish grin. "You're kind of enjoying this wild ride you walked right into, huh?"

I croak out a sound. "It's not like there's been a boring minute lately."

"Admit it, of all the guys on that hockey team that you could have woken up married to, you're happy it's Connor."

"Relieved may be more like it," I admit.

She chuckles as she stretches her arm over her head. "Mark my words, Hadley Crews Spears. That guy isn't your accidental husband, he's your forever husband."

Before I can think of an answer, Isla tips her head to the door. "Speak of the devils." Isla offers a funny smile as my mom and Brielle enter my studio, along with two other ladies who join the class.

My mom walks to me and gives me a hug, along with Brielle. "You shouldn't be here, you should be on your honeymoon," my mom mentions.

"That will come later, I guess."

She waves a finger in front of me. "I know. But since you made the choice to elope *without* your parents present…" There is that disproving tone, and here comes her bright cheery smile. "Brielle and I have taken the liberty to explore options that something is done to celebrate your marriage."

Brielle hands me an envelope. "For you and Connor."

I examine it with curiosity and see it's a fancy envelope that's closed by a traditional stamp that requires melting a stick of wax that I used to do as a kid at the craft station at Pioneer Park nearby. My eyes nearly bug out when I notice the letters H & C engraved on the stamp.

Taking the card out, I begin to read then stop. "Did you two seriously just hand me an invite for my own wedding?"

Brielle bounces her shoulders. "We're just presenting options. We can't do *nothing*. It's not a wedding, per se, it's a celebration, wedding-ish."

I read out the card. "'Mr. and Mrs. Spencer Crews and Mr. and Mrs. Ford Spears warmly invite you to celebrate the *unexpected* marriage of their children Hadley Crews and Connors Spears at the Dizzy Duck Inn in Lake Spark.'" My jaw goes slack. "You even put hockey sticks on the invitation?"

"I thought it was a nice touch, actually. It was Brielle's idea to add that little phrase at the end." My mother is in her element.

"'He was always waiting to win her heart.'" I read it aloud in utter disbelief that they mocked up an invite and made it so sweet that I might get a toothache… but I'm grinning.

My mom turns to Isla. "I think the bridal shower is off. We're going bigger with a party if they agree. We'll meet for the second round of invites."

Isla bursts out laughing.

I have to fan myself because, as ridiculous as this is, my mom and Brielle look deliriously happy.

I hold the invite up. "We'll talk about this after class, now get to the barre."

Heading to my little table where I store my phone, I quickly send a text.

Me: Options for a real wedding-ish. Our moms created an example invite.

I take a photo of the invitation and send it to Connor.

Instantly, he types back.

Connor: What are the chances they actually booked the venue already?

Me: Probable. They've gone a little loco, but they seem so ecstatic.

Connor: I bet you my dad would order a tux for the dog.

Me: I guess this might be better than them planning our honeymoon.

Connor: Rumor has it that's a work-in-progress.

Me: Uh oh… Well, I gotta go teach.

Connor: Sure, hey… the invite is for well in the future, you know…

I still for a second. I did notice it's in a few months but didn't think much about it. Connor and I spoke of a timeline, but I'm not sure something ever connected that we have one.

I type a lie.

Me: I didn't notice…

Connor: Liar. Guess I'll just have to spank you later.

A goofy grin hits my face, and I set my phone on silent and hit play on the dance class playlist.

THE NEXT DAY, I find myself with a sandwich wrap sitting near the gazebo at the end of Main Street with my dad next to me. His request for a quick bite and walk wasn't unusual considering we always do stuff together, but the last few days he's been a bit distant. This chat over turkey and honey mustard feels a little more stiff than normal.

"Ashton is bummed he is missing your husband's charity game with puppies, but I have tickets for a baseball game in the city and need to make an appearance since it's my old team." The way my dad says husband causes my cheeks to raise.

"Puppies make people happy," I state blandly.

My father tosses the paper wrapper from his sandwich in the nearby trash can then turns his attention to me. "You okay with your mom going a little overboard with pushing a wedding-ish, if that's what we're calling it?"

I laugh. "Sure, she can plan away, but that doesn't mean it will happen. Are you okay with her acting crazy?"

"Sure. In this fictional wedding, would I get to have a dance as father of the bride?"

I interlink our arms. "Of course. Is that what has you down? Missing your father-of-the-bride responsibilities? Because if you say that's what has you in a mood, then I might not believe you."

"You didn't have the wedding I would have expected, but you're right. I'm just worried that you married for the wrong reasons."

I quirk my lips out. "Stop scowling, it's bad for your age lines. Besides, I thought you and Connor had a little chat the other day. Are you worried about something?"

My father's eyes glaze with a mood that I can't quite distinguish. "He never asked me for your hand in marriage, never went through my vigorous tests, and I needed to be sure that he will do anything for you."

"And?"

He pauses for a second. "It's nothing. Can you blame me for being protective? How are your first days as husband and wife? Wait…" He recoils when he realizes what he asked. "Don't answer that."

I chuckle and hold his arm tighter. "You know I think I've been lucky. You gave me the best life, kind of a breeze. The only thing that was a surprise was when you met Mom. I guess what I'm saying is I finally threw the unexpected at us. Surprise!" I splay my hands out.

He attempts to smile, but it slips, and he dips his gaze down. "Nearly gave me a heart attack too, and I'm not even fifty, so thanks for that."

"I'm your favorite daughter, you'll forgive me," I tease.

"You're my only daughter," he reminds me.

In the corner of my eye, I see Connor approaching us. I had mentioned via text that I was going to grab a bite with my dad today.

I offer him a curt wave to let him know that I see him. His eyes land on my father, and like every man who sees my father when they ever tried to enter my life, his eyes fill with a humorous fear.

My father stands to greet my husband. "Connor," he states.

"Spencer."

Lines furrow on my face because these two together are far too much testosterone, even for them. Connor kisses my cheek, and I swear my father is still adjusting to the scene, and truthfully, so am I, considering this time last week I would have swatted Connor away with a growly comment.

"You two should maybe go do a gym session or something together," I suggest to them. "You used to do that. One trip to Vegas and it feels like I need to lock you two in a room or something. I know, what about golf?"

"Golf isn't a sport," they both say in unison.

My hands fly up to calm them. "Okay, well, at least you both agree on something."

Both men stand taller, and my dad puffs his shoulders out. "We agree on a lot of things, Hadley. Like we both agree that you are something special and deserve only the best." He slaps a hand on Connor's shoulder. "Don't we, *son*."

Connor is amused by my father's expression. "Absolutely."

"I think I'll leave you two love birds alone. I need to pick up your brother from a friend's house." My dad steps to me and offers me his arm for a hug. "Let him take care of you," he mumbles. Our embrace breaks, and I see the sincerity in his eyes that throws me off. I realize that he and Connor are more alike than I ever thought; they are kings of mixed messages.

He gives a nod to Connor who returns the gesture. A secret code that only they seem to know.

I watch the man who was always my number one walk away as I stand next to the man who takes that spot in a different way. The profoundness of this moment stings my heart. I guess this is what growing up feels like. Because we never stop, even when we're in our twenties. We constantly evolve and change…

Even the ones who broke your heart the first time around.

They may not be the same, which is why another layer falls to the ground as far as Connor is concerned. Because what if he really was right the other day? If I let down a wall or two, he could be everything.

No better time than now to discover if he's right, especially since he's already my husband…

13
CONNOR

I'm not used to eating this late, but Hadley mentioned earlier that she would be finished at eight tonight, and after meeting her at the park earlier, she seemed a bit more distant than normal. Not frosty around me per usual but lost in thought.

I was in town, running an errand, when I texted to ask if she wanted to grab a bite, and she mentioned she was already at the park. I took it as an invite, but arriving, I saw that I was interrupting a moment between her and Spencer, and I have no clue what. She didn't say much after, and I accepted the silence when I walked her back to her studio.

Glancing down at the stove, I can see the vegetables and chicken are tender for the curry that I've made. I grab the small bowl of cashew nuts and toss them in when I hear the door to the garage open, and a minute later, Hadley enters.

"Wow." Hadley's voice sounds different. She walks slowly to the other side of the kitchen island and sets her giant water bottle down; the lines on the bottle indicate she is right on track for her hydration scheme. "You cook?" Her brows raise.

I smirk to myself because I aim to impress. "I do. Need to ensure I'm eating good macros during game season. I figured you might have skipped dinner."

Her brows stay fixed in an arch as she seems taken aback. "You waited for me?"

"Yeah." I turn the stove off. "It's a mild yellow curry and rice."

Her eyes relax, and a warm smile forms as she sits down on the bar stool. "It looks delicious." A sound rumbles in her throat. "Is this your good-husband thing? Cooking?"

"Maybe." I wink at her before I dish out the food. I figure we can keep it simple and eat at the counter.

She bites her inner cheek as she watches me place the plate in front of her and remains somewhat in awe that I cook. I find my spot next to her and hand her a fork.

"Okay, here I go, I'm digging in," she announces before she brings a forkful of food to her mouth to blow on then carefully takes a bite. Hadley stalls as she chews, watching me, because she knows I'm waiting for my appraisal. She swallows, and her face stays neutral. "It's… good." Her facial expression relaxes.

"I know."

"I don't even want to know what you do when you actually try to impress a girl," she mentions before her fork dishes up another bite.

I study her for a second while I eat my own bite. "Not this. This is casual-weekday Connor."

"As opposed to puck-bunny Fridays?"

Ah, so she's fishing into my dating history.

"Cute. And no, cooking is reserved for wives."

"You've only ever had one wife."

I point my fork at her. "Smart."

Hadley sets her fork down and her look of hesitation returns before she surveys the room. "More gifts?"

"Ridiculous, huh?"

"Depends. Are there any big water bottles? I could use a new one."

I laugh because I appreciate that she doesn't care for fancy things, she's all practical.

"You know, other than your ridiculous request for birthday cakes, party dresses, and a dance studio in your house, contrary to what people would assume, you're not a spoiled princess."

She rests her chin onto her propped arm. "First off, cake is important for the soul, so it better be good. Second, dresses are key for many situations; weddings, birthdays, proms, impromptu elopements. And finally, the small dance studio in my parents' house was all my dad's idea when I was six."

I scratch my end-of-day stubble on my chin at the mention of her father. He gave me the father-of-the-bride speech the other day, nothing I wasn't prepared for or couldn't handle, but our relationship is one of understanding —ensure Hadley has the best life.

"You okay? Seemed like you were kind of out of it after seeing your dad," I pry.

"I'm fine." She's lying, but I let it go.

We stew for a few beats in silence, just playing with our food. I'm not sure we're that hungry.

But then she does something that catches me off guard. She lunges forward on the chair, cups my face with both hands, and plants her lips on mine.

It takes a moment to digest what is happening, but then I close my eyes and give back as much she gives, which is a lot. I snake my arm around her middle to keep her close. Her lips nearly suck the life out of me, it's a bruising kiss, and we both moan a sound of satisfaction. She's fervent and determined, I'm not sure of what, but I'm sure as hell along for the ride. I'm lost in this kiss that she owns.

The sound of our lips parting is what causes me to open my lids and see her swollen lips.

"I'm deciding," she states. My eyes widen slightly because she has my full attention, and her eyes meet mine. Hers filled with adventure and mine filled with hope. "About you. This husband-and-wife thing, as if we could actually work."

I swivel my stool to allow me to have her in full view and for my fingertips to rest on her lower arm. "Why not go all in and see if we can prove ourselves wrong?"

An audible breath escapes her lips. "People change, but I don't want to be on the receiving end if you haven't. I wanted to make you suffer, and I'm sure you had some other plan too. But the difference between you and me is that I can't survive you hurting me a second time around."

I squeeze her arm, because nothing I say will rewind the clock, all I can do is be honest. "I want to prove you wrong. Maybe waking up married was our odd way of getting a fresh start."

She slides off the chair, leaving my fingers vacant. Hadley walks a few steps before throwing her arms up in the air. "I'm cautious and still deciding," she gripes and leaves me with the hope that maybe she's softening to me.

Circling around the Range Rover, I open the door for my wife. She's busy typing away on her phone, and it kind of annoys me. "I might throw that phone somewhere. You've been on it non-stop since we got in the car," I tell her.

Hadley tosses the phone in her bag, a Spinners tote. "I know, I know. It's my little brother. He has some biology project for his summer science club he's taking part in that I need to help him with." I relax because we both have a soft spot for little brothers.

Offering her my hand, she gently shakes her head and smirks at my effort to be a gentleman, before she slides her palm onto mine and we begin to walk. Although we parked in a quiet spot behind the training center, in about one minute, we'll be surrounded by my dad's marketing team, hockey guys, and puppies.

I'm wearing my jersey, and I'm thankful that she got her jersey less than twenty-four hours after our marriage was announced, because the marketing department acted quick and sent over something for Hadley, and now she's wearing my number 19 with the word husband on the back. Paired with her jeans and hair only partly up thanks to her sunglasses, I can only conclude that I'm lucky to have a sexy-fox wife.

"I guess it's a few photo ops, then I'll go change for the friendly hockey match. We're only going to do a one-period game." It's for charity, the local shelter where my parents adopted Puck from. A few guys from my team are here, along with a few veterans, including my dad and uncle.

Hadley snorts a laugh. "Isla and the marketing department are geniuses. I'm positive this setup got every female from the 18-35 demographic here within a fifty-mile radius."

I shrug a shoulder before I open the side door. "Happy to oblige using my good looks if it means it helps a little furball find a home."

She stops and tips her nose up, giving me a knowing look. "As much as I could call you out, I know that you are actually being noble here. We both know you're going to milk the attention for the sake of a good cause."

I bring my hand to my heart. "Most definitely isn't for the female popularity. I'm a taken and tied-down man now."

She chuckles under her breath, and I follow her in. Instantly, we see the main entrance covered in balloons and a table to one side with various cookies, both for humans and canines. There is a pen of dogs playing with toys on the other side of the hall.

Already Briggs is holding a yellow Lab puppy, and Shawn is holding a mixed breed that doesn't appear to be a puppy at all. They smile for the photographer, yet the smile on their faces is purely natural, because how can you not be happy right now?

We are quickly ushered by one of the coordinators to one of the dog pens, and before we know it, I'm holding a mixed Labrador breed that is older, but a hundred pounds is easy for me, so I cradle him like a baby. Hadley is cooing and rubbing his belly, but the dog just looks at her with a blank stare.

"This dog is way too chill," I note.

"He seems to be one of the few on this earth that enjoys your company. Isn't he lovable?" She scratches his chin.

Glancing down at the dog in my arms that's wearing a bandana and this guy is sucking me in. "I need you to pull the wife card."

"Wife card?" Hadley wonders.

"Rule the house, tell me no, remind me that we don't need a dog," I explain.

She giggles, and the way her hand touches my shoulder feels good. But the last few days she's been softening around me, and we just... flow.

We ignore the camera going off around us.

"Oh, I have no problem saying no to you," she jokes.

"But I also see cookies over there, so I dunno… priorities." She slants her shoulders up.

"You two are adorable!" Brianne, one of the wives of a veteran from my dad's years, says as she greets us, with her meticulous blonde hair. She was young when she married then; I can imagine she still isn't pushing forty yet.

"Hey, it's been a long time," I greet her and bounce the dog gently as I cradle him.

She turns her attention to Hadley. "I'm Brianne O'Shae, my husband is playing today. He used to play for the Spinners. Congratulations, you two! Did the team reach out about the wives' club? You are in for a wild ride at games. A few rules, but mostly everyone is decent."

Hadley glances sidelong to me, slightly panicked. "Someone will be in touch, I'm sure," I say.

She awkwardly smiles to Brianne. "I'm sure we will be fine. I watched my mom handle my dad for a few years before he retired from baseball."

The bubbly woman in front of us touches Hadley's shoulder. "Oh, that's right. You'll be a pro then. Okay, well, you two are the cutest. Loving the social media boost that it's giving the team." She shimmies away, and her burst of sunshine makes us need a second to come down.

Briggs arrives next to me, now dog-free. "How's married life, you two?"

"Joyous," Hadley answers, with smile fixed and one-tone voice.

Briggs chuckles, and we both watch Hadley meander on over to the cookie table where Isla is busy checking her tablet.

I make faces at the dog in my arms, and he opens his mouth as if he wants to talk but then nuzzles into my chest.

This guy knows how to give marketing what they need; social media will go crazy for this.

"Not going to lie, it's a little strange seeing you two together and being kind of sweet. I mean, you both always flirted, it was some serious foreplay we all witnessed, but this is… damn. You're completely into this." He speaks low so only I can hear.

"I am," I admit honestly without hesitation.

My friend grins at me. "Maybe this will help keep your head in the game next season." He nudges my arm because being an ass sometimes is our play.

"I'll be better. You just need to get laid, and then you can play at my level," I joke.

"Yeah, this is why you shouldn't have eloped. I was counting on a hot bridesmaid who needed her night rocked."

One of the volunteers comes to take the dog out of my arms, and I kind of miss him already as they walk away.

Briggs and I begin to walk toward the locker rooms. "I'm still debating how we can turn this all around and still have a bachelor party post-'oops I got married,'" he comments.

My lips quirk out. "Are we talking like beers with the boys or full-out 'Hadley would rip my balls off' kind of party?"

"You lost your right to strippers when you signed your name in Vegas. Doesn't mean we all have to suffer," he teases, but then he turns serious. "Nah, we'll check out a brewery or something. Your dad and I have already been texting to maybe arrange something."

"I'm happy my life is turning around everyone's social calendars," I quip.

"I bet. Now let's go play some hockey."

An hour later, after getting on my equipment, some warming up, some photos with dogs on the ice, and waving to some fans who came out, I find myself near the center line to the right. This is low-key friendly, so no fancy lights, more of a practice than anything. I'm playing against my dad and Shawn, plus a few others, so nothing like making this an easy game.

I skate toward my position on the ice, and my sight sidelines to Shawn who is skating next to me.

Shawn begins to speak to me. "I've been trying to figure out what wedding gift to get you. I'm thinking a vibrator is probably what your wife needs since she's with you."

My blood begins to boil, but I know I need to take the high road. "Classy. Aiming low at a charity game."

We both line up. Me as right defense on the blue line and Shawn on the opposite side as left defense.

The referee blows the whistle, and my sight focuses on guarding his ass, following him is not my ideal, but I have dogs to save and a wife to impress.

Telling hockey players to play for fun is kind of pointless. The retired veterans have a point to prove that they're still young, the new players want to show enthusiasm, and wingers just want to be an ass.

We're five minutes in and every block and chase is making me work.

My only relief is when I notice Hadley sitting in the stands watching me. It feels like extra support, makes me focus better, and she could be part of my formula to always win. I ignore any flag in my head about timelines or next season, especially when she wiggles her fingers at me because she caught me looking.

But now we're going into another play, and Shawn is pissing me off again with his radiating aggression.

"You know, I'm confident if I'd gotten her drunk enough that she would have married me too."

"Fuck off. That's not what it is," I grit out.

"Right. She'd probably spread her legs too."

I drop my stick and shove him without thought, my protective instinct in full swing. "Do not speak of my wife that way." My gloves come off.

"Touchy, Spears. I would be too if I had girl with a tight body like that."

I push him again before all hell breaks loose, and we take turns in headlocks. We scuffle, and the referee blows the whistle before players are ripping us apart.

"Box," the ref informs me as he brakes on his skates next to me. "Instigating, two-minute penalty."

Great. I got sent to the penalty box during a charity game.

14

CONNOR

Briggs sits on a sofa in one of the spare offices, with a yellow Lab puppy on his lap as he attempts to be the peacemaker after the game.

"Seriously, it may be the off-season, but if our captain or coach were here, then you two would be dead. What kind of shitty sportsmanship was that out there?" Briggs continues to lecture us as he continues to stroke the puppy.

"Dude, are you seriously going to keep that puppy on your lap as you attempt to get us to listen?" I point out the obvious as I adjust the ice pack on my shoulder and lean into the lounger.

He doesn't stop. "Yep. This fluffball is like therapy. We should totally get a team dog."

"Well, why don't we have Connor ask his uncle since we know he has the connections," Shawn throws out the shade as he touches his roughed-up arm.

"Fuck you, man, I earned my spot."

"He kind of did. We need his skills," my friend says, supporting me.

Shawn looks between us, completely unamused.

"Don't say anything about my wife, and then we won't have any future problems," I suggest.

"Fine. But you realize I could say she's standing over there in a turtleneck and you would lose it. You are so fucking whipped it's unbelievable. You better get it together before next season or I will have no problem highlighting to the press about your Vegas accident, considering they are all shipping your romance as if it was years in the making."

"Go ahead. We'll be the proof that you're lying, you'll see," I promise.

Right on cue, there is a knock on the door and Hadley peeks in. "Sorry to interrupt, I came to check on my husband."

Hearing her say husband, meaning me, is good. I'm already used to it.

Shawn shakes his head and stands. "You know, it doesn't matter if you have a ring on her finger, you would have ended up in the penalty box for her even before." He walks out, giving Hadley a fake smile.

"He might have a point," Briggs adds before he too leaves.

Hadley patiently waits for them to exit before closing the door behind her. She approaches me with caution, reaching out and debating if she should touch my shoulder when I stand.

"You ended up in the penalty box during a charity game for puppies," she states the obvious, with underlying amusement in her tone. "Was it because…"

I peer down at her as I adjust the ice pack, but she takes over with her hands and holds it just right. "Doesn't matter."

"Kind of does. Besides, Briggs already texted Isla about why you went berserk out there, so I know."

I shake my head gently. Of course he did. "Siblings."

"Want to know a secret that I really hate to admit?" She moves so she is squared off with me, our middles flush and her voice raspy.

I'm fully invested to discover her secrets. "Go on."

"I don't condone violence in any shape or form… but knowing you were maybe defending my honor slightly, then well..." She kisses my cheek. Who does that? The woman who knows any touch can send a man spiraling, that's who. "It's kind of hot," her voice husks.

"Oh yeah?" My voice is mixed with desire, because her saying that motivates both my heart and cock.

I should kiss her, but her eyes twinkle in a way they did the other night, with adventure and chance glazing her eyes. I should let her lead this moment.

"I'm being cautious," she states softly, with vulnerability seeping into her voice.

"As in?"

A slow delicious smirk begins to stretch on her mouth. "The husband-and-wife thing. We can try and see where it goes. The whole letting down our walls as if we actually enjoy one another part. I'm just not jumping fully in without hesitation, but okay, might as well make it bearable between us."

I give up on the ice pack as it falls to the floor. "What are your conditions?" I grin because she wouldn't make it this easy, and she shouldn't, considering our history. I bring my hand to the back of her neck so I'm in position to slam my lips down on hers after she answers.

She steps forward and rises on her toes, drawing me in, bringing our mouths closer. I feel her breath, and it encourages me to brush my lips along her cheek.

"We might have consummated the marriage, and we might be sharing a bed." Her sultry tone is a killer. "I might go to bed every night in next to nothing." The image sounds like heaven. She's reeling me in, and my thumb blots her bottom lip.

I swallow. "Uh-huh."

"But Connor, no entanglements until you work for it. Woo the hell out of me. Show me why the women peg you as their romance hockey guy. Until further notice, you get nada except a kiss."

My stomach sinks. She's brutal. Vicious. And fine, I'll do it because I want to see where we'll go.

I groan a sound. "Fine."

"Fine?" She doubts me.

"Yeah, fine. Are spankings off the table?" I tease her.

She hums. "I guess one or two would be fine." She flashes her eyes at me. "Now kiss me."

I slam my mouth onto hers and ensure that it's firm, deep, and long. Inescapable is what I'm aiming for.

I love when she kisses me back. It only reconfirms that I'm not delusional, and maybe I'm right. I might have pushed her away over the years, but she always wanted to be mine, even if she couldn't admit it.

Reluctantly pulling away, I enjoy how her arms hang around my neck. "You're going to go all out at bedtime, aren't you?"

"You mean wear your jersey and nothing else? Absolutely." Her saccharine tone is already misery. Her chin tips down, and I know she's looking at my hard cock. "Oops. Poor guy." She fakes concern with that gorgeous grin of hers.

"We so need to adopt a therapy dog now. My dick is going to be so turned on by you constantly that I fear I may go blind since he has to wait."

Her head falls back in laughter, and it is music to my ears.

Hadley unhooks from around me, and all I can do is admire her, as I feel it in my bones that this has to be our time.

She glances over her shoulder on her way out the door. "I'll give you a second and meet you out by the dogs."

"How giving of you." I roll my eyes.

A few minutes later and I find her by the same Labrador mix that I held earlier. Before I get a chance to tease her that she's attached, the woman in her thirties who volunteers notices me.

"I was just telling your wife about Ace. He's one of our older dogs. Only four, but too old for most. He's up to date on his shots and he is chipped. He was abandoned in an apartment a few towns over."

Hadley's face turns sad and my own heart tugs. "That's horrible. We also had a dog growing up that my mom adopted when he was older." Hadley pets Ace's head, with his eyes sullen.

I swipe a hand through my hair then pull at the back, struggling to walk us away. "I-I mean, surely, he could…"

Hadley shoots me a hard stare. "Don't. You travel during game season."

I shrug. "You wouldn't be alone if we got a dog."

Her eyes bug out. "Dogs are as big a commitment as marriage." She ensures only I can see that her eyes flash, indicating that we're already in new territory; why bring another into life to it?

"You're right," I calmly voice.

Her eyes bounce between the dog and me. "Maybe my mom and dad would be interested. They are surely ready to get another dog, my brother wants one."

Ace wags his tail and angles his head to the side.

"I know, buddy, you had a connection to Connor." Hadley's melting. It's made worse when his eyes travel to me.

"Boy, he likes you two," the volunteer states the obvious.

My voice cracks because I'm caving at high speed.

"No." Hadley pinches the bridge of her nose. "I'm supposed to use the wife card." She winces as she says that.

The volunteer pipes in. "If it helps, you wouldn't be able to take him home today. We have a required waiting period to ensure that new owners think through their decision. During the waiting period, he is on reserve. But he also has to finish his basic training that all our dogs take part in before adoption, and that doesn't end for a few weeks."

Hadley's eyes shoot to me with hope, but she doesn't want to admit it.

A dog wasn't really on my radar, but this guy is calling to us with his wagging tail and pleading eyes. Maybe Hadley's right, her parents are better suited.

"Come on, we should go." It pains me to say it.

She nods, and we begin to say goodbye to the dog, but he stands on his back legs and rests his front paws on the pen.

Hadley and I look at one another, and in unison we blurt out, "Maybe."

"I MEAN, even if we don't work out, we can share custody. During the hockey season, I'll take care of him." Hadley speaks while she's in the bathroom, with the door ajar to the bedroom as she does her nightly routine, which I noticed a few days ago requires a lot of creams.

I scoff as I scroll through my phone in bed, shirtless. "If we don't work out. Thanks for the vote of confidence," I call out.

She emerges through the door, turning the light off to the bathroom. I drop my face into my hand because this isn't fair.

Hadley is wearing an old cut-off Lake Spark Summer Festival shirt and panties, and the best part is that she doesn't even make a big deal about it.

"Well, we can't get Ace for a while, so maybe we will come to our senses," she mentions as she crawls into bed.

"I feel like I'm betraying Puck." I'm completely serious. He's the family dog, although he has a special kinship with my dad.

She smiles at me as she fluffs her pillow. "By the way, I was kind of curious what that hockey wife said, so I checked my email and realized like three different coordinators from your team e-mailed me. Welcome emails, protocols, schedules, and they need a copy of my passport."

"Yeah, probably for booking travel. Remember, I travel to that great country to the north for games," I explain.

"You mean during game season, which is *after* the off-season." The way she says that has me worried, and I turn my body to her.

"I thought we no longer have a timeline." I narrow my eyes at her.

She slithers lower into the bed to get comfortable. "I said I'm being cautious and let's see what happens if we make somewhat of an effort," she corrects me.

"Well, I'm not worried."

Hadley rolls to lie on her side. "I noticed. We are heading into dog-parent territory."

I follow her indication and get into the same position in bed, facing her. "You're in the lead here. Nothing beyond kissing, *except* you didn't specify where." I squint one eye.

She playfully shoves my arm, and I grimace from slight discomfort. "Shit. Forgot about your shoulder and defending my honor."

"You said it was hot."

"It was." She hooks her leg over my hip and begins to stroke her fingers gently over my biceps. "You for sure earned cuddle time."

I snort a laugh. "If that's the only thing on offer then get closer, Sprinkles."

Hadley shimmies nearer until our bodies meet, and she guides my arm over her. "Shh, don't make a big deal that I've traded in ripping your throat out for cuddling."

"It'll be our secret. I have good arms for this, though."

"I remember." Her words hit me because I know she means all those years ago when we had a special night—up until the point I initiated our war.

My lips twitch. "It's a different time now," I promise softly and kiss the top of her head.

I'll woo her like she requested and win, but I would just throw her over my shoulder kicking anyhow, because I have no plans of letting her go again. Our marriage may have been an accident, but divorce won't be in our cards.

15

HADLEY

I count the number of bee-print leotards in the box that was just delivered. This has been my day today. Sitting on my knees, checking on all the costumes that came in for the upcoming summer show, after my doctor's appointment for my annual checkup this morning. Slamming my pen down after I cross off my list, I glance to Isla who writes down a number on her list, as I roped her in somehow since she was working from home this afternoon.

"I think everything is here," I confirm.

"Cool." Isla swings her feet to enable her to sit cross-legged on the floor, and she takes a sip from her water bottle. "Did I tell you that Ford said he is sending me to a conference later in the year down in Florida? It's especially for organizing sporting events, it should be good."

"Sounds awesome. If it's near a beach, then I might just tag along."

"Tampa or nearby, I forget the exact location. Perfect for my bikini that I intend to pack. I actually checked the schedule, and I think the Spinners have an away game there the same week. Assuming you're still in your wife glory, then you should totally come."

A line stretches on my closed mouth at the way she said that. "Assuming?"

Isla flicks her hair behind her shoulder and smiles. "What's going on with hubby? Don't blame the canines, you two were completely easy and in your own bliss the other week. Thank you too for giving the marketing department enough material to break the internet."

I begin to pull my hair up into a bun as I recall how Connor and I are falling into a routine. He makes me my breakfast smoothie, we check in during the day, we laugh over late dinners, and go to bed not to sleep. "It's nothing. The hockey game was fun, minus Connor ending up in timeout like a toddler. You did a great job organizing it. We might even adopt one of the dogs or convince my parents to."

Isla begins to fan herself. "Oh my, if you adopt a dog together, this would absolutely blow up our socials. That's me being 'trying to advance my career' Isla. Your best friend has to point out the obvious…" She trails off, and I look at her, entertained and waiting. "You are totally committing to making this work between you and Connor. What in the world changed?"

I slide a box to the side. "It's more… I don't know. I owe it to myself to try and make it work since we're married. But something my dad said made wheels in my head turn toward where we all deserve a second chance, and maybe my brain got fried when we kind of, you know, the other day."

Her entire face blazes with so much interest. "What now then?"

"He has to prove to me that I won't get hurt. I'm not jumping full swing in, I'm dipping my toes in a little bit first," I attempt to justify. My feelings are there, but I've built a barrier.

Standing up, I pretend to wipe dirt off my legs, as I'm satisfied that I got through the boxes and can start handing them off to the dancers in the coming days.

"As long as you believe you are making the right move. I mean, despite watching you two over the years nearly murder each other, I don't think Connor would ever let anything happen to you, not then or now."

My jaw goes slack, and I touch my cheek as I listen to her state the obvious, what everyone, including myself, has always known. "Anyhow, we're married and kind of living together, so I might as well see him give his best shot."

"What is his version of best shot when it isn't hockey?" she wonders.

My face screws. "No clue, but he texted me earlier that I need to be ready soon, which is fine, as I'm letting one of the teenagers take on more responsibilities with teaching."

"What's the dress code?"

My shoulders bounce. "He didn't say. I'm sure in his mind less is better, zips are preferred, and my purse should be able to fit handcuffs."

"I dunno, is there also room for the blindfold?" Connor's voice takes over the atmosphere from where he's standing behind me. Is it possible to already see his smug smirk? I'm positive he has one.

Isla attempts to hide her smile. "That's my cue to leave."

We both stand and she walks by me while I remain frozen, not because I'm mortified—I'm not. It's because a flutter travels through me, and my heart thrums from excitement that Connor has plans for me.

I give Isla a nod in acknowledgment before I spin on my feet to face Connor who is leaning against the doorframe as if he owns the place, and his mouth confirms the image that I had in my head.

"I'm sure you'll keep her in line." Isla snorts a laugh when she walks past Connor, leaving us alone.

"You're early," I say, attempting to steady my voice.

He does that move I like, where his eyes dip low, then he bashfully glances up with a suave grin. "I don't know the rules around kidnapping since we're married. Is that kidnapping then? Anyway, there has been a change of plans."

"Oh?"

His hand that was resting behind his back comes up, and I chuckle instantly because a blindfold is dangling from his finger.

"What can I say? You know me so well," he explains.

Now I'm anticipating what he is up to.

I'm kind of disappointed that Connor hasn't used the blindfold yet. Not exactly thrilled that I didn't get a chance for a shower either, but he insisted I was fine in jeans and a t-shirt.

We're driving along the winding road around the lake, and we are not heading in the direction of the house. He has "Follow You" by Beyond the Horizon on his speakers, and I could see him training to this.

I attempt to meander my gaze to the backseat, but immediately, he tsks me. "Eyes forward," he demands as he focuses on the road. "Or you get the blindfold early."

My fingers tap on my thighs. "I have no clues to work with."

"That's the point of a surprise."

I scoff as I lean against the window of the car. "Haven't we had enough surprises lately?"

A grin tugs on his lips. "This one is planned."

"Give me something to work with."

"I can tell you what we're *not* doing." He glances sideways toward me then back to the road.

I give him an unimpressed look. "Helpful." Nothing is further from the truth, but I'm curious. "Go on."

That confident look plays on the corner of his mouth again. "Well, no Dizzy Duck Inn, because that's your parents' and my aunt and uncle's spot, for reasons I don't particularly want to know." I smile because he is so right. "The lagoon is like sacred territory for my own parents, so I can never take anyone there," he adds.

My smile vanishes, and he notices. "Uh, I mean, not that there are a lot of anyones, just… yeah, can't save myself there." He gives a pained expression before he tilts his head. "I thought about taking you to the city, looked for tickets to the Joffrey Ballet, but they're not in season in the summer, except for a public show in Millennial Park, plus we don't get much privacy in the city."

My eyes nearly bug out because he put thought into it, and I'm surprised he even knows where to look for ballet tickets; surely, he must have an assistant who helps him. "So, where does that leave us?" I ask.

"Back to our own place."

We drive a few minutes more, and he parks off the road next to the woods. I'm fairly confident that we shouldn't be here, but Connor isn't one for rules.

He indicates for me to wait a second when he turns the engine off, and I patiently stay seated until he circles the car to open the door.

Connor holds up the blindfold with a cheeky smile. "It's

time."

I can't even attempt to give him a scowl because the stirring emotions are running wild inside of me, as there is significance here. It's been a hot minute—okay, months—since I was on a date with anyone, and what woman wouldn't be in good spirits when her husband tries to surprise her? I'm not immune, even I know that.

My hand molds into his palm and I stand, turning on my heel to allow him to wrap the black fabric around my eyes. Connor knows how to tighten a knot, and my brain instantly registers that fact with heat swirling inside of me.

"I didn't blindfold you on the road because that's pure hell on the turns, but you won't be this way for long, although we can keep this blindfold for other activities later tonight if you want," he casually mentions, and I feel him step away and hear the hatch of his car open.

"Wishful thinking," I call out.

He returns, and next thing I know he is guiding me. The ground feels uneven and rough, and occasionally I feel long grass against my ankles or I step on a large pebble.

"I have an inkling where we are, but really, where the hell are we? Don't we need to worry about, I don't know, foxes or raccoons? The old lady from the grocery store mentioned the coyotes in the area are getting bold," I list.

Connor just chuckles as he helps me step up a rock. "Isn't that what you want? You can feed me to the foxes."

"That was before we got drunk and reckless. You might be growing on me a smidgen since then."

"I think I'm growing on you a full nine inches," he retorts.

I giggle, and without notice, he hoists me up and throws me over one shoulder. I can feel he is carrying something in his other arm. Damn, I love his arm strength.

It's a few steps, then he twirls me around for effect before plopping me down on a spot. I can feel him step away for a few seconds, and I wait, noticing the somersault in my belly and the way my pulse has changed in the last few minutes; it's eagerness.

His fingers feel like feathers, yet they leave a gentle imprint on my shoulders as he half turns me in one direction before his digits sneak under the cloth to untie my blindfold. "Open your eyes, Sprinkles," he whispers as the fabric falls.

It only takes the flick of my eyes opening and two blinks for me to be awestruck. I'm overwhelmed about where to look because there is the backdrop of the lake and woodlands below since we seem to be up on a hill, and right here in front of me where Connor must have been earlier because there's a blanket and a few lanterns. I notice the box that keeps food warm and realize that must have been in the back of his car the whole time.

"Oh." It softly escapes my lips before I turn my head to find that Connor has been watching me this whole time, with his foot on a log and face stoic.

"Uh." He shyly strokes his jawline with his thumb. "Doesn't this place seem familiar? Although, last time we might have stayed in my car."

Looking around, I *knew* this place was familiar. I know why too. A profoundness hits me, and I do my best to keep it in by biting the inside of my lip. "You mean, do I remember being here at night with you once?" In truth, this brings up mixed emotions, and I'm not entirely sure if this is the place for us to be.

A fondness hits him, and his head tilts low while his eyes perk up. "Yeah." His voice is soft. It seems he chose this place for a reason.

A silence floats between us because we don't need many

words in relation to the significance of this place. It was a beautiful night, but it started our years of hate too. I glance around again at the view. I think I'll choose to remember the good, which is why I turn back to him with a small half-smile.

"I haven't even pulled out the big guns yet," he says.

I cross my arms. "Oh yeah? What might that be?"

He indicates with his head to go sit on the blanket, and I easily follow instruction.

He is busy grabbing items from the food box. "We're not really supposed to light anything that burns here, but I'm sure the forest ranger will let me off when I get him season tickets."

I can't even tell if he's joking. My eyes trail down to see he is holding a small tinfoil-wrapped casserole dish, and it looks familiar, the writing on the top anyways. "What is that?"

"My gamechanger for tonight."

"Leave it to you to think food can sway me."

Connor takes a seat next to me, with our elbows grazing, and he hands me the box. "You're mom's famous mac 'n' cheese."

"Really?" I'm completely thrown off because it's such an original and sweet gesture.

He nods, with his subtle smirk permanent, because he's satisfied with my facial expressions. "I know how much you love that stuff, and since you're not living at home anymore, I figured you might miss it. I asked for her help for dinner, and yeah, the squeal and aws nearly burst my eardrums."

My cheeks hurt from how much I'm smiling. I can picture it all in my head. "I bet. She probably went overboard too."

"Oh, she did," he confirms. "We also have zucchini

pancakes. There is no logic to the menu other than she said they were your favorites."

It's thoughtful that he reached out to her.

A silence takes over as our eyes catch and silly looks grace our faces. I decide to pipe up and admit the truth. "You might get points for how this night is starting."

"Does that hurt? Giving me a compliment?" He nudges my shoulder with his.

I touch my arm, then my stomach, followed by my legs. "Everything seems to be okay."

"That sucks, I was kind of hoping you needed me to tend to your wounds."

Reaching out, I hook a finger under his chin to bring his mouth in my direction. Our foreheads touch and our eyes connect. I could kiss him, but I enjoy keeping him captivated like this. He's partly in suspense if I'll bring my lips to his or if this location is a good idea at all.

Dance has been the passion of my life. The best dance, however, is the one where Connor and my lips trace and brush one another's, with our breathing entwined, while our noses nuzzle the lines of our cheeks. The most unchoreographed dance is my favorite, and that's him.

"You're making it hard, Connor Spears," I rasp. "I'm supposed to make you work *really* hard."

"Well, Hadley *Spears*, sometimes a clear shot appears, and you take it." He returns my tone.

I'll let him off on the hockey reference because the sport is part of the blueprint of who he is, and I don't mind. I kiss the corner of his mouth, nothing too sensual; it would be respectable enough for my grandparents, but it drives this man crazy.

Giving us some space, I retreat and decide to get our conversation moving and enjoy this picnic that is in a prime location for the upcoming sunset to the west. "You'll always play for the Spinners?"

He shrugs before he reaches to the side for a bottle of wine. "My contract is actually for one more year. I'm an unrestricted free agent which means next year it's about the right contract and whichever team offers it. I would like to stay with the Spinners, but I'm not sure my prospects are great. Nobody here wants me to be captain considering my family connection to the team. Careerwise, it will be better if I find a new team."

Oh, away from Lake Spark.

I touch his shoulder to comfort him while he works on the bottle, because he has talent, and it would be a loss if people thought only of potential bias. "I can see that… uhm… I guess your wife would follow you where your team would be?" I never thought about that, and I'm not questioning why I seem invested in the topic, but then again, a timeline kind of vanished somewhere in my head.

His fingers still on the bottle mid-pour. "I would hope so. Then again, I travel for more than half the games. Hockey is a lot more grueling on the schedule than other sports."

"Yet you want a dog," I state the obvious.

"Between our families, I'm confident he would have plenty of places to stay and be happy, even if I'm away. It's better than living at the shelter."

"You really want him, huh?" I have to gush because Connor is like a kid waiting for Santa, and it's all for the sake of saving a cute dog. Some people would call that being a man of character or having a heart of gold, and in this case, it's all true.

He gives me a pointed look. "Even if you want me crucified, I know you would take care of him."

"Kind of correct. I'm used to hectic families, with pets included."

Connor hands me a glass of red wine. "It's kind of cool."

I nod. "Considering I don't have many cousins, then yes, I'm lucky that our little family provided the full effect. Twins run in my father's side, but he lost his twin brother young. My mom was an only child, though."

He pauses for a second and looks at me with interest. "Twins? So, we're having like ten kids." He looks into his glass of wine, nearly somber.

"Whoa, relax, twins means two, not ten, and I'm still years away from wanting to swell my ankles to push out a baby or three. But anyway, I guess you and I are family people. Didn't Violet make you godfather to her daughter?"

His brows bounce. "I'm sure she and Declan argued over that one, but yeah, I'm Willow's godfather. Happy to be the stellar influence she needs." He isn't afraid to put himself in a different light if it means humor.

Connor's soft smile returns. "We have something else in common." He holds out his glass for a toast. "We now have the same last name, and I think it's the next best thing to a leash for keeping you tied to me and in line."

I chortle yet clink our glasses. Possession is completely a turn-on for me, and I have no problem admitting that, which is why it's worthy of a toast. The sweltering in his sentence creates an ache between my thighs too.

Leaning my head against his shoulder, I interlace our arms and let a relaxing breath escape while we look forward at the horizon.

I'm beginning to wonder if our whole situation may actually be luck on our side. Because right now, he feels like the Connor that I kept locked in my dreams, but this time, I open my eyes and he's still there.

16

CONNOR

She's easing into me, tearing off a few layers, and right now I feel like I'm being the man I should have always been to her.

I'm following her lead, but I would kill to lay her down right now, but that's not what tonight is about. Tonight is a sort of truce to move on, with the possibilities endless.

The thing is, I've always been the guy who can be charming when dating someone, but tonight is confronting that maybe I've always done it for show, because with Hadley, it's very different. My entire body comes alive, and I truly mean every romantic gesture that I'm making.

We eat dinner, and it must be true that food brings comfort. It dawned on me earlier that even though Hadley is a grown woman, our situation kind of called for an impromptu move in a flash. She doesn't seem to mind, but still, I wanted to do something for her to remind her of her old home.

With the sun setting, the orange hue fades, revealing a starry sky. The lanterns were a nice touch if I do say so myself.

Lying down on the blanket, we look at the sky with hopes

of finding a shooting star. She gently jabs her finger into my hand, and I can tell she is testing the waters for me to weave our hands together. I follow her cues and slip her fingers through mine.

"Maybe we're idiots and should get out of Lake Spark. See the world. Or maybe that's why we do stupid things, we were out of our habitat," she muses with humor mixed in her tone.

I chuckle and sling her leg over mine. "Speak for yourself. I'm on the road half the year, although mostly I don't see much. Besides, nobody bothers us here except our parents." I'm happy she asked about my career earlier. My schedule isn't for the faint of heart, though she doesn't seem deterred. Then again, I'm not sure what timeline for us exists in her head.

She sighs but it seems peaceful. "Do you think having memories together from our younger selves is a curse? Like, it's hard to differentiate between adult us and younger us?"

"I fucking hope not. I promise, I look at you and only think about those tiny tattoos on your skin that I can explore before my tongue runs up to your pussy." Fuck, I'm supposed to keep us above board, not get us sidetracked.

"Is that where your mind is at?" she teases.

I huff out a breath and flip us to ensure she is under me. "Yes and no. You are a feisty woman who I kind of admire, who can dish out what she takes and isn't afraid to knock me down a peg or two."

"I'm only feisty when it's you."

"I noticed. I'm only pulling out ridiculous moves in the romance department when it's with you, so congrats, we bring out the best in one another," I promise.

Her body writhes under me, and my cock instantly reminds me that he's alive and waiting. "Even though we get two timelines," she says, "I have one little fantasy years in the making that you kind of need to make come true."

"What might that be?" I play along.

She reaches out to claw her fingers into my shirt. "Kiss me under the stars again, just like last time we were here."

I pretend to debate her request, but then I'm lowering my mouth, happy to oblige. Kissing her is an addiction. It doesn't matter if she's in a foul or pleasant mood, I want her mouth both on mine and wrapped around me. I want my name to escape her lips as she pleads, and her mouth should always look like I've ruined her in the best possible way.

I groan as she runs the tip of her tongue along mine, and she pulls her body up, pressing her breasts against my chest. It can never be just a simple kiss with her, Hadley must know that.

"Let me make you come." I scrape my teeth gently below her ear because it always makes her shiver from the tickle of my short scruff.

A chuckle rumbles in the back of her throat, but it only makes her neck elongate, and she's offering me more opportunity to trail my mouth on her body.

"You seem very eager," she hums.

No shit. I'm scolding myself that I'm not better behaved.

I slip my hand between our bodies to enable my fingers to search for the zipper of her jeans. "Hadley, whether we were arguing or perfectly content with each other, making you come is the best way to leave you speechless."

She isn't stopping me, and my fingers dip into her damp and warm panties, and I rumble a sound when my fingers get drenched in her arousal. I'm already going dizzy from the thought of my tongue enjoying every drop of her.

"We're in the middle of nowhere, and I swear I just heard an owl or some wild creature," she observes.

I continue to stroke her, feeling her tremble under my touch. "I'm the fucking wild creature, so let me have my way." My voice is filled with reverence.

"Are you about to have a hissy fit?" Hadley has the audacity to taunt me right now.

My response is to spear a digit inside of her that instantly causes her breath to halt and her internal walls to wind tightly around my finger. "Depends, do I get to have you coming all over my hand?"

She struggles to form words as I slip my thumb between us to ensure her clit continues to receive the attention it deserves. Her breath hitches again, and her mouth parts open as her body responds to my touch.

"I guess it's the least I can let you do since you did arrange a romantic picnic under the stars. You're such a softie when it comes to dating."

"Whoa, you have the audacity to tease me right now? I'm by no means soft." I'll show her.

In a flash, I yank down her jeans and panties until they're stuck around one of her ankles, then knock her knees to part to give me a canvas because I'm on my stomach in no time, with my arms hooked under her thighs. My mouth covers her pussy, my tongue flicking her clit before drawing circles. I could get high just from the taste of her. I'm trying to ignore how hard I am, but it just makes me determined.

"Connor," she bellows out, her fingers clawing my hair.

Briefly, I glance up. "You will come all over my tongue and you will not look away while I do it."

Her eyes drop to watch me. "Fine, yes, don't stop," she nearly slurs before another moan escapes her.

My fingers dig into her thighs while I keep her splayed open, and I continue to lick her senseless. I could spend hours feasting on her and I wouldn't get bored.

"Remind me who this pussy belongs to," I murmur as I grasp for air.

"Someone who managed to get a ring on my finger." Her voice strains as she pieces a sentence together.

I still my tongue on her pussy before retreating my head back.

Hadley giggles, and with her face flushed and highlighted from the lanterns, I'm only wanting to devour her even more.

"Say my name," I grit out in demand because I hate leaving her pussy unsatisfied.

She touches herself with her finger and my eyes have a full view of Hadley playing and ensuring I watch. Her finger swirls where my tongue just was. "Hmm… I think my pussy *might* belong to this guy I kind of woke up with."

"Hadley," I snarl with an uncontrollable grin.

"Connor," she says matter-of-factly. "In this moment, my pussy is all *yours*."

"It always was."

Her hips buckle from the work of her finger. "Debatable."

I shake my head and growl before I push her hand away and continue on my quest. I don't ease her into her oncoming orgasm; I lick that spot and repeat over and over until she's convulsing on my mouth. I don't stop even when she's shaking. I continue to lick her relentlessly as her body pulses and she curses my name. Only when I feel her weaken do I finally move back to enjoy the view of her body completely spent, with a drowsy smile curling on her lips. I help slide her pants back up before I dip my mouth down to kiss her, knowing she's tasting herself on my lips.

Ignoring my dick that wants to break free against the fabric of my jeans, I take the high road. "Should we swing by Jolly Joe's for a sundae on the way home?" I pretend the last few minutes didn't happen, just to rile her.

"Was I not your dessert?" She throws on a pout for effect.

"Not even close. I need you swallowing me, before you insist I come inside of you so you can watch my come drip down your thighs, then you take your finger and swipe it up into your mouth while I watch you suck it all off. That's dessert."

Her jaw drops open, and her eyes grow into saucers. She has no clue the dirty thoughts I harbor for her.

Reaching to my side, I pick up my wine and take a sip before getting cozy on the blanket and welcoming her back in my arms, because I'm a fucking gentleman.

―――

WALKING BACK INTO THE HOUSE, I don't understand why Hadley is so quiet. We laughed some more while we looked at the stars and talked about wanting to visit Iceland or Norway. By the time it was midnight, we realized that ice cream wouldn't be in our cards and instead drove home on the dark roads with good music playing in the car.

Maybe I should have been concerned that she didn't say much in the car, but a permanent half-smile was glued to her face when she occasionally glanced my way.

But as we walk into our bedroom, she seems stressed.

She pivots to face me and points a finger to confront me. "I detest you!"

What the fuck is this turnaround?

"No, you don't, but enlighten me. What have I done now?" I scratch my cheek and remain calm, ignoring the whiplash that I should be experiencing.

"You were romantic and giving and everything I shouldn't enjoy." She seems angrier with herself than anything.

My lips quirk out as I step closer to stand off with her; we're good at this. "That's a bad thing?"

"Yes! I shouldn't let you have it so easy," she nearly squeals.

I take hold of her wrists by wrapping my hands around them. "Are you making it easy? Because we have two very different interpretations."

The spark in her eyes is beautiful and promising.

"You should have to work harder, but…" Her lips roll in, and she appears frustrated, yet her demeanor is folding.

I raise a brow because victory is mine. "Uh-oh, was someone affected by my date planning?"

She rolls her eyes to the side. "You do not get to win."

Releasing a wrist, I snake my arm around her waist to pull her flush to me. "Right, someone wanted me to make them swoon and go slow."

"I never said slow," she corrects me. "Be an asshole right now. Don't be the guy that I kind of really want to pounce on, nor do I want to wait," she bites out.

Leaning in to whisper with purpose, I notice goosebumps form on her skin. "Babe, you know we can always fuck angry. But my money is on that you want me to fuck you like we matter, because we do."

She attempts to push me, but my hands are quick to cup her head while her eyes lock with mine, the twinkle not fading but now mixed with recognition. Her frown disperses into history and the corner of her mouth tugs.

"Do we matter?" She's breathless from my simple yet true statement.

"Yeah," I answer softly.

We stand there, nobody making a move because we're waiting for her internal debate to end. It doesn't take long before she jumps onto me with our mouths sewing together.

It's a bolt of lightning that causes me to stumble back a step or two.

"It's not fair." She speaks against my lips, as neither one of us wants to part. "I crumble around you in no time."

I carry her a few more steps before I toss her onto the bed, and I peel off my t-shirt. "Welcome to the club."

I'm over her with my hands running wild all over her body, letting her work her clothes off because she'll do it faster.

When she's down to her bra, she leans up while I dip my mouth down to capture her in another kiss. Hadley is busy yanking her panties off, and I reach behind to unclasp her bra. I love her naked, but it's distracting, and right now, I just want to plunge right into her.

Luckily, we are two minds alike, and she wraps her legs around my waist to help gravity pull me to her faster. I brace myself over her and bring the tip of my cock to glide around the proof that I make her crazy. She moans when the head of my cock rubs friction against her sensitive spot, and I groan from the fact she's soaking.

Our mouths fuse at the same time as I align myself and enter, sinking into her and feeling instant relief because she's tight, warm, mine, and if I have it my way, nobody else will ever touch her again.

I pump in and out, slamming back in until I'm balls deep, and a sharp moan escapes her lips.

"Shit, did I hurt you?" I study her face with concern in my voice.

A playful dazed look appears on her mouth. "The contrary. It's okay, you can go hard. I just need you inside of me."

I place a gentle kiss on the corner of her mouth and skim my lips down her neck before I continue my thrusts that have me feeling like I'm incapable of breathing unless I get to come inside of her.

Her skin feels searing under my touch, and I'm tumbling toward a release too damn fast. Her hands come to gently hold each of my cheeks while our eyes lock, and I'm deep, with nowhere else to go. She tightens her legs around me to hold me in and clenches her walls. Everything magnifies in intensity when the corner of my eye catches the sight of her wedding ring on her finger, and it makes me go feral.

I'm so far gone that it feels like an explosion when we finally get there together.

It takes a solid minute or two before I'm even capable of rolling off her, only to drag her with me because we are sweaty, our breathing rapid, and I want her head resting on my chest with my fingers combing through the strands of her hair.

Instantly, her fingertips begin to draw lazy patterns along my pec, even though our hearts are racing.

Hadley purrs a sound against my chest that vibrates against my heart, especially when it turns into a drawl of low laughter.

I squeeze her closer. "Yes?"

I notice her looking at her wedding ring. "Nothing. I'm just… content, I guess. Didn't think that was possible with you."

I contemplate what might be going on in her head, and I narrow it down to our first bad experience. I once laid with her and promised that we could see one another again, I would find a way to make it work I said, only to backtrack hours later for reasons she can't know. I shake that memory out of my head, ignoring the consequences of that night, and choose to focus on the present.

Kissing the top of her hair, I inhale the scent of fresh

lake air mixed with sex. "I'm actually quite enjoyable when you break a wall down or two." She makes a sound and stays molded to me in a perfect fit. "But seriously, you don't, what was it… detest me?" I tickle my fingers along her arms.

"Ha-ha," she mocks mundanely. "I'm getting used to this. Us being like this. It feels very natural, yet kind of… exhilarating."

"That's a positive," I point out.

"I realize that." She peers up to greet me with a unique wonder, and I respond by giving her a quick kiss.

"You're beautiful, you know that?" I whisper right before I steal one more kiss.

She makes a funny face because she goes nearly shy. "Don't throw classic lines at me."

"I wouldn't dare. I'm just giving you the truth."

Hadley buries her face against my chest before planting a quick kiss against my skin. "Tell me something that's true and I don't know."

I think for a few seconds. "Even with no Vegas, we eventually would have found our way to one another."

A sound of doubt escapes her lips. "Why are you certain?"

"Because that's just the kind of chemistry we have. We're right for one another in love or hate, and I'm not sure the barrier between us was never going to be long enough to keep me away forever." I speak to myself more than her, maybe she notices.

"I think we need sleep. You make it sound like I wanted to keep you away, but it wasn't always like that, and in this very moment, I want you as close as possible." She snuggles against me, letting out a relaxing sigh, and even though I can't see, I know her eyes are gently closing.

I stroke her hair and stare at the ceiling, with my thoughts running rampant.

I always knew one of us would have caved at some point, even though I had my own private vow when it concerned her, she just doesn't know. Now, a knot twists in the pit of my stomach that we'll be okay because she is taking a step with me, and I broke my internal vow.

17

CONNOR

The way Hadley's lips twist when she's watching videos of my old hockey games is spellbinding. Games where I lost my cool seem to be her favorite. Nah, who am I kidding, it's me in my pre-game suit that she loves the most. A sort of smirk tilts on her lips, as if it's typical of me, yet she finds it irresistible. The best part is that she has no idea that I've caught her yet again watching in what she thinks is secret.

She sits on the couch in the living room with her knees tucked under and ear pods in while she holds her phone screen.

Here comes my favorite part.

Walking on my toes, I sneak up behind her and reach over the back of the sofa to shake her shoulders. Instantly, she shrieks and brings her hand to touch my arm that's wrapping around her as I playfully bite her cheek.

"Connor," she squeals my name.

I hop over the back of the couch because I'm smooth like that and land next to her on the cushions, only to encourage her to swing her legs over to rest on my lap.

"This is classic. My very own superfan, and it's none other than you," I note.

She pinches my arm. "Simmer down that ego, I'm just… curious."

"It's not a little bit that you're wondering why everyone is obsessed with our team? Or maybe you love that interview I did with a nine-year-old which melted the hearts of many." I bring a hand to my chest.

She rolls her eyes. "I never realized that *perhaps* you play kind of a cool sport, plus once you watch one video, then the app's algorithm sends you down a rabbit hole of more videos." It's cute the way she tries to play this down.

The last few days we have talked about aspects of our careers that we probably didn't realize. We went off track when I caught her glancing at photos of me in a suit when traveling between games; her bottom lip always gets attacked when she stares at those photos.

I stroke her thigh with my hand as we just relax together on the sofa. "The guys will be here any second, then I'll start the grill." The goal is to hang out, but I'm sure we'll end up re-watching a few games from last season.

"Cool. I'll stay for a drink then leave you guys be." She gently combs the hair behind my ear, a soothing touch that I love.

"We have cake at least. Our moms dropped off a box when I was in the shower and you were at the store." I flash my eyes at her because I'm entertained.

She giggles. "They did a wedding cake testing without us, didn't they?"

I grin. "Just in case, plus they're getting ballsy."

"But they are happy, and they would shut it down in a heartbeat if we asked them to. I'm convinced they enjoy messing with us. *Yet*, I really want to see how far they'll go." I couldn't agree more, which is why I smile. Hadley gets more comfortable on her spot. "Which cake are we having?"

"No clue." I shrug.

Just like that, we fall into a moment. One where our eyes linger and the lines on our mouths are in a permanent tilt. This is when I enjoy gliding my thumb along her cheek that causes her eyes to flutter at me with a glittery ember glazing in her eyes. Lowering my head, I gently nip at the tip of her nose, eager to get us lost in a deep kiss.

But the sound of the doorbell causes us both to groan because we can't stay in our moment of bliss.

Struggling to get off the couch together feels good because she's here, in my house that we now share, and we just move around one another in a perfect pattern.

Apparently, we are good hostesses together too.

Hadley set the television to the right channel, while I offered beers. I worked the grill, and she tossed a salad.

"You're okay if I steal him away in a few weeks? Bachelor day and all," Briggs asks Hadley as he refills his plate with food as we put one of our late-season games on pause.

Hadley stabs another cheese cube with a toothpick to snack on. "Yeah, sure. Just don't tell me what happens on it, okay?"

"I would say relax since your dad and Ford will be there, plus your one neighbor is invited too," he explains.

"Hudson Arrows? Yeah, he's friends with my dad, and our street is small," I explain.

"Those guys are legends and know how to party if needed, so you may want to be afraid." He winks at her.

"Oh, I know, I've witnessed far too many holiday parties. By the way, what is with the hate in this room for Vaughn? I don't even need to look at the screen and I know when he's on, as you all say, '*fucking Vaughn*.'" She attempts to deepen and lower her voice.

I grab another beer from the fridge. "I get along with him, but he and Briggs don't see eye to eye. Rumor is that next season is his last down in Tampa, then he will either retire or maybe come back to us. Our current coach likes him."

"But Vaughn is past his prime. A complete douche too." Briggs crosses his arms, agitated. "That asshole got me out of the game in our playoffs. I couldn't play the last four minutes."

I slap a hand on his shoulder. "Relax, we'll worry about him next season."

One of the guys sitting in the living room calls out, letting us know they are going to press play again. Briggs grumbles his way back, and I take the opportunity to quickly check in with Hadley.

"You good?" I ask as my eyes narrow in on her, and I step close enough that I can bring an arm around her.

She checks the screen behind me then focuses on me again. "Totally. I've been sipping on Chardonnay while you guys swear at the screen every two seconds."

I laugh. "Are you tipsy?"

She tilts her head to the side in doubt. "Maybe." She leans in to pretend to whisper, "I get kind of handsy when I'm tipsy."

"Oh yeah?" I'm very interested in this side of her.

She nods and a droll sound escapes her. "Like full-on 'I'm making plans in my head for how to mount you later' handsy."

I snort a sound, as she's definitely feeling light right now. "I will gladly take part in this."

Hadley stands up on her toes and brings one leg high up

above my waist. Those dancing skills are a gift from the heavens.

"I'll leave you guys to enjoy the game. Me and my wine will be in the bathtub soaking and preparing for later." She kisses me sensually on the lips and my entire body feels aflutter with anticipation.

"Get a room," someone calls out, and I only grin more.

Hadley gives me a sultry look before she touches my chest with her fingertips in parting and walks away with an overdone sway that looks perfect on her.

I can't wait for later when I can plunge into her warm heat and see stars when I come while she screams my name.

I blow out a breath to recenter myself and turn my attention to the TV screen. Picking up my beer bottle, I walk back into the open living room to join the guys.

It's a slew of expletives and commentary right off the bat. I'm able to get into the game until my phone vibrates in my pocket. Pulling it out, I see that it's a reminder for next week.

Hadley has a summer dance show, then we're having dinner with her parents after.

I don't remember discussing this, but the joint calendar doesn't lie. It's a sacred tool for any marriage. I may be young, but I realized that quick.

The difference is that most people don't fear dinner with the in-laws the way I do. Because Spencer Crews may just be the reason that I lose it all.

18

HADLEY

Pride hits me as I watch little girls in tutus and bumblebee wings wobble back to their parents after having performed to a crowd of *awws* and *ohs*. We performed in the outside theatre here in Lake Spark for the summer festival. I somehow knew the little kids would be the ones to steal the show. The teenagers on their ballet pointe shoes performing elegantly to a *Midsummer Night's Dream* theme didn't really hold a candle to the cuteness overload of bumblebees twirling.

Still, I made sure we performed five numbers of various dance genres to please the crowd on this weekend mid-afternoon. One of my girls was sick, so I had to fill in on the dance front too. I was kind of hoping to have stayed choreographer today, because I didn't want my dance company to feel like I was stealing their thunder. I did my best to stay in the back.

A pair of hands that I've become accustomed to and that blaze excitement at every touch sneaks up around me and winds around my waist. Like always, I sink into Connor's touch. What a wild contrast to before Vegas.

"These are for you," he murmurs against my cheek before placing a respectable peck on my lips. His other hand holds out a single peach-colored rose. "Well done."

I gladly take the flower and feel my cheeks blush at the same time. Sweet Connor is, well, cute, but strangely eerie in a wonderful way. I'm not used to him this way, but it's nothing to complain about, especially when my eyes trail up to watch him lift his sunglasses off his eyes. Gosh, he is extra sexy when he's been sitting in the sun all day.

"Thank you." My eyes travel back to the rose that I twirl between my fingers. "I'm all done here. Dancers have been returned to their respective owners," I joke.

He raises a brow and a gleam that melts my panties graces his face. "Including you? I'm on board with being your respective owner."

I chuckle at his ability to send us on a train of dirty thoughts. "Easy there. My parents are somewhere around here."

"I know. I was sitting with them. We were thinking instead of going out for dinner that maybe we just pick up some takeout from Catch 22 and head to our house for dinner. Sound good?"

"Perfect. I wasn't really in the mood to sit in a restaurant all night."

He brings his arm around my shoulders, and we begin to walk side by side. "Cool. I'll call them with our order, and we can pick that up on the way back. Your parents will grab the wine."

"You bet we will," my mother announces. My parents and little brother walk toward us with bright smiles on their faces.

I'm quickly met with hugs. "You were magnificent as always out there," my dad mentions.

"So beautiful," my mother adds.

The compliments stop when I look at my brother who is busy on his phone. It only makes me smile, though. I bet this was his idea of the worst Saturday ever. Ashton is at that funny age where you're no longer a kid but hate being a teenager.

"Thanks for your kind words," I tease him.

He glances up from his screen with a scowl. "I didn't say anything."

"I know," I deadpan.

"Hey, can you help me with my biology project later? Won't take long," he requests.

I shake my head that we fly past into new subjects. "Sure," I promise.

"How about we meet in an hour or so?" Connor suggests while he studies his watch.

"Sounds good," my father agrees.

"I'll send you the alarm code in case you get there before us," Connor adds.

My eyes whip to him with an awkward look plastered on my face. "Do we really want them to have the code?" I mumble, knowing my parents can hear, and they're entertained.

My mom gives me a fake unimpressed look. "You mean so we can unexpectedly show up at random times and ruin your newlywed phase?"

"*Yeah*, I think you guys can wait a few minutes. It's lovely weather," Connor comments.

After one more round of hugs, we divide up. Connor and I are on our way to the parking lot, but he takes hold of my hand and yanks me in another direction.

"What's up?" I wonder.

"We have a few minutes to spare." He begins to tow me in the direction of the Ferris wheel, and a twinkling star inside of me travels from my heart to my stomach. "Come on. One time around."

It would be impossible to scrape the giddy look off my face, from the time he suggests his romantic scene to the moment that I'm sitting next to him in one of the cars on our way up to overlook Lake Spark.

Interlinking our arms, I cozy up close to him and rest my head against his shoulder and a deep long relaxing breath escapes me.

"Connor Spears, what am I going to do with you?" I say softly, with my words sounding floaty. Probably, because I need to pinch myself that this isn't a dream.

"I could give you a list of about a hundred options if that helps you," he offers.

I rest our connected hands on my lap and admire our wedding rings. A happy accident in the end. I was supposed to be watchful and cautious around him, but I only seem to be falling in the best possible way.

"It's not so bad… being married… to you," I state flatly, but I mean so much more.

His deep, smooth chuckle rumbles in the back of his throat. "Why thank you, I think."

We glance briefly at one another with sheepish smirks. Then our balloon that kept us at a distance bursts when he leans down to kiss me like it always matters. Soft to start, then his lips take me on a journey to being commanded. I love every second of it.

"Mmm," I hum because I feel as though I'm drowning in a pool of glitter. Inside, everything sparkles. We're being sappy, but our nights in bed are anything but.

Getting comfortable in my seat, we approach the top of the wheel and both look out ahead when the car stops. Something tells me he may have bought us a little extra time up here.

"It's hard to imagine living anywhere else," I note. Connor makes a sound but doesn't answer, and I feel his muscles tighten slightly. I realize why. "If you transfer teams in a year, then… we will figure it out." That's the best that I can say.

He kisses the top of my head affectionately. "Someone is thinking long run," he teases, but I hear the vulnerability.

"Maybe I am." It comes out faint.

"You know, the off-season is when I should be relaxing and resetting my mind and body for next season. I was *deeply* concerned when we woke up in Vegas that plan went out the window." I hear the humor drenched in his sentence. "But I think it's worked out quite all right." Now that part was just honesty, and it causes me to ensure our eyes meet and lock.

"I think so too," I agree.

We both lean in, with our foreheads touching, and I've never felt so alive.

"What kind of guy would I be if I don't kiss you at the top of a Ferris wheel overlooking the lake?" The desperation in his voice causes my cheeks to heat up.

"I don't know, you've been the guy to not kiss me before," I taunt him.

His response is to growl and bring his hand to cup my cheek, demanding my full attention. "That was another time. Tell me we're past that."

I slowly nod without hesitation that we are. It must make him happy because before I can register, his lips are on mine, and I'm certain it's his way of sealing my confirmation.

No going back.

But it doesn't cross my mind anyway.

Sitting outside at the table on the deck of the house, we all are in a filled-belly slumber. Dinner was delicious, partly because I didn't have to cook, and the bottle of wine that my mom picked out was a perfect pairing.

Now we're taking a rest before ice cream for dessert.

My eyes break away from the candle keeping mosquitos away and draw a line to my mother.

"Okay, so I've planned for a wedding dress fitting in Chicago just in case, and of course, your grandmothers and Isla could join us," my mom casually mentions.

I squint an eye, debating if she is just riling me up or if she is dead serious.

"Already married," I say one-toned.

"But don't you want a princess wedding dress?"

I look to my father for help and to simmer her down. He gets the clue and touches my mother's arm. "Relax. Tonight is just dinner, no party talk." I mouth thank you. "So, what's the plan, kiddos? For the rest of the summer before hockey season? With the summer show out of the way, you have fewer dance classes to teach."

"I just want to take it easy," I say before taking a sip of my wine.

Connor squeezes my other hand that he hasn't let go of. "We should go somewhere for vacation. I'm thinking island, tropical, cocktails, bikini—"

"That's my daughter," my father adds on the list in a stern voice.

I can't control my grin because these two together are kind of hilarious. A perfect team if they allow it.

"We'll see. Also, depends on if we adopt a dog or not," I add.

My mom holds up her hand. "I'm all for babysitting the pooch, but we're just not keen on getting a dog right now."

"I know. Besides, I could use some company when Connor is off on the road for games. Maybe a dog is exactly what we need. If he's calm enough, then he can come to the studio with me." I flash my eyes at Connor, as I'm sure that news will make him happy.

I can see the hint of a victorious wry smile on his lips before they wrap around the rim of his beer bottle.

Looking around, I feel lucky in this moment. Or at least content. We're all enjoying the little things in life, with some form of elation on our faces. It's a perfect night too, as we can see the stars.

"Hadley, come on," my little brother groans from the patio door.

I stand, holding onto my wine glass because no way am I forfeiting this delicious vino for a biology project. "I'll be back. I promised to look at his project for summer science club," I announce.

I quickly lean down to kiss Connor's cheek and leave them to talk amongst themselves. I hear the mention of visiting a casino for the bachelor party, and it only makes me grin more.

Walking into the house, I head straight to the sofa where Ashton is scrolling on his tablet. I flop onto the cushion next to him and prepare myself for a doozy.

"All right, show me your wizardly knowledge," I tell him.

He begins typing away with his finger. "I need your blood type," he orders.

"Oh, uh… I don't know… wait, actually, I do know. I had bloodwork done recently for my allergy tests." I grab my phone that's resting on the charging station on the side table. "Can I see what you're working on?" I ask, curious.

"Nothing special. We're going over blood groups and pairings. I'm filling out a family chart. I've just been waiting on you, but you've been too busy being married."

I roll my eyes because he loves Connor. Who wouldn't want a superstar hockey player as their new brother-in-law?

"Mom told me hers, and dad's I found in his wallet," he further explains.

"You were snooping again?" I call him out on his admission.

He is quick to defend. "So? It's educational."

I shake my head as I pull up blood test results that produced nada on the allergy front, which is a good thing.

"I'll be back, nature calls." He hands me the tablet and disappears down the hall.

My curiosity gets the best of me, and I begin to look at the chart. There is a list of possible and impossible combinations. Huh, interesting. I remember studying this all back in middle school, but it is purely a blip in my memory.

Reading between the tablet and my phone, I search for my blood type then return my sight to the scientific table on the screen. I double-check then triple for good measure.

But my face falls, right before my heart quickens and an uneasy feeling stirs in my stomach. I freeze, and it feels like a crack is forming somewhere.

It must be a minute or two until I'm shaken out of my daze. I peer up and find Connor looking down at me.

"I'm just grabbing dessert. You okay?" His relaxed facial expression disappears when he looks into my eyes.

I toss the tablet to the side and stand up, ignoring Connor. I walk into the kitchen and begin to pace.

"What's wrong?" Concern is apparent in his voice.

"The mosquitos are getting vicious," my mother points out as she and my father enter through the sliding door.

The mood vanishes when they notice me standing in the kitchen, mostly in a bewildered state.

"What's up?" my father asks.

I stare at him for a long second. "Ashton's biology project. Have you seen it?"

He shrugs. "No, he mentioned it, but I haven't seen it yet."

I'm unable to blink or move, I just stare at him. "It's about blood types. How if your father is one type, your mother another, then their kids will have X type." I study him to see if his eyes change, but it feels like we're in a standoff. "I got my blood type the other week when I went to the doctor, routine tests, nothing really. Surprised it never came up before, actually." There it is, a heaviness glazing his eyes, fear combined with revelation. A bitter laugh escapes me. "According to my little brother's project, you have type O blood, but the thing is…"

I vaguely hear my brother walk into the room, but my mother ushers him away to somewhere else, grasping the gravity of this situation.

"Hadley." My father says my name as if he's carrying the weight of years on his back.

Connor steps closer to me, but I step back, as I need space to process.

"If both parents are type O, they can never have kids who are type A. Since my birth mom did do something right and left us with her medical history, then we know her type, which means it can't be possible that I'm type A… but I am."

I never knew it was possible to hear glass breaking if no glass is even present. But that's what is happening in this very moment as my father's face falls and tears pool in his eyes.

"It's not what you think," he says, his voice breaking.

Connor steps closer to me to touch my arm. "Hadley, why don't you sit down."

"Sit down!" I squeak out with so much strain inside my body. "Oh my God, it's true, isn't it? You're not really my father." I begin to lose my footing as panic takes over.

"I am. It's complicated," he admits.

I shake my head in disbelief. This isn't happening. "No, no, this is some joke."

"Hear him out," Connor pleads softly.

My eyes snap to him in surprise, why would Connor say that? He should be as astonished as I am. I yank my arm away from his touch. Something clicks in my head. "You knew!"

The immediate pain in Connor's face is my answer.

"Since when?" I ask, with a tear falling down my cheek.

Connor swallows and his fists hang by his sides. He glances to my dad then back to me. "For a while." He's avoiding the answer.

I push him out of frustration. "Tell me the truth."

Connor grabs my wrists, softly, tenderly, as if he can see I'm fragile and he won't be the one to break me. "A few years." His jaw tightens. "The morning after we…" he whispers.

But his attempt fails because I break.

19

CONNOR

I am a con.

It's not just a nickname.

I kept her away when all I wanted was to have her closer.

Now she's in front of me combusting from life-altering news, and my heart is breaking for her.

Hadley's eyes blaze with fury as they slowly travel between me and her father. She's not sure what to do with this information.

Her hands find her hair and she claws the strands as she shakes her head. "W-wait, I don't... where the fuck do I begin right now?"

"Hadley, it's really not what it seems," her dad attempts to soften the blow.

"Not what it seems?" she yells. "Are you kidding me? You're not... and my husband knew this whole time!" Hadley is enraged, and she has every right to be.

I step to her, but she moves farther away, giving me a warning glare to stand back. "Let him explain," I attempt to suggest.

She shakes her head, hysterical from this news. "I don't understand," she cries.

"You're my daughter. In every way that matters, you're my daughter. But if you really want to look at biology, then we are related, just not as father and daughter. My brother was a twin, just not identical. Technically, you're my niece…" Spencer drops the bomb.

Hadley stares at him blankly, connecting dots in her head. "You mean my uncle, your brother, the one who died?"

He nods. "He wanted me to raise you as my own, and I did just that since you were barely able to walk, and I never looked back. My brother never wanted me to tell you. Still, I thought about telling you, but I was scared because you're *my* daughter." The agony on his face is apparent, and I feel for him in this moment.

Tears stream down Hadley's face, and I try once again to reach out to her, only to be rebuffed quickly by her taking another step back. I just want to hold her in my arms right now. She doesn't need to stand by herself. I'll take care of her.

"Unbelievable… I had a biological mother who didn't want me, a dad I never got to know, and only now I learn of this," she wails.

"I'm so sorry. You must know it's from love." Spencer swipes a hand across his jaw before wiping a tear away.

Hadley looks at him with pure hurt. "Who else knows?"

"Your grandparents, Mom, a friend, lawyers… and apparently Connor." He sighs.

Her sharp gaze returns to me. "Why does he say it like that?"

My shoulders sink, and I know nothing I say will ease her pain. "A few years ago, when I came to you that morning, I snuck in to surprise you, but I accidentally overheard your parents talking. They didn't realize I was there, obviously, and they were debating telling you since you had just turned eighteen. Spencer didn't know I knew until I told him the day after we got married."

A gasp escapes her lips and fresh tears form. "That's what you two were talking about so intensely?"

"Yes," I whisper.

She lunges forward and takes hold of my shirt in pure rage. "Were you ever going to fucking tell me? Or were you just going to stay married to me and keep this secret?"

I take hold of her wrists and ensure our eyes engage. "Hadley, you have to understand—"

"No," she interjects firmly.

"What can I do right now to make this better for you?" Spencer requests with sadness in his voice yet standing strong because he won't ever let her go.

Her sobs fill the room. "Go away," she whispers with deep pain flooding her face.

"Hadley." He tips his head to the side, hopeful the conversation won't stop.

"I can't be here right now." Hadley's voice cracks right before she just flees the kitchen, leaving us there.

I want to go after her, but I feel she needs a minute. Instead, my hands slam down on the counter from pure anger that she's hurting and I'm not even sure who's at fault.

"You'll keep an eye on her?" Spencer requests faintly with his voice unsteady.

I only half glance over my shoulder. "Of course." He doesn't even need to ask.

"Take care of her. I'll be back," he promises.

I do my best to give him a comforting look. "I know, Spencer. I think right now she needs space to take it all in."

He sniffles and stands there for a long heavy minute before leaving me to ponder how I'm going to support

Hadley in this very moment. I'm not exactly in her good graces, but she deserves to know the entire truth.

I reach for the liquor cabinet and pour myself a shot of bourbon, down it, then pour another, but this one is for Hadley, to help calm her nerves.

I head straight to our room to find the door closed and locked. I knock gently with hope she'll let me in. "Hadley, your dad is gone. It's just you and me. Let me in."

She doesn't answer, but I hear her crying into a pillow, the sound muffled.

I take a deep breath, step back, then use my weight to press against the door to break it open. It's actually easier than I anticipated. Only a little of the alcohol spills over onto my hand in the process.

My move takes her by surprise, and she sits up in the bed, her face red and puffy. She may be a mess, but she is still a beautiful disaster.

"Get out," she demands.

I hold up the glass of alcohol. "No." I walk to the bed and set it on the bedside table. "Here. This will help you calm down."

She goes quiet again, and I make no effort to sit on the bed with her, as I'm waiting for her clues for how to approach her.

Her eyes are sunken with pure sadness. "You knew," she states, still in disbelief.

"Yeah."

"Is that why you came to my room and said I was a mistake?"

I lick my lips, because the truth fucking hurts, and I hate saying it all out loud. It's like a knife wound when you hear the words. "Yes."

"You're an asshole."

I agree, but I felt my arms were always twisted. "Hadley, it wasn't my truth to tell. You know that too."

"So you just pushed me away?"

I laugh bitterly to myself. "Don't you see?" I sit on the bed and take hold of her face between my hands because she has to understand my reasoning, I won't have it any other way. "I've been trying my damnedest to break your heart all these years to actually ensure it stays mended." My voice breaks because I'm aching too.

"That's why you hated me?"

"I never fucking hated you. The opposite. But I couldn't have you close because I didn't know if I could keep the secret. It's not my place to tell you, and your relationship with your dad is everything to you."

She laughs then takes hold of my hands to remove them from her cheeks. "What was your big plan, Connor? Never tell me, even though I'm your wife?" she snarls.

I stand up again and pinch the bridge of my nose. "Truthfully? You want the honest truth?"

"Yes," she bites out.

"I wasn't going to tell you. I just knew that if you ever found out that it would be harder for you to leave me if we are married." I raise my voice because the truth is confronting.

Her jaw goes slack from my admission, and it feels like the air in the room evaporated.

"Wow." She huffs a breath before she looks to the side then brings her sight back to me. "Get out."

"No." I stand there, defiant.

"I can't be near you right now," she volleys.

I grab the throw blanket from the end of the bed and lie down on the floor. "Tough luck. I'll sleep on the floor, but I'm not leaving you alone."

Hadley goes speechless at my move.

I pretend to get comfortable on the floor, then after a minute peer up by the edge of the bed. "Will you throw me a pillow? You know you want to." I'm trying to see if a glimmer of relief is deep within her somewhere.

She just sits there frozen, aware that I'm serious. I won't be moving an inch from here. I'm staying firm.

Slowly and unsure, she tosses me a pillow.

We both lie down on our spots in silence for a solid ten minutes, because that is what she needs right now.

Until I break our silence. "Deep down, you know it's true. It wasn't my secret to share."

A new round of sniffling tears fills the room. "Maybe you're right, but it doesn't change the fact that I'm broken right now."

I sit up to observe her. "I won't let you break," I softly confirm.

Hadley props herself up on her elbows to look down at me. "I don't know what to think right now. But Connor…"

"Yeah?"

"Just hold me," she sobs.

I'm lying next to her in a flash, curling her tightly to my body as I swipe away the tears with my thumb and stroke her messy tear-drenched hair. There is no place I would rather be.

"Did we ever have a chance to be something real?" she asks as she buries her face into my chest.

I continue to touch her in hopes of soothing her. "It's not a chance. We *are* something real," I assure her.

"I'm so confused," she mumbles into my shirt, and I can hear that her energy is nearly gone.

"I promise you, we'll get through this. I'm not leaving you."

Then I hold her all night, not sure what tomorrow may bring.

20
HADLEY

Numb.

That's what I feel.

Not long ago, I woke up in a Vegas hotel room with no recollection of the events of the night before. This time, my body is in a similar state physically, but make no mistake, I remember every second from last night.

A ton a bricks didn't hit me; they came crumbling down around me. It's no wonder I struggle to gather energy to move from this bed. I attempt to stretch, but my hand pokes a firm body.

Connor.

I have two things to process; my dad who lied and my husband who lied. I'm not sure where to begin.

My eyes widen to take in the view of Connor perched on the edge of the bed with a mug in his hand. He must have been waiting for me to wake up, as he looks showered and dressed in a fresh t-shirt and jeans. His hair has this ruffled wave that screams he has an edgy side.

"Hi." His greeting sounds so delicate.

I drag my body up to sitting and sigh. He offers me the

mug of tea, but I indicate with my hand no. Instead, I opt to bring my knees to my chest to hold onto.

"Tell me it was a nightmare," I whisper.

"I can't say it didn't happen, but I don't believe it's a nightmare." He sets the mug on the bedside table and brings his hand to my knee, but I flinch. I'm uncertain what to feel, and he must pick up on the signs. "I'm so sorry."

I glance away, choosing not to say anything, but I do listen, and I hear a man whose voice is filled with remorse.

He continues, "Hadley, you have to know that I did what I thought was right. Spencer loves you more than anyone, only ever puts you first, and it wasn't my secret to share."

I scoff as fresh tears pool in my eyes, and my stomach twists because his point may be valid. "I have so many reasons to be upset. My da—" Why can't I say it? I move up the list. "You knew and pushed me away by making me feel like I was nothing."

"It fucking hurt, trust me."

"Oh, poor you," I mock before sliding angrily off the bed, feeling wrath building inside of me, and it's ready to bubble over. "You know, maybe we would have had something amazing if we didn't lose those years when you decided the best policy was to treat me like the enemy."

Connor stands, my words clearly hitting him hard. "I realize that. I can't turn back the clock, and we will still have something amazing. I *want* to have something amazing with you."

A sob escapes me because I'm so damn torn between the deceit and the emotion that I feel right now when he looks at me. He believes in his pleading words.

My fingers tangle into my hair as if I'm grasping at straws. It's frustration. "Connor, I don't have the strength to deal with you and also my da—" Another sob escapes me.

Connor is in front of me with his hands on my shoulders in no time. "Your dad is still your dad. You know better than anyone that biology doesn't mean a thing. Look at April, she's your mom, and you think nothing less. Spencer is even more of a parent because he's all you've ever known, and you are related in some way. Your real dad wanted it like this because they all love you so much."

I sniffle. I understand his logic, as it floated into my head a few times when I woke during the night. "I just don't know why he never told me or why he never planned to tell me if it hadn't been for a stupid science project."

The pad of Connor's thumb swipes a tear off my cheek. "Because he only sees you as *his* daughter, and he didn't want to lose that connection. He was scared."

I snuggle my cheek into the palm of his hand. "I just need to process it all."

He nods gently and guides me to muffle my snotty tears into his chest without a care in the world that I'm destroying his shirt in the process. "I'm not going anywhere. You can push me away, but I'll only return," he promises.

A new overwhelming flood hits me, with thoughts racing into my head from all directions. I step out of his hold and throw my arms up. "This is such a mess."

"It doesn't have to be."

I sneer at the humor in that. "Connor, it is. You and I are married because of a drunk night in Vegas. A night that I don't even really remember. Do you know how messed up that is? I didn't even have a wedding dress or a big cake or so many things—"

"But you had the groom who would do anything for you," he cuts me off, and the glimmer in his eyes is there. It's more than caring, it's... dare I say love? I see it for the first time, a gleam of hope and insistence. Maybe it's always been there, but I only really see it now when I'm trying to cling to anything to keep me from falling.

The bedroom feels smaller as our eyes stay connected, and the thumping of my heart returns. A beacon that maybe one day everything will be okay surfaces purely because of his damn eyes.

It just won't be okay today.

"How do I pick up the pieces?" I ask softly.

Connor takes one step before he drops to his knees and wraps his arms around my thighs, with his ear resting against my belly. "You let me do it."

His selfless words strike me, and I run my fingers through his hair. I'm clearly affected but still unsure if what he did is noble or plain fucked up.

Lucky for him, right now, I won't push him away. It doesn't mean I'm fully committing either.

We stand there for a solid minute as I try to connect dots. The truth was clearly always there. Little clues that now make sense. It just wasn't obvious at the time. The lack of baby photos, the photo of my uncle on the mantle, the timeline and story of when he passed away due to an accident, or when my parents had Ashton and it felt like pregnancy was something new for both of my parents. There were signs in retrospect.

The best thing I can do right now is take a hot shower alone. I begin to shuffle out of Connor's hold. "I'm going to shower. Alone."

He slowly stands, observing me and doing his best to assess me. Good luck with that, because I don't even know what I'm feeling or thinking anymore.

It's an hour later when I emerge from the bathroom in a towel and find that Connor is sitting on the bed with his arms resting over his knees and feet firmly planted on the floor.

"You don't need to be waiting on me or watching my every move," I comment.

The corner of his mouth tilts up. "Since when do I listen to you?"

A slither of amusement attempts to break through my darkness inside. "I thought you had a meeting for the summer camp for kids that you're volunteering at?"

Connor leans back on his arms, his body now half splayed on the bed. "You're trying to get rid of me, but that ain't happening. I told them that I wouldn't be in today, that something came up."

"Oh." I stand on my spot, now studying him.

This will be my life until I find some form of closure surrounding the men in my life. Connor won't relent until I'm at peace, even if he's part of the reason that I'm in this state.

But in my shower, it kept circling in my head what he has repeated several times. The truth wasn't his secret to tell. I've attempted to imagine myself in his shoes, and to be honest, I'm not sure what I would've done.

So, I've decided for now that I'll have a temporary truce in my head when it comes to Connor and focus on my dad. Doesn't mean it's back to roses and sunshine with Connor, but I'm not going to run away.

And right now, Connor is before me trying to help.

I need him too.

To hollow the numbness.

I take a few confident strides to him, stopping short of his knees. He brings his body up, as I have his full attention.

Dropping onto his lap, I swing my leg over to staddle him. I settle in his lap and feel his length twitch and grow hard against the apex of my thighs. Connor doesn't move, including his eyes that are pinned to mine. He's going to let me lead because he knows this is what I want.

Bringing my hands to cradle his face, I splay my fingers along his jaw and cheek while I press my body to his and take command. "I don't want to think right now, just… feel alive," I rasp in desperation.

"Then use me," he whispers adamantly.

I bring my lips to his and kiss him with intention. It's warm and sensual, grounding me, and it stops the spinning in my world right now. I press harder against his lips with a force that causes the towel around me to loosen and fall gently. Ignoring it, I begin to ride on top of Connor, my hips moving in waves to feel friction against my pussy.

Connor gets his shirt off before our lips are glued to one another again, and his hands run down the sides of my body to find a home on my hips.

My arms rest on his strong shoulders, and our position only encourages him to lower his mouth to my breast. With the towel now fallen to my waist, he has prime access to my breasts, which is why he is eager to swirl his tongue around one nipple. I moan, with my entire body feeling extra sensitive, except for the pounding ache of my clit and the dampness between my thighs.

I'm turning greedy too, and I guide his mouth to my other breast. I want his mouth and fingers everywhere; it won't be enough.

When he's done teasing my hard nipple that only intensifies my senses, he leaves a trail of hurried kisses up my neck to find my mouth again. I close my eyes and let myself get lost in this momentary ecstasy.

Keeping my legs wrapped around him, he rolls us until I'm underneath him, and the towel gets lost in the process, leaving me naked. He drags my arms over my head, pressed against the mattress as our lips skim one another and stay in a dance.

"I'll do anything you want." His voice is full of lust as he traps my bottom lip with a featherlike brush of his lips.

My hips tilt up to feel his hard shaft, and I can't get a release fast enough.

"I just need you inside of me," I whisper as we thrust our bodies together.

"Then I'll take you."

I break my wrists away from his hand that had them pinned and find the zipper of his jeans, urging him to undo them, and the desperation inside of me to touch his bare cock is overwhelming. He slides them off in record time and then I receive my wish, with my hand wrapping around his long length, enjoying his gasp that vibrates against our open mouths that touch.

Taking charge, I urge him to his back and crawl on top of him.

I plunge down onto his cock with pure abandon, closing my eyes and focusing only on the feeling of being full. I move up and down, finding the right angle that hits the spot I like.

My hair falls over my shoulders as I tip my head back and close my eyes. I don't dare dip my gaze down to see Connor. It would make it far too intense.

Too real.

And I need an escape.

But I ignore my internal warning because fire builds below my navel, and I feel like I'm at the edge of a cliff. Glancing down, I'm met with a pair of protective eyes that sends a flame up to my heart.

Connor watches with pure admiration as I fuck him. As if I'm a queen.

He has patience because I know it's a struggle for him to let me lead when we're intimate like this. I don't mind, I like it like that, it's kind of a turn-on. But right now, I need the control.

I slide up and down, dragging from his base to the tip, knowing it gives him pleasure as much as it does for me. At first, I thought that I needed slow, but I have frustration swirling in me, which is why I need to work out some stress, and I pick up the pace.

Connor uses his upper body strength to sit up, which allows me to wrap my arms around his neck, drawing his mouth back to mine while I swivel my hips and tighten around his length, every thrust more charged than the one before.

My breath turns to a near pant, and his answer is to cover my mouth with his, as if he will give me air, but it only causes the passion between us to intensify.

We move together, with my breasts pressed against his chest and his arms tightly wound around my middle, bringing his length deeper inside of me. His own breathing turns heavy as he follows my cues and meets me on every thrust.

A shade of contentment hits me, because in this moment, my mind goes blank, and my body feels alive. I quickly spiral into temporary relief when I convulse around him, not even noticing that he chases his own release to the end. My body goes weak, but he has me. He stays inside while his hand rubs soothing circles on my back, and he kisses the curve of my shoulder.

Connor doesn't say anything, he just holds me because my body is spent and filled.

I lose track of time, but he eventually kisses along my jaw

before gently flipping me so I'm on my back and he can pull out. Connor grabs the duvet and brings it over my body while he leans on his side to observe me again. However, I only feel his eyes on me, since I stare at the ceiling.

His finger, like a feather, traces the lines of my shoulder to the base of my neck. "I'm not leaving you."

"You've mentioned."

"I'll make sure nobody bothers you today if that's what you want."

I turn my head to the side to look at him. "You mean my father?"

His lips purse out. "He wants to see you."

A scornful yet humorous smirk curls on my lips. "I forgot that you two are close now."

Connor's head falls, and he rubs the back of his neck. "I did what I thought was right."

A long silence overtakes us.

"You and me? I'm cautious still. I'm here and not running away, but that doesn't mean I can forget. That's where you and I are," I clarify.

He drags his thumb across my bottom lip before his fingers dive through my hair to the back of my head to bring me to his lips for a confirming kiss. "I'll take it."

A SHORT WHILE LATER, I'm dressed in a hoodie and yoga pants when I stall at the entrance to the kitchen to find my father sitting at the kitchen counter.

He attempts to offer me a gentle comforting half-smile, and he holds his hands up in surrender. "I come in peace. Connor let me in. He ran to the store."

My husband clearly isn't following my instructions for

the day. I walk to the coffee machine, but I give up because I doubt that I will be able to taste much due to the irrational amount of crying that has transpired today.

"I needed to see that you're okay," he laments.

I lean against the counter and feel defeated. "I'm alive."

A long breath leaves his lips. "This doesn't change anything. You'll always be my daughter. I was the one who watched you grow, raised you, and love you more than you can even measure."

The sting in my eyes returns, which informs me that tears are coming. "You and I have always been close. Why didn't you just… tell me?" I feel so hopeless.

"I promised my brother Camden. It was his dying wish that I raise you as my own, and that meant never telling you. He thought losing another parent since your biological mother was never in the picture was the right move. We're not identical twins, which might explain why we don't have the same blood type." His head gently lolls to the side. "I owed him his wish, and it was the best gift I ever got… just don't tell your brother that," he says, attempting to make me smile. "I don't want anything to change between us. I'm still your dad." I notice it now, how his eyes look as though he hasn't slept in days.

"How do we move on?" I barely whisper.

"Whatever way you want. Either way, you're just as much my daughter now as you were before you found out," he promises.

It makes me break into a sob, mostly because I hear how much it's true. This man loves fearlessly, and I've always been lucky to be his little girl. I just can't figure out if my identity is now different.

I wipe away a tear with the back of my hand and sniffle. "I believe you, but I just need to process."

"I get that. I'll follow your lead, but I'm not going anywhere."

I can't help it, the corner of my mouth tugs with a need to smile through my tears and aching cheeks. "Damn, you and Connor are too alike. I keep hearing that sentence."

My dad smirks to himself. "He's a good guy."

My eyes nearly bug out. "Did you just say that?"

He scoffs and a droll smile forms. "After you both got married, and he told me he knew, I was scared. Took me off guard, but then he promised that you wouldn't get hurt, and it turns out we're on the same team. Then when you arrived for the photos for that article, we both looked at you, so beautiful, and it was apparent that he will take care of you the way I would expect."

I would say that it doesn't make sense, considering Connor hated me then, but it turns out he never hated me at all. He's been harboring his feelings for me, and everyone could see except me.

My dad continues, "I attempted to give him a lecture when he informed me that he knew, but no shit, your husband literally told me, 'Don't bother with the lecture, Spencer. I have every intention of ensuring she's well taken care of and has a happy life. I'll do whatever it takes. Hadley's heart is mine, so get used to it.'"

I chortle because that sounds like him. "Always assumed you weren't his biggest fan."

"I don't like hockey players. There's a difference."

"News flash, that's his career." I appreciate that our conversation moves in a comforting way, as though we may be all right, even if we're not there yet.

My dad scratches his cheek. "He's one of the good ones. Connor kept the secret for far too long to protect you, so he is as good as gold to me. Because he sees exactly what I do.

You adore your family, and we adore you. We thought it was the right thing to do."

I notice that my tears have subsided and I'm at last blinking normally. "Time will tell if it is."

The sound of Connor coming in through the garage door brings our attention to him. He walks in carrying a tray of coffees and a bag of what is probably pastries. Connor's eyes bounce between my dad and me, unsure of the scene.

Connor clears his throat. "Hey." It's an awkward greeting, probably because he knows he conspired.

I give him a pointed look. "Ambushing me?" I indicate to my father.

Connor sets the tray down and his face stays neutral. "He wanted to talk to you, and I thought it would maybe help."

My father stands up. "I think we've talked enough today, as I know it's a lot to take in. I'll leave you two alone." He walks to me and brings his arm out, hoping for a hug, but I don't move and his arm falls, his face disappointed. "I'll check in again tomorrow. I love you, Hadley."

I nod that I heard him and watch him leave, touching Connor's shoulder in passing. My heart cracking but not broken.

Connor steps in my direction with that look that is pure confidence. "You're not angry with me. Even if you don't want to admit it, you needed to hear from Spencer."

It wasn't horrible, better than last night, just… it's raw.

I grumble a sound before I begin to stomp out of the kitchen. "Space and time, Con. That's the only way we'll all come out of this," I declare.

21

CONNOR

Skating across the ice, I hate that I left Hadley at home. Well, she might be celebrating. She's been itching to have some space for a few days now. I could tell that she is growing tired of my constant check-ins and chivalrous gestures, like bringing her favorite coffee from Jolly Joe's or cooking for her even if she isn't that hungry. The only thing she doesn't seem to mind is when I'm inside of her.

I just didn't want to leave her alone, considering how the past week has gone.

But she insisted that I stay committed to my duties of volunteering at my dad's summer hockey camp for developing skills, plus I need to ensure that I stay in shape by keeping up with my workouts, as the new season is fast approaching, and I don't want my mind out of the game.

Briggs skates around me like a shark until he brakes. We both helped earlier with the kids, but now it's our time to run a few drills. Nothing too strenuous.

"Do you think Vaughn will retire or trade next season?" my friend asks as he bounces the puck on his stick.

I swivel my skates back and forth as we talk in place. "Does it matter? He isn't that bad of a guy, and we might need him if we want a chance at the cup. We won't know until end of next season. He's still signed with Tampa."

"Easy for you to say. You get along with the guy, and it isn't your position that they would trade."

"I can be off the team. It might be for the best," I admit.

He glances up, taken aback that I said that. "What's up with you?"

I hold my stick out to circle my wrists. "I'm just saying maybe getting away from Lake Spark would be good for me, for Hadley too." A bit of fresh perspective, change of scene, no parents around us.

Briggs laughs. "Nah, you two are complete family people, plus your uncle would be pissed if his team loses their star defender."

I give him an unimpressed look. "It's not always up to him." I'm kind of offended he said that. He's always had my back while I proved my abilities.

"Sorry, man, just being honest with you. Ready for the bachelor party?" He grins.

He wasn't joking, it's happening. In two weeks. I have no clue what the hell is up, and I'm kind of scared. Never underestimate Briggs, or my dad. My entire life my dad has attempted to be relatable and cool due to having me young. I can only imagine that he'll put in the extra effort to hang with the boys.

My head falls and my nose squinches as I debate if I can figure out any hints. "I'm fucking terrified."

"Also cool if the father of the bride comes? Spencer sent me a text that he wasn't sure he should be there."

That doesn't really surprise me considering what's gone

down. "It's totally fine." I mean it too. Hadley loves him, and although they haven't spoken much lately, I believe they will be okay. His intentions have always been pure. "All is good," I confirm again.

He touches my shoulder as we skate to the rink exit. "I fucking love ya, man, which is why I can tease you that your mom is here with your juice box."

I laugh to myself and smile at my mom who is, in fact, standing by the rink holding up a bottle of water, indicating that she has brought me a drink so we can talk.

"Playdate's over, buddy," I reply in good jest.

"Good. I'm going to hit the spa at the Dizzy Duck Inn for a massage. That new masseuse they have is magical with her hands and her mouth."

"I didn't just hear that, Briggs Chase." My mom smiles sweetly, and I have to chuckle.

Briggs gives her his signature grin. "Sorry, Brielle, you know I'm just trying to find a woman of your caliber, but the pickings are slim here." He's just purposely annoying me now, because yeah, I've heard the guys mention how they think my mom is hot, which causes me to cringe.

"Such a charmer as always, Briggsy," she replies with her arms crossed.

He brings a hand to his heart. "I save it all for you in another life where Ford doesn't exist."

"Fuck off," I tell him.

He and my mom both laugh because annoying me is a pastime they enjoy.

Shaking my head, I get busy on my skates, taking them off, then head toward my mother to sit with her.

"I was visiting your dad in his office and saw my first-born, so had to stop to say hello." Her voice is breezy.

I lean in and pretend to scan the room. "It's okay, you can say I'm your favorite son."

She feigns an unimpressed scowl. "Funny. Seriously, I feel like we haven't touched base much lately, and I know when you get married that your wife becomes number one, just don't forget about me."

"Couldn't if I tried," I assure her. "And sorry, I've just been tied up in a few things."

My mom touches my shoulder with affection. "Everything okay? I thought everything is going fine. I mean, I've never seen you so happy. Marriage suits you."

"Really?"

"You have a glow."

I roll my eyes. "You and Dad need to work on these sappy speeches."

"Fair enough. But all good? Hadley had a substitute for her ballet class this week, and April seems out of sorts too, but I get the feeling that I shouldn't press." Concern is apparent in her voice.

I blow out a breath and briefly look down at my hands where my wedding ring sticks out. Marriage *does* suit me. "All good. She's just under the weather," I lie. It's not my place to inform anyone about Hadley and Spencer, and I don't think Hadley wants anyone to know. She mentioned not even telling Isla.

"Flu or…" It trails out of her mouth.

An exhausted breath now escapes me. "Relax, we meant it when we said that we're not with child, nor plan on being in the near future."

She gives me a sympathetic look. "Sorry, my mind tends to go there." I get it, I do. Being pregnant at eighteen must impact you in many ways. "If there is anything I can do, then just tell me," she offers.

"Thanks, but I've got it covered." My mom chortles, and it causes me to look at her peculiarly. "What?" I wonder.

She wraps an arm around my shoulders and keeps me locked in a side hug as we look out over the empty ice. "Of course you do. Love is when you put someone else first, and that's all you ever do when it concerns Hadley Crews, now Spears."

A proud partial smile attempts to break out on my lips. Reflecting on all my choices, although not always ideal, my mom is right, because I'd make the same choice again. Ultimately, putting Hadley first is my only goal.

"If only she saw it that way," I softly say to myself.

Not quiet enough, as my mom looks at me with alarm before she eases into advice that I know she is about to dish out. "Marriage isn't easy. What does help is ensuring you remind the other how much you love and care, say it over and over, louder if you can. Don't ever assume it's clear. We need to be showered in proclamations of love."

I bring a hand to my forehead and shake my head slightly side to side. These heart-to-hearts with my parents are killing me. Way too saccharine for my liking yet ridiculously informative.

Because if I look back at it, I've done many actions to show how much I feel for Hadley, yet I haven't stated the obvious. Maybe I took it for granted and never told her how I really feel, assuming she got the hint.

I can't afford to get it wrong now. Not when she's uncertain of how to move forward.

"Duly noted, Mom," I comment. "Great talk as always." I give her a little fist bump.

"Go. You have a wife waiting for you."

"Yeah… yeah, I do." My words linger in the air.

When I arrive home, I'm relieved to see that Hadley ate something, as there is a half-eaten sandwich on a plate in the kitchen. That's what I call progress. Especially since she told me that she was going to check in at her studio and go for a walk. She's attempting to find some normalcy again.

Heading to our room, I know she's there since her car is here, and her phone was downstairs by the charger. The moment that I'm standing at our bedroom door, I see her resting on her side with an e-reader on the mattress.

"Hey," I say as I walk into the room and remove my watch at the same time. My intention is to get comfy with her and have a relaxing evening.

"Hi." She sounds deflated. I guess maybe we haven't made progress.

I slide onto the bed to spoon her from behind. She's wearing a light summer tank top dress which means I have ample opportunity to brush my lips along the curve of her shoulder. "I was thinking… maybe we should get out of Lake Spark for a few days."

Hadley glances over her shoulder at me, and I take the moment to capture her chin with my crooked finger. "What do you mean?" she asks, curious.

"One of my teammates is back in Sweden for the summer and invited me to his family lake house there. Maybe it would be a good escape. The summer is ticking, and I'll have to start preparing for the season soon."

"Sweden?"

"Why not?" I shrug then tip my mouth down to trace her lips with mine.

"I'm not sure. Kind of feels like I'm running away."

"Sulking around here isn't the answer either," I point out.

Her eyes turn into saucers. "Really?" She's unimpressed. "I think I have valid reasons."

I do something that I know will calm her down. My hand journeys along her oblique around to her belly, stopping just below her navel, causing her dress to creep up slightly. Meanwhile, I drag my teeth on her skin as I travel down her neck with the occasional playful nip. I feel the goosebumps spread against her warm skin.

"Think of me holding a puppy, think happy thoughts," I tease her. I circle my fingers around the sweet spot below her belly button that drives up her anticipation for me to go lower and makes her hum in response. I turn serious again. "Did you talk to your father today?"

She growls but stays put against my body. "Why do you care so much?"

"Because you and I have a good thing going. It will be even better if you are at peace with him."

She throws a scowl in my direction. "Don't be noble," she demands.

I smirk in response. "I'm not. I'm being a selfish motherfucker who wants to see you completely content." I kiss her shoulder, determined to drive her wild.

"You need me happy so I don't ruin this marriage and your image and hockey season and our parents' hearts…" she lists.

I huff from frustration that she doesn't seem to get it, and my head falls forward for a second to gather my strength. "I don't care about any of that, and if you didn't get that memo, then I'm failing somewhere. Sometimes you just want to stop the world for someone because you put them first."

"Why would you do that?" she volleys back.

"Because you love them." It slips out of my mouth.

Her head instantly perks up, and her eyes blaze with realization.

It hits me that I'm confessing it all. I own up to it because the words come too easily. "Yeah, Hadley… I love you." Might as well state the obvious.

Her frown disperses, and the corners of her mouth curve up, with her eyes lighting up and softening. "You love me?"

My eyes bounce side to side because she is full of questions tonight. "Yes." I bring my palm to her cheek and encourage her face to move in my direction so I can entrap her with a kiss. I lean down and kiss her slowly, ensuring my tongue dips into her mouth to make this memorable.

I enjoy the way she sinks into my touch, allowing me to kiss her the way she deserves. We have history and a future. It was always going to be her.

Pulling away, I notice her eyes mesmerized and a wry smile on her lips. "You love me," she echoes.

It causes me to chuckle softly because she seems to be in a daze, but I'm not complaining about that. It feels exceptional that for the first time in days she seems happy, and it's my doing.

I'm not expecting her to say it back, and I don't give her the opportunity anyhow.

Dipping my head down, I capture her lips again while my fingers urge her cotton dress up. I don't drag this out; I pull her panties to the side and slip my fingers between her thighs and stroke her bundle of nerves that has her whimpering into my mouth. My proclamation did something to her, because she's slick with want, and it's easy for me to plunge my finger inside of her.

"Shall I prove it to you too?" I rasp and trail my mouth along her collarbone to the middle of her cleavage, recognizing the way her body shivers. "Show you that your pussy is mine?"

"Connor." Her body writhes.

My answer is to add another finger inside of her while the pad of my thumb softly rubs circles on her clit. In response she begins to ride my hand.

But when she breathes my name, it always makes me a little untamed.

"I love you," I whisper against her skin and begin to take my cock out. I'm eager to be inside of her heat, filling her up, letting go because I'm free from hiding anything from her. "I love you," I repeat as I bring my body over hers and align myself.

"Connor." Both of her hands come to frame my face in a tender manner.

Hadley lifts her knees high, offering herself to me, and I settle right where I belong. I start slow, keeping our eyes locked as I begin to make love to her, which is new for me. This is different. Very different.

Something inside of her jolts like lightning, and she lifts up to kiss me hard while I thrust in and out of her. I move deeper and harder in response, with her dress now tangled and loose around her body and revealing her bare breasts as she lies back. My mouth kisses any spot that I can find.

"You like this? Me inside of you because it means something?"

She burrows into my forearm planted next to her head on the mattress, gently biting, me with a beautiful droll smile on her lips.

"Answer me," I grit out.

"Yes," she gasps.

"You can be angry at me whenever you want," I begin as I pick up the pace. "Just remember that I've always been waiting for you, you're my end game." Her toes dig into the cheeks of my ass as she tightens around me, trying to bring me deeper. "Don't you see, beautiful girl…"

Her moans and the way her body vibrates beneath me tells me that she's close, which is good because for this round we have to come together. I grab her one arm and pin it above her head then bring the other between us, and she knows exactly what to do as she begins to touch herself.

"Don't I see what?" Her voice strains as she tries to balance breathing and the moan that rips through her.

My body tightens and fire spreads through me. A satisfied smirk appears on my lips. "It may have felt like a game all this time, but I've been purposely waiting," I manage to grunt out, as my own release is impending.

We kiss once more, a messy kiss.

"You're the only game that I've been waiting to win," I whisper into her ear.

And it sends us down the spiral of ecstasy as I come so hard until I collapse on top of her with my heart about to burst.

I do my best to roll us to our sides and stay inside of her so we don't lose our connection.

We lie there, in silence, staring at one another, letting our fingers roam.

Then it's there. Her lips twitch and her eyes flick up to meet mine while her arm snakes around my neck.

She fails miserably at trying to hide her smile, especially when I kiss the tip of her nose.

Her mouth cracks open with a sound, but the words don't follow until a beat later. "You're something special, Connor Spears."

I grin with smugness. "I know I am." Being cocky makes her smile, and right now she doesn't want to return my declaration, which I don't mind. You need a clear mind when you say it.

"I think we'll be more than okay," she whispers a promise.

I brush a few strands of hair away from her eyes. "Only when you make peace with *everyone*," I remind her.

Because otherwise, she may break, and if I can't fix that, then it feels like I didn't protect her at all.

22
HADLEY

Staring aimlessly into my coffee mug, I dive my spoon into the drink in search of my jellybean. That's why people come here, after all—for the jellybean in their coffee. I hope it's purple, they normally bring luck.

"Hey, girl," Isla's voice causes me to look up and see she is standing over me with a to-go cup in hand. I wasn't expecting her, and I haven't been the greatest friend lately.

"Hey." I softly smile back. "Want to join me?"

"For a little bit. I need to get back to the sports complex, as we are getting ready for our pre-season marketing strategy." She slides into the booth across from me. "I'm happy to see that you're still alive. I was getting worried."

I tilt my head slightly to the side and my smile feels strained. "Sorry about that. Had some family stuff."

"Everything okay?" Isla inquires before her lips purse on the rim of her cup.

I thought about reaching out to her many times. The support of a friend is key to a friendship. But the secret that put me in my current state is one that I don't exactly want to share. The fewer people who know the truth the better, because if I'm honest to myself, I understand my dad's logic. I wouldn't want any reason for anyone to think he is anything less than the dream dad he is. Not to mention, I have someone to share this all with… Connor.

A soft smile toys on the corners of my lips at the thought of him. I was taken aback when he told me he loved me. It was a beautiful moment and stirred a lot inside of me. While I didn't say it back, he was at peace with that, and it didn't alter our mood. It's not that I don't feel strongly for him, I do. More than anyone. Just in that very moment, I felt being lost in his embrace was the only answer.

My smile stretches, though, because wow, he said it first. Not only that, but it also lightens the gray that's been looming over me lately.

"Earth to Hadley." Isla waves a hand in front of my face, and my gaze zooms to her as she laughs. "Wow, your giddy look is hopefully contagious, and I hope I find myself a hockey player who sends me in a daze like you… preferably after a *long* night."

I bring my hand to my cheek and attempt to hide my blush. "What can I say? I scored myself a good husband. Besides, you're surrounded by hockey players, you have options."

She wiggles her long finger back and forth. "No. The ones that hang around Lake Spark are too close to where I work. They are a no-go." I bounce my shoulder up in agreement. She changes the topic. "Are you getting nervous for game season? It's a long and exhausting one, with pre-season games and potential playoffs later in the season."

I bite my bottom lip. "Truthfully, it hasn't crossed my mind. At least, it probably should a little more. I've just been distracted."

"I can tell."

"I kind of originally didn't plan to be around for game season, but now… that plan has changed. I also just assumed it would be kind of like my dad when he played baseball."

Isla's face goes crooked. "Hockey is a totally different realm. Longer season, more games, more injuries, a hell of a lot more fights. Connor will need the emotional and mental support for sure, and you'll need to get used to him not always around." She speaks from experience with her brother.

I take in her suggestion and recognize that I can add it to the list of trying to figure out how to move forward with my current life.

"Damn, I should have gotten a cinnamon roll while I'm here." Isla peruses the menu on the wall behind the counter.

"They are delicious," I note.

She studies me for a second and seems to debate her words. "You've lost a little weight. Are you sure everything is okay?" Isla reaches across the table to touch the back of my hand. "Or is it just that you're working out a little extra with your partner?"

I snort a laugh. "Something like that."

I feel someone arrive near my side, and they tower over us. "Oh hey, Mr. C," Isla greets him.

My dad offers her a warm smile. "Hey, Isla."

Isla scoots off the seat. "You can steal her back. I actually just popped in for a coffee on my way back to the office."

"Thanks," he replies.

Isla waves goodbye to me, and I promise to text her soon, but my stomach flips when my father replaces Isla in the seat across from me. There is no way around it. In plain terms, I've been avoiding him.

His eyes carry a seriousness and love combined. "Saw you sitting here when I was walking down Main Street."

I hold up my mug. "Caffeine. The code word to open the door to my soul."

The corner of his mouth tilts. "Not long ago, you would sit here and demand a sundae after your ballet classes."

"Hmm, I still demand sundaes." I do my best to keep our conversation bright because I believe we will eventually be okay.

"Hadley." He breathes a long breath. "I can't keep repeating myself, but I will if that's what you need."

My fingers curl up and my palm faces him low on the table to stop him. "I would rather we didn't rehash what we both now know." The truth and his reasonings.

He nods in relief.

I lean over the table. "I think I'm beginning to realize that sometimes life gives us a boost in the direction of unlocking a truth."

"It does," he agrees.

"I'm living two parallels right now. With Connor, it was a Vegas wedding that led to more. With you, it was a science project that led to a change in our dynamic."

"I don't want there to be a change," he protests in a low gritty voice.

I scan Jolly Joe's and see we are basically alone, as it's a weekday, except for some tourists over by the jukebox taking photos of the interior.

I blink several times to ensure tears won't fall. "You are my dad, but I don't feel anything for the person who is biologically my dad, you know? And I think what I struggle with is... I feel guilty about that."

"Hadley, you don't need to. It's what my brother would have wanted," he assures me.

"Isn't that twisted? He gave me away so easily."

My father shakes his head. "It wasn't like that at all. He

knew he wasn't going to make it, so he made the choice to give you the best life, a selfless choice."

I lick my lips as my mouth feels suddenly dry. "I'm trying to wrap my head around that."

My dad sulks, as he is balancing patience and wanting to scream, I can tell.

"You know, Connor seems to think that we should get out of Lake Spark for a few days for a change of scene," I inform him.

"I think he might have a good suggestion."

"He wants to go to Sweden." I half laugh because a simple bed-and-breakfast somewhere warm would have sufficed.

It causes my father to grin. "I would say I should be concerned that he wants to take you far away, but I know he has to be back here before he starts training for pre-season."

I puff a breath from the reminder of my husband's career and what it will entail for me. "I remember watching your baseball games—well, the snacks might have been my highlight, but I remember. I was so proud, and you would always come say hi before a game. Something tells me hockey is a little different. I'll be clenching my seat every time they get out of line."

"I'll be there holding your hand then," he offers in a tone of pure affection.

A closed-mouth smile hits me as natural as a breeze. "I would like that. I might be cursing half the time, but we abolished the swear jar many years ago."

There it is, a natural laugh and ease between us. "It's okay, I'll join you. At some point, we get past things that are no longer what they always were. No more Pioneer Park that you loved to go to, no more tooth fairy bills, and no more treating you like a kid. But I promise, the moment you come to me and say you need anything, then you'll still be my little girl, and I'll take care of you."

Emotion floods through my veins. Spencer Crews is a good man. I glance away to try and hide a tear. "April is my mom, and I never even think of my biological one. It's just, I know my biological dad didn't think the same way and wanted the best for me, which is why I feel so guilty that I wish I didn't know because I'm perfectly content that you are my dad in all aspects. But I *do* know, and it just lingers in my thoughts." I feel like I'm repeating myself, but at least I'm being open.

"Trust me, I wish I could make you feel better," he swears.

I quickly wipe a token tear away. "I know."

A long silence hits us. What more can we say? We'll be going in circles.

"Want me to order a sundae? The one in the kitchen sink? It always used to make you feel better." My dad tries to capture my gaze with a sympathetic half-smile on his mouth.

God, I appreciate that this can't be easy for him and that he's trying.

"Go on. Just make sure they add peanut butter to the banana part."

"Oh, I'll steal the jar if they don't," he promises.

Sometimes an old-fashioned heart-to-heart over ice cream is what we need.

RETURNING HOME, I overhear Connor in discussion with someone in the living room, and I slowly approach, only to stall before the corner so they don't see me.

"I hate being in this position as both team owner and your

uncle. I don't enjoy having the sense that you want to sign to another team after next season, especially after your marriage news is really spinning your image in a positive light." It's Declan, I recognize his voice right away.

"Look, my heart is with the team. But I'll never get to be captain of the Spinners, you know that. Everyone will assume bias," Connor explains.

"Just play like you are worthy, then it isn't a problem," Declan reminds him.

Connor scoffs. "We both know that isn't true. Besides, if our coach doesn't shape up this season, then it's another year of my career where I miss the opportunity to skate during playoffs and for a cup. I have career goals."

Declan growls, and when I peek around the corner, I see he is rubbing his face in aggravation. "Look, I shouldn't be telling you this, but we're off the record as family right now. I doubt we'll have the same head coach or general manager after next season. Not if I have anything to say about it. Just hang on a little longer. You even have a wife now, and I'm sure Hadley doesn't want to leave Lake Spark."

I clear my throat, announcing my arrival. "Hadley can speak for herself."

Both men whip their attention my way. Declan appears guilty, as if he was caught, and Connor smirks because he enjoys when I have a backbone.

"Sorry. You know where I'm coming from," Declan apologizes. "I'll leave you two be." He tips his head to Connor while he stares at me. "Talk a little sense into him, will ya?"

I grimace. "I think we both know that Connor will do what Connor wants to do."

Declan sighs. "Story of my life."

With Declan leaving us, I stride in Connor's direction, carefully, as I can tell he is sailing on rough waters right now.

"All good?" I ask, even though it feels like a pointless question.

"It's fine," he lies and walks to the kitchen. "This happens a lot. The lines get blurred between me and him." Connor grabs a beer from the fridge, and I hop up to perch on the edge of the counter.

My sympathetic look hasn't faded yet. "I think you and I have had a day."

His eyes narrow in on me with intrigue. "What happened to you?"

"My dad and I talked. It was needed, but I still feel a little overwhelmed. Need to find my bearings, I guess," I explain and stare at my dangling feet.

"It will get better," he assures me.

I sit tall and throw on an overdone smile. "I'm sure it will. Especially since I think I will take you up on the offer to get out of town. It seems that you could use a getaway too."

Connor sets his beer bottle down and approaches me with a smoldering gaze. "Oh yeah?"

I nod and quirk my lips. "Yeah. I figure you have two more weeks before you really hit the gym and ice hardcore to get ready for the season. A last-minute trip. No Sweden, though. I sent my passport off for renewal and it isn't back yet. Can we settle on, I don't know, Florida Keys or something?"

Connor brings his hands to the counter on either side of my body and leans in to bring our mouths within touching distance, but not quite. An agonizing move, but also enticing for me to attempt to brush my lips against his.

"You in a bikini, it's a deal."

Our lips meld together for a delicious kiss, which leads to him pulling me to the edge and using his hands to guide my legs around his waist.

This is what we need. A new setting to bring some clarity.

23

HADLEY

The feeling of lips grazing along my naked spine and moving up tickles, yet I respond by humming a sound of approval. I'm lying on my stomach, tangled in a sheet that isn't even covering half of my body.

Morning light floods into the room since the balcony doors are open to our own private little beach down in the Florida Keys. I've slept in pure bliss, but someone felt the need to wake me up in a delicious manner, with his hand now journeying up the back of my thigh.

I attempt to push him away playfully. "Sleep. It's more important."

Connor's answer is to take his fingers and sneak up under the sheet to claw my ass instead of spanking me. "Wake up. I have things I need you for." His voice is pure sin.

I decide to flutter my eyes fully open, and I flop over in bed. I'm greeted with Connor ready for the day ahead, with a subtle glean of sweat on his skin. He must have gone for a run or did his thousands of push-ups this morning.

"You don't need me awake for that. I might actually enjoy

it when I'm in my slumber and you take me from behind," I tell him in a drowsy state.

He leans down to give me a kiss. "Oh, I'm familiar, but I meant breakfast arrived, and you wanted to walk around Key West today."

I slowly crawl up to my elbows. "Ah yes, vacation things."

He slides off the bed and begins to take his tank off. "I'll grab a quick shower then we can get going."

"Okay, I'll throw on some clothes if I must and attack those pancakes that I see over on the breakfast tray." I begin to scooch out of bed and abandon the sheet in the process. I stand up and stretch my arms overhead, releasing a long comforting sigh.

My husband stares at me with hungry eyes and arms crossed. "As much as I love watching you display your tits to me, I love seeing you relaxed and happy even more."

I grab the silk robe hanging off the back of a chair. "I guess… I am." The tropical way of life seems to suit me or at least destress me.

We've been here only a few days, but the change of scene has helped a lot. Only at the airport leaving Illinois did someone recognize Connor, and since it was a ten-year-old, Connor agreed to sign something for him. After that, we've been in our own bubble in an exclusive tiny resort in the middle keys and taking day trips to Key West or snorkeling. I've noticed since we have some distance from Lake Spark, our families, and hockey that it isn't just me who needed a few days of shutting off. Connor has hockey on his brain far more than I realized. Not in a bad way, but in an ambitious manner. He's determined to conquer his goals.

Connor peeks out around the bathroom door with the shower now running. "Want to join me?"

I'm in a faceoff with the pancake on the tray, wondering if it's a good idea. "Nah, you go ahead, otherwise we'll never get out of here."

Pushing the cart of food outside and parking it next to the table, I sit down and enjoy the quiet morning and the gentle breeze. My eyes lock down on my wrist, and something connects in my brain for what might be a great idea. For months, I've wanted another tattoo, but I want to make it more significant. It's a good while of contemplation and nibbling on food before Connor emerges with sunglasses in hand and ready to go.

"See? You could have joined me in the shower since we're still not going to get out of here on time," he teases me, but he leans over from behind to kiss me upside down while he slides his palm down the middle of my breasts.

I tip my head up to give him a better angle for a kiss. "You're right," I murmur against his lips.

His response is one more peck on my lips, and then he circles around the table to sit down. "It's all good. We can go hang by the pool if you really want."

I smile. "What do you want to do?"

"Nothing in particular, just to see where the day goes." He pours a little pepper onto his eggs.

"Connor, you seem less anxious about hockey too while we're here," I say, being honest.

He runs his tongue along his inner cheek. "Maybe so. It's not that I'm apprehensive, I just want to feel that my career is going up, not stalled. It's hard when your family is so involved."

I grab my glass of freshly squeezed orange juice and lean back in the chair. "I admit that the last few years, I didn't always follow your career other than wanting to throw something at the screen if I saw you on TV. But since I now admittedly pay closer attention, I can without a doubt say that you have talent. You're not just the next-door neighbor who played hockey; you are the man destined to rule hockey."

His lips twist at my observation. "I like hearing that."

I snort a laugh. "You like hearing anything that boosts your ego."

Connor's smoldering grin comes out in full force as he rests his elbows on the table, but his eyes pin to me with a heavy gravity sinking him down. "Hadley, we'll be okay if I sign to another team after next season, right? I mean, it's rare that a player is with the same team his entire career, it's pure numbers that don't lie. I know how close you are with your family, and you have your dance studio…"

Without hesitation, I slide off my seat and circle the table to land right in his lap where I loop my arm around his neck. "All of our beach walks and visiting eclectic boutiques has had me thinking about a lot of things." A soft reassuring smile hits my lips. "The dance studio is a non-issue. I can manage it from afar with other teachers in my place and teach during the off-season. I can also dance anywhere. Our family will also always be there waiting for us. I never imagined that this would be a conversation that you and I would have."

He's listening to me but worry fills his eyes. "What do you mean?"

"I can't say we're happening fast because we've known one another our whole lives. We're doing a lot of things out of order too. No matter how hard I try to shake it, the idea of you and me just stays glued to everything in my body."

Relief hits him. "Still not 100% sure what you're trying to say."

I kiss his forehead. "I'm open to whatever gets thrown at us."

He offers me his mouth for a kiss and our lips meet. A life

with Connor is one of the clearest things in this moment of my life.

"Don't make a big deal about it." I might sound blasé. "But I love you too." I haven't told him until now.

But I feel as though this is my moment to do so, I want to. He follows my lead and pretends that we didn't just seal our fate.

"Thought you did," he answers, casual as can be, trying to hide his smile as he grabs a stick of bacon.

We're not going to make a big deal about this, because that's just us. We accidentally went full speed ahead, only to retrace the steps to that end point, and that's okay.

WALKING hand in hand down the busy street of pedestrians, bikes, and occasional roosters pecking around, I ignore the fact that I'm only slightly buzzed from the afternoon margarita that I just enjoyed with my burrito. We are having such a good time. There are literally no hours on the clock down here in the Keys. We don't plan and just follow the trail of what takes our interest.

"Should we send a postcard to your dad?" Connor jokes when we pass a tower of cards, but I know that it's his way of starting the conversation of the topic that he hasn't pressed me on since we've been down here.

I stall, and it causes him to turn his body to me. That shallow feeling in my stomach returns, but it feels more faded than recent weeks. "I really don't want anything to change between my dad and me."

Connor reaches up to tuck a few strands of my hair behind my ear before running his fingers along my arm. "Then it won't. It's up to you."

"It's just with the truth there and having told him how I feel, I'm not sure we can bury this all. Am I overthinking this?" I try to string my thoughts together.

"Hadley, you can bury something, but it will always be there in the spot that you left it. Instead, we do things to prove that we've moved forward, and then what you buried suddenly feels less heavy and behind a hidden wall. You're staying married to me, that shows we've moved forward, hasn't it?"

My lips press together because I admire his thoughts. I would never in my wildest dreams have anticipated him having this train of thought, but he's a lot more than a hockey dude and the former villain of my life.

I step to him and rest my hand on his shoulder while his arm snakes around my middle. "I'm kind of lucky to have you, but I think you realize that."

Connor tips his nose up in a cool kind of nod of recognition.

"The past few days and the ability to clear my head a bit has me realizing that I do want to move forward. Spencer is my dad in all ways," I declare with ease.

Connor's face softens. "That's wonderful to hear."

"I just need to find the key to help us confirm that."

Connor brings his arm around my shoulders, and we continue to walk. "You'll think of something."

It's a few blocks farther when we are confronted with a tattoo parlor, one that I've read about with rave reviews. I pull on Connor's arm, indicating for him to stop.

"I want a tattoo."

His eyes nearly bug out. "As in… now… or…"

I chuckle and lick my lips. "I've been thinking about it for a while. Remember? Vegas? I was going to get one there but got really sidetracked."

Connor indicates for me to stop. "Watch it, Wifey, you gained a husband, which I consider the best sidetrack shenanigans there are."

A bright smile spreads on my mouth. "Couldn't agree more." I interlink our arms and guide us straight to the door. "But I still want my tattoo, and this place is supposed to be phenomenal. Just a small one, a special one."

It makes sense for me. This isn't a spontaneous thought, but the meaning has changed.

I get yanked back when I realize that Connor isn't following me. Glancing to my side, I see that he appears nervous or agitated, with his feet rooted down. "Are you okay?"

"Why don't I just wait out here?" he offers.

"If they can see me now without an appointment, then it might be a good hour."

"I'll go grab a drink or pick out some souvenirs, I don't know. Anything other than looking at needles."

My face blazes with realization. "How did I not know that you're afraid of needles?"

He shrugs. "No big deal. I mean, you should do this. It's in an appropriate spot? I won't need to punch the artist after because he's seen your pussy or something, right?"

I giggle and point the side of my wrist. "Won't even see me half-naked," I promise.

Connor leans in and kisses my cheek. "I'll be waiting for you then."

I grab the back of his neck and yank him forward so I can crash my lips onto his in a bruising kiss. He deserves more than a delicate kiss goodbye. I slip my tongue in and swirl while I press my body against his, holding us tight. "Go pick out something for tonight when I can't touch the bandage of my tattoo but can lie in bed at your mercy," I purr.

That puts him in a good mood.

Sitting in the hammock next to our hotel room, Connor stares down, hypnotized by the clear bandage as we sit side by side with our feet on the ground and the sunset fast approaching.

"I can take the bandage off later tonight. Since it's only black ink and small, then it doesn't need so much time," I explain.

He hasn't stopped glancing at the design since he picked me up. The tattoo is visible through the Saniderm bandage. It's a few stars along the line from my wrist bone and up my forearm. They're small, and you would only notice if you were searching or happened to catch a glance.

But it isn't the stars that has him sentimental. I added tiny letters and numbers inside the stars. One is the initials of my dad, SC. Another star has the number 19; my husband's jersey number when he became my husband. That was a bit of a surprise for him, and me too, as I wasn't planning on it, but it felt right.

"I'm speechless," he reiterates again.

"I've noticed," I tease him.

Connor cups my cheek with his hand, drawing a circle on my skin with the pad of his thumb, holding my gaze as he kneels down before me, his eyes full of intention. My heart is on a rollercoaster, as he has me transfixed.

"Hadley Spears. I know you are kind of already my wife, but marry me for real. Let's have a real wedding, the kind you wrote about in your diary when you crushed on me when you were seven."

I bring a hand to my mouth and gasp fake shock. "You

mean a wedding with a unicorn theme and a magical cupcake tower?"

His laugh is deep and magical. "Okay, we may need to re-examine a few things… but a *real* wedding? One that you deserve to remember."

My hands frame his face, and I dive my head down to kiss him. "I absolutely love that idea." It's always kind of bugged me that I don't remember when I said I do or missed out on a few wedding traditions.

I throw my arms around his neck, and he falls back onto the sand, taking me with him. It doesn't take long for Connor to lead us inside where we tumble and miss the bed, opting to fall on the floor without a care in the world. He finds his way between my legs, first with his mouth and then with his cock. Screw the fancy bed, we just need the floor when we're this delirious with happiness.

Afterwards, we don't move from the floor and remain in a tangled mess. "The moms are going to lose it," he mentions, nearly out of breath.

"Oh, but we love it."

It's our last day of tropical life, but we can't wait another night to speak to our parents. There is no sugarcoating it, Connor and I are family people through and through.

Connor and I get cozy around the breakfast table to ensure we both fit in the phone screen. It takes two rings before my mom answers, and not so surprising, Brielle is with her, as they normally have coffee on Saturday morning together.

"Hey! You two look like lounge lizards," my mom notes.

"You both look good," Brielle adds as she attempts to equal the screen share with my mom.

I smile. "Thanks. Look, we're going to be quick. Don't make a big deal about it, but I kind of know you both probably have been plotting this anyway," I begin.

"We want to do a real wedding," Connor finishes my sentence in a melancholy tone to mess with them before swiping a few fingers across his jaw.

The sound of shrieking instantly causes me to lower the phone and stare at Connor who is shaking his head ruefully. Bringing my phone back up, I throw on a polite smile.

"Say no more. We can get invites out, confirm our reservation at the Dizzy Duck, and ask Piper to design a dress that she may have already started," my mom lists, and it causes me to burst out laughing because of course she had our neighbor designing a dress.

Connor gives them a thumbs up. "Cool. Just remember the father of the bride pays," he jokes.

"Connor," Brielle scolds him.

I see my dad peeking over their heads, attempting to see the screen.

"Can I talk to dad?" I request, and my mom hands him the phone. Connor takes my hand in his under the table to give me a comforting squeeze.

"Hey, princess. We're going on the real wedding train, huh?"

"Yep. I can see Mom is going to be busy the rest of the day." I indicate over his shoulder, as I can see in the background my mom already discussing plans with Brielle. In a strange modern-technology way, we have a bit of privacy. "Uhm, so I kind of did something while we're down here." I swallow.

My dad gives Connor a hardened look. "What the hell did you two kids do now?" He's messing with us.

"This one is all her idea," Connor promises.

I hold my wrist up to the camera so my dad can see. "It turns out my husband is a horrible replacement for tattoo partners. You are a lot better at going with me to get tattoos together, but I needed to do this one on my own and in my own time."

My father squints his eyes. "Is that—?"

"Connor's hockey number and… your initials." His mouth falls as the magnitude of the meaning overwhelms him. "Because you're my dad, the one and only, always a part of me," I confirm.

Tears swell in his eyes, and I notice that my mom quiets down as she observes. All eyes are on my dad and me. "No need to wait. We'll be okay," I tell him in what must feel like code words to the outside world.

But right now, everything fits perfectly. A fleeting few months brought a lifetime ahead of us.

24
CONNOR

The room erupts in low cheers as I arrive at the Vegas hotel penthouse. A mix of friends, teammates, and in an odd twist to the traditional bachelor party, my dad and his friends, including my father-in-law, are in attendance.

This should be completely awkward, especially since Briggs played a role in organizing this evening. But I know there will be no strippers or anything questionable since, well, I'm already married.

Instead, the room is set up with poker tables, a private bar, and a buffet of food to finish off our night. Because all day we've been on the go. A helicopter ride over the canyon, car racing at the speedway, and a scavenger hunt that led us back to the chapel where I got hitched yet don't remember.

Briggs grins as he walks over to me with a bottle in one hand, offering me his hand to pull me into a bear hug. "Keeping it real and giving us a little déjà vu. Oh, and I controlled the guest list, so, sorry, I did not invite Vaugh."

"That's kind of a dick move. He'll be at the wedding, you know. Unlike you, I consider him a friend. He volunteered once at the summer camp for kids." It's a lost cause, and Briggs takes a swig of his beer bottle. "We're going to play poker?" I ask.

"Yeah, and I'm going to give a not-safe-for-the-dads speech." He winks and cheekily grins, leaving before I can protest, but my half-glare and grin are apparent.

Briggs passes my dad who is approaching me with a whiskey in hand. It's kind of unusual to see him letting loose a little. He's always been easy to hang out with, but he's more of a BBQ type of guy.

He pats my shoulder. "Enjoying your day?"

"For sure."

"Your brothers are not thrilled about missing out, but they are way too young for this. Your uncle wishes he was here," he comments.

My lips quirk out. "I get it. Kind of inappropriate for the owner of the Spinners to be at my bachelor party if word got out."

My dad rubs my shoulder. "He did ensure we have the best whiskey available and sent some cigars our way."

I chortle. "I think you're living in your element right now. You didn't have a bachelor party when you eloped. Plus, you're off the hook from dad duty for the weekend."

"Whoa there, Son. I'm never off the hook from dad duty. I'm here to ensure you keep it respectable, as I know you will." His tone is humorous.

"Lies," I joke. "I'm a good cover. Now go, go enjoy owning the night."

His response is to chuckle.

As soon as he's off, Spencer is before me. Except, unlike my father, Spencer's smile is subtle. "This is a bit opposite to the lady's high tea bridal shower," he notes while he looks into his scotch glass.

I laugh. "I don't think Hadley minds. Besides, she had a wedding dress fitting today." We are throwing together a wedding in record time because pre-season games start soon, and we didn't want to wait until next summer, because that's what the calendar will do to us, make us wait. Luckily, our moms were ready to go, and this ship is sailing.

Spencer now breaks out in a grin. "Want my advice?"

I smirk shyly. "I'll hear it anyhow."

"Next off-season, take it easy."

I clap my hands together, eager for a drink. "Oh my God, I couldn't agree more."

One of my teammates brings me the scotch bottle to freshen up my drink. I've been pacing myself all day, and luckily, we had a big lunch too.

Someone turns the music down, and Briggs hits his glass with a cocktail straw to draw silence into the room. "Gentlemen, the sun has set, and we're heading into the night. Bring your A-game to the poker tournament that we have planned and enjoy the drinks. We're all here because of this man right here." Briggs points his glass in my direction. "Back in May, a bunch of us came out here for my birthday. What we didn't expect was that our boy Con would decide to ditch the party, carrying his future bride out over his shoulder."

A bunch of guys begin to cheer while I stand in the middle of the room, patiently accepting the roast that my friend is about to give me.

"For those of us lucky enough to witness the many quarrels between the love birds, then you will know that the bride and groom have *very dirty* mouths." Some guys begin to whistle, but my eyes bug out and signal to Briggs to mind the dads. "We can only imagine what that wedding night was like." More woots, but my jaw tightens, and Briggs notices before he glances to my dad and Spencer, but his smug grin doesn't fade since they're just eating up this speech. "Apologies, Ford and Spencer. Kids these days, am I right? Getting to the good stuff before committing to their vows."

My head falls as I give up, but I appreciate that everything is in good jest.

"But seriously, Connor, man." Briggs's tone turns serious. "I wasn't going to let you be shackled down without a good sendoff, so here we are. I've reluctantly called off the strippers, except for two, but they're heading straight to my room, since we're going to keep this classy. Let's open some champagne and have a good night. Cheers."

Everyone clinks their glasses before the music gets turned up again. Over the next few hours, we play poker, smoke cigars, and feel light thanks to the whiskey.

I appreciate everyone turning out and the effort put in to tonight, but somewhere between two and three in the morning, I decide that the DJ can play on without me, and I head back to my room.

I don't take much notice when I open the door, as I am busy unbuttoning my shirt, but I'm startled when a light flicks on, and I see Hadley sitting in the chair in the corner.

"You may want to lock the door." Her tone is pure sultry, and my eyes fill with desire as I give her the once-over.

It can't be the alcohol that has me imagining that she's in shorts that barely pass as clothes, a bra top, and her ballet pointe shoes that she dyed black. The ribbons lead a path up her calf.

I'm fully invested in this moment. "What are you doing here?" She should be back in Illinois.

Hadley propels from the chair and strides my way with a sway to her hips, drawing me in and building the need I have for her inside of me.

She reaches out to claw my shirt. "Decided I wanted to

surprise you, so I flew out. Now sit down." Her stern demand swelters desire between us, and this dominant side is new to me, but I'm all for witnessing it.

A smirk toys on my lips, and I exaggerate the way that I sit down, informing her that I'm listening.

She walks back to me and leans down to chase my lips with hers, ensuring they never touch, but I feel her breath cascading down my chin and neck. "If we're going to have a real wedding, then you should have a real bachelor party… lap dance included."

My eyes widen, as I'm impressed that this is the angle she's going for. "I agreed to no strippers, so my wife decided she would fill the role?" I cock my head to the side.

"Something like that… but I've also never danced for you."

I grab her wrists, and I'm eager to take charge, even though this is her show. "You have, you just didn't realize."

The corner of her mouth pulls. "Well, this time it's with intention."

She drops low into a squat, balancing on her toes, before slowly slithering her way up my body, ensuring her breasts rub against my body, creating friction to my cock in passing. Next thing I know she's straddling me, with her upper body falling back in a curve because she's flexible and wants to offer me her body.

My eyes survey her like a canvas, eager to press my lips on the cleavage of her breast, but just as I lean in to scrape her skin with my lips, she sits up and brings her hands to her long hair. I get completely lost in her flawless transitions, especially when she rests her hands on my shoulders and reaches one leg behind her to the sky while she leans into me on one foot. She stays in this position while her mouth travels lower down my chest, pausing when her warm mouth covers my hard cock through my jeans.

I would love to be inside of her right now, that's the only clear thought that I have in this moment.

She peers up at me with mischief and flops around with her back now to me as she grinds against my body, grabbing my hand to part her thighs open. If we weren't alone, then the entire room would see her covered pussy on offer.

Taking the liberty, I unhook the bra top, and she leans forward to cover her breasts when the fabric falls. But she doesn't just gently push her body forward, she brings her ass to the air as her palms land on the floor.

I shudder from the image and the growing ache my dick is experiencing. Hadley is erotic in this moment and magnificent, but most of all, she's my wife.

I spank her because her behind is screaming to be touched, and she responds by swinging her hair over as her body draws back up. Hadley does a little turn on her toes to face me, and my eyes wander straight to her breasts with pebbled rocks peeking out at me. I fucking love her eyes that are filled with a sexiness that's new.

My hand finds her hip, and she drags my palm up to one of her beautiful globes while her hips move in a wave. I'm going to enjoy my prize, which is why I squeeze her breast, and her head falls back with a seductive smile.

I'm entranced by every inch of her in this very second, and when she tips her body forward and drops down to another squat with her knees out, I'm tempted to pull her onto my lap.

Her tongue darting out to lick her lips has me intrigued, especially when she begins to unzip my jeans and force the fabric down.

I bring my hands behind my head as I watch her fingers

wrap around my length to give me a stroke and then her breath is on the tip of my cock. My eyes hood closed as I take in the feeling of her lips wrapping around my tip.

"Such a good girl," I praise.

She hums a sound as she takes me farther into her mouth, her nails digging into my waist to keep her steady as she brings me deep, only to drag her tongue back up in her wet mouth.

"Damn," I breathe heavily.

It only encourages her to repeat that move a few times more until she gags once, then she finds a rhythm by bopping her head to pick up the pace.

"I'm positive this isn't how a lap dance should go," I state.

The sound of Hadley's lips popping off my cock has me glancing down, and I fist some of her hair as I admire her swollen lips with a little drool on the side of her mouth.

"Positive you want to fuck me too," she says, being sassy.

I cock a brow. "Be a good girl then and ride my cock."

She smirks slyly and slowly stands when I reluctantly let her hair go. Once she stands, she pivots which means that I am unable to see her face. She hooks her fingers under the band of her flimsy shorts, and she leans forward, with her ass in the air as she drags the fabric down her thighs to her ankles, and she steps out of them. The entire move, allowing me to see her glistening pussy and the crack of her ass.

My body buzzes with heat and a swirling desire to plunge inside of her.

Hadley steps back and sits on my lap, with her back tight to me and her pointed toes against the floor. Her hands find my fingers, and she drags them through her arousal. "Am I ready enough for you?" she rasps.

I growl into her cheek then playfully nip her skin before I

drag my teeth to scrape the lobe of her ear. "Perfectly wet. Now slide down on top of me, you fucking bad girl."

The feeling of her heat taking me in sends my eyes to the back of my head because she's snug and mine. My little vixen rides me slow until I square her hips and guide her to bounce. Then it turns wild, with our relentless effort to go harder and faster. She squeezes tighter, and my answer is to flick her clit with my fingers to drive her crazy. Her moans entice me to take control of her body and throw her on the bed, but I let her stay on top because she is the initiator tonight.

But then she glances over her shoulder and buries her head into my neck, with her heavy breath mixed with her moan. Her body is about to crumble in my arms as she vibrates around my cock from an orgasm. I hold her tight as my release ripples through me shortly after.

We're a couple tangled on a chair, and I didn't even get to kiss her lips yet.

I hook my finger under her chin to guide her to me and kiss her with passion and appreciation. When I pull away, I smirk when I whisper, "You are some surprise."

"I'm only here to please," she says, sarcastic.

It's a few minutes later when we crawl into bed naked, and Hadley finds her way into my arms, with her head against my chest. I begin to stroke her hair, because as much as I'm exhausted, I don't want this night to end.

"I'm happy we remember moments now with each other." I laugh under my breath.

"It's better." Her nail traces my pec. "Kind of sucks that I don't remember if we were handsy with one another when we got married."

"We'll make up for it. Besides, if it didn't happen this way, then I'm sure you would have cut my hand off that night and never ended up as my wife."

Hadley half-laughs. "Ooh, that would have been bad. The world needs your hand. I need your hand."

"Ha-ha." I squeeze her tighter.

She looks up at me, and it's sentimental. "I love you."

"I love you too." I kiss her real quick. "Not that's it's a competition or anything, but I did say it first, and we should note that," I tease her.

Hadley's answer is to pinch me. "Not everything is a game, you know."

"If it was, then I would just win," I answer blankly.

"Lucky me." She stares at me intently for an extra second. "No really, lucky me." Then she cements our lips together.

Because she is everything that I knew was worth waiting for.

25
HADLEY

Okay, I'm doing this again.

I stare at myself in the mirror. I'm in a white dress, this time for a real-ish wedding.

My wedding.

The white dress is fitted and just long enough. The lace and silk are subtle, simple yet elegant. My hair is down except for one side pulled up slightly, with a peach rose in my hair, and I skipped the veil. I'm confident that the extravagant wedding and reception downstairs at the Dizzy Duck Inn will make up for my lack of a princess gown.

Any minute now, I will walk down the aisle to marry my husband again, with memories to replay in my head for the future ahead.

I needed a moment to myself before my dad comes to collect me and bring me down the aisle. My mom agreed a few moments of reflection would be a nice idea. Who am I kidding? She needed to go shed a tear and yell at the caterer to ensure the cupcake tower is taller.

A smile already hits me from everyone being so happy.

The gentle knock on my door puzzles me, as I thought for sure I had a few more minutes before showtime.

"Hadley, let me in." Connor speaks low, as if he doesn't want to be discovered.

"Connor?" I sound surprised.

I open the door, and he slides right through the crack, only to close the door and gape his mouth open at the sight of me. I steal his breath as he admires me, and I mirror his sentiment, as he always looks suave in a suit, like the man he was always going to be.

"Beautiful," he rasps before he strides a few steps in my direction.

I already feel the butterflies, every cliché for a wedding spinning through my body. "Here we are, Mr. Spears."

"Again… Don't worry, everything is going smoothly. Isla is your maid of honor extraordinaire, with 90% of the single hockey players here eyeing her like crazy. My mom quickly checked on Ace." Because we adopted him when the shelter phoned to say that he still didn't have a family. The little dude loves his life with us, plus he's good company when Connor will be away more and I need to cuddle in bed. "Our brothers have managed to be respectable ushers. Everything is in check."

"Then what brings you here?" I sound very curious.

He begins to chuckle as his lips stay closed, then he waves his phone up in his hand. "I kind of have a pre-ceremony present." Connor indicates with his head that I should follow him to sit on the end of the bed.

"Really? You want us to go at it right now? It took a solid two hours to look like this," I feign disbelief.

He gives me an odd glance. "That's not it. This is something…" Connor swipes his screen and shows me an email. "Significant."

I read the email from Briggs.

Con,

Only you could get me to give you two wedding presents for two different weddings in the span of a few months. However, this is perhaps going down as legendary. We're all idiots. You know those Elvis chapels? They save videos for six months…

…Yeah, I watched. Isla too.

Briggs

My eyes snap to Connor who has a grin. "Our… first wedding?" I'm unsure how I feel about this.

He nods. "Yep. Do you really want to watch it? It isn't long."

"Uhm… is it a good idea? Did you watch it?"

"No."

I roll my lips in and debate for a millisecond. "Who the hell are we kidding? Press that play button."

Connor laughs and does what I say. I squeeze his arm and keep him close as we sit tight to get a full view.

Then my brows furrow when he presses play.

The screen shows me that Connor is handing over a paper and his credit card to the chapel clerk, while I am on his back piggyback style.

"Ah yes, I think we had to get a license at the county office which is conveniently open late, and there are about ten chapels within a three-block radius."

"So, we just walked across the street?" I wonder.

We both angle our heads as we try to figure out how we found ourselves in such a predicament. "Sounds about right."

On the screen, he sets me down when the lady behind the desk indicates for us to walk down the aisle. My head now falls to my hands when the video shows me jumping onto Connor's front, straddling his waist, with my arms linked around his neck. Then he walks us down the aisle in that very position.

"Wow, you were eager." He smirks at me. "Oh look, we're getting to the good part. Elvis is making an appearance."

We both watch the video as we arrive at the end of the of the aisle, with a man in a costume ready to seal the deal. Connor lowers me, and we look at one another.

Suddenly sound begins on the video.

"Should we be questioning this more?" I ask Connor, clearly under the influence of tequila and holding fake flowers.

"Were you when we were making out with my hand up your dress in the elevator at the hotel after we fought then gave in?" he challenges, and it doesn't sound like he's sober, not by a long shot.

I shrug my shoulder. "Meh, you're right." I face Elvis. "We can do this. He has already told me he doesn't hate me… I think. Wait, did I admit that I want him too?"

Connor scoffs a laugh. "Damn straight you did, you pushed me against a wall to kiss me again."

I smile and point a finger at Connor. "I totally did. After you told me you didn't hate me at all, and I should be yours."

"You should be, Sprinkles." Connor nearly sounds offended.

I coo a sound. "You called me Sprinkles."

We share another affectionate look before we grab one another's faces with our hands to kiss hard and fast, not taking notice of the man trying to marry us.

Elvis observes us blankly then gets into character again, complete with a chuckle and voice that clearly isn't his own. "You kids ready to shake it? We'll make it quick so you can take this to the marriage bed."

Connor and I pull away from one another in a state of buzz and realization.

"Be mine forever," Connor states.

"Do we get to have a dog? I can wear your jersey too, right" I ask far too seriously.

Connor wraps an arm around my middle to keep us close. "Anything you want. I'll get a diamond ring after in the hotel store. We should totally get another bottle of tequila to celebrate that we're doing what we were always meant to."

"Yesss, tequila. Naked too. Naked tequila for our wedding night," I agree with excitement.

"You two seem like cool cats. But I gotta keep this cruising, we have another couple waiting in some medieval costumes, and we try to keep this short." Elvis is doing his best to move us along.

"Fast version," Connor snaps at Elvis then returns his gaze to me.

Elvis chuckles again. "Take her to be your bride?"

"Yes." Connor's answer is quick and sharp.

Elvis directs his attention to me. "Take him to be your husband?"

"Yes," I reply with vigor.

"I pronounce you husband and wife. Love her tender and love lives forever." He leans to the side to grab rose petals before he throws them at us. "Crystal at the front desk will take your picture. Have a blast."

Then we kiss and nearly skip down the aisle.

I lean my head against Connor's as he turns his phone off and the room is silent.

"That was…" he begins.

My eyes widen and my lips curl in as I'm struggling to come up with words. "Kind of a trainwreck."

He kisses the top of my head as he nudges my arm.

"We're not watching that ever again, are we?" Connor seems to be on my wavelength.

"I don't think so, unless we're playing naked tequila."

We both let a laugh escape.

"You were totally into it, though," he points out.

I gasp at his accusation. "You were the one leading us. It was completely you pushing that wedding," I lie and try to control my grin.

"Who the fuck cares how it got us there. We're married and where we're meant to be."

Our eyes lock in a sentimental gaze. "So we are."

"We get a redo today."

I gently shake my head. "Thank the heavens for that. I have a feeling this wedding is the one that I'll always want to remember."

"No Elvis in sight," he promises.

I huff a sound. "But we're getting Briggs instead," I deadpan, because we don't actually need someone official since that deed is done, but it's just as scary as a fake Elvis but equally perfect too.

Standing up off the bed, I smooth my dress, and Connor joins me as he adjusts his tie.

"My wife," he whispers.

"My husband," I reply.

We both lean in for one last soft kiss on the lips before Connor walks to the door, and just as he opens it, my father is standing there with his fist up, about to knock.

My dad swims his eyes between us. "Really, you two? Couldn't just give your parents one traditional element for this wedding?" He is half serious but maybe kind of annoyed.

Connor and I both shrug as my father brushes past Connor then turns to lead my husband out. "The groom isn't supposed to see the bride before the wedding. Bye now."

I try to suppress my laugh and so does Connor.
We only follow our own path and rules.
Always have.

EPILOGUE

HADLEY—A FEW MONTHS LATER

Squeezing my dad's hand for dear life, I wince when I see my husband scuffling with the winger from the opposite team against the boards. I do my best to return to my neutral face, hence why my dad's hand is getting ripped off.

I should have stayed up in the wives' room where nobody would be able to witness my observation of Connor during a game. But I need to feel closer, and it's kind of, well, exhilarating next to the ice.

That is, until my husband gets the whistle from the ref for cross-checking the other team's winger, Vaughn Madden. Just great, now I'm going to hear Briggs complaining about this for days, while Connor just takes the high road.

I breathe softly to stay calm. You never have any idea when a camera or fan might catch you.

Thankfully it's a home game, so my dad, keeping to his promise, stays close. Ford and Brielle are sitting up in a private room with Declan to watch the game.

"Number 19, two minutes," the ref calls out Connor's trip to the penalty box.

I bite my tongue, as I can tell Connor is now more pissed, and he will be sulking in the penalty box in the minutes to come.

"It's fine. He already scored twice, and we still have a period to go," my father leans in to assure me.

I huff. "He'll be grumbly later." Never with me, though. Connor may be an aggressive cocky ass on the ice, but he is the polar opposite when at home.

Grabbing my purse that I had set on the floor, I search for my lip balm, only to smile softly to myself when Connor's wedding ring hanging around my neck swings in the air. He's not allowed to wear rings during games. He brings it with him on the road, but when it's a home game, it's safe around my neck until after the game when I'm waiting by the locker room.

My dad rubs my shoulders as the next two minutes fly by, and then Connor is whizzing across the ice, outskating the other team that is eager to block him.

"What did I miss? I heard booing," Isla asks as she slides back onto the seat next to me.

"You picked the worst moment to go to the bathroom, which by the way, are you okay? You do that a lot," I'm a little curt, but the ref's earlier call has me livid.

"Feisty. Sorry if nature calls," she defends.

"I'll give you two a minute, and I'll go grab some snacks." My dad seemed to have a hint that Isla and I need a little space.

My eyes travel from the ice to Isla who looks a little pale. "What's up with you?" I wonder.

"Nothing." She's lying.

Drawing a line from her to the ice then back, it registers to me that we're playing Tampa tonight.

"Nothing to do with who's on the ice?" My brows raise.

She shakes her head, but it feels as though it's a struggle.

I touch her arm. "Spill it."

It feels as though the floodgates are opening and her face relaxes. "You know how I had that conference in Tampa a while ago?"

"Yeah, the one where you got stuck there because of a hurricane."

She nods. "I wasn't exactly alone when I safely rode out the storm in a hotel."

Excitement spreads through me. "You were riding someone else during the storm, weren't you?"

Isla bites her bottom lip. "It's not ideal."

"Why not? It's great. You are allowed to have fun. Who was it?" I inquire with deep curiosity.

She laughs nervously. "The guy who just put your husband in the penalty box."

My jaw goes slack. "Vaughn Madden?"

Guilt floods her face, and she brings her hand to her forehead. "Nobody can know. Especially since my brother isn't a fan. It was a one-time thing."

"Really? I mean, he's not hard on the eyes. Long-distance isn't ideal, but it's no different than if he played here in Lake Spark and had to travel for the season." I feel like I'm getting carried away.

Proven by the fact that Isla places her hand over mine on her arm. "Take a chill pill. It really was a one-time spur-of-the-moment kind of thing. He wasn't even there when I woke up."

"What an ass." Now my sour mood has returned.

"Can we forget about it?" she pleads.

I roll my eyes and feel frustrated for her. "Fine. But give him a piece of your mind after the game. You're entitled to that."

"No, Hadley. We're all entitled to a no-strings night. Now, will you focus on your man who is back on the ice and already intercepted a pass?" She smiles softly.

My attention moves forward to watch the ice where my husband has rejoined the game. "Damn. He has talent," I comment in awe, because it never gets old, the way he always goes straight back into it.

The game is a win for us, and I find myself waiting outside the press room, staring at a television screen mounted on the wall, watching as reporters ask my husband questions for post-game analysis.

There's something about Connor slightly flushed from the exercise, mixed with wet hair and a grin, that has my panties melting.

"Look, off the ice, I consider Vaughn Madden a friend. We played together before, and he was at my wedding. On the ice, we're not always friends, but that also means we can push one another's boundaries more easily, as the trust is there. It just happened that tonight the Spinners played better, with a tight defense, partly because I wasn't afraid to go in strong," Connor speaks into a mic.

Another reporter asks a question that I can only hear a mumble of.

It causes Connor to grin. "Yeah, we have a few days off for Christmas, but I'll use that to do a mini reset. I don't want my head out of the game since we are back next week playing, but it is my first Christmas as a married man, so I intend to enjoy that with my wife."

I love that answer. Even more, I love that it wraps up the

round of questions, and Connor is walking straight to the hall to me, with the cameras still following him.

He kisses me real quick while I take my necklace off to return his ring. "Good game," I congratulate.

"Would have been better if I didn't get that penalty," he rumbles a sound.

I massage his shoulder. "Relax, forget about it as soon as we're out of here. Besides, you have a turkey to roast tomorrow."

He half-laughs. "Thanks for volunteering us to host."

"It's tradition that the newlyweds host," I counter.

"Since when?" he challenges.

"Mmm, since I made up that rule." I interlace our arms as we walk toward the players' parking lot underneath the arena. "Besides, we have a dog at home that would hate to miss out."

Connor chuckles again. "Sure, we'll host dinner for twenty because our dog might have hurt feelings."

I rest my head on Connor's shoulder as we walk, enjoying our post-game routine. Especially since I know hard and fast sex is coming later.

STARING down at the kitchen counter, I give Connor knowing eyes. "See? Christmas dinner is easy as pie."

He removes more foil with a grin. "That's because your version of cooking is having your mom do everything and bring it over in tin dishes."

I splay my hands out. "Delegating is cooking."

Connor walks a step toward me to pull me close, and his fingers entwine in my hair as he jerks me forward for a kiss. "You're a genius. Briggs is bringing beer, my mom pie, and our little brothers will be annoying shits as always. Not to mention my aunt and uncle will bring my cute little goddaughter and her persistence to ask one hundred times if a turkey is an animal." He loves it, he does.

"Sounds wonderful. Isla already brought the wine and is changing out of her yoga pants. I'll go change too since your hoodie doesn't feel like festive attire."

He draws me in for another kiss just as we feel Ace jump at our feet. We both look down, and Connor sighs. "I'll give him a quick walk and keep him out of the kitchen."

"Great."

We both part to head our separate ways, but he tows me back since he doesn't let go of my hand. "I love you," he reminds me.

"I love you too." I blush every time.

A minute later, I'm upstairs on my way to find a sweater dress, but I hear a sniffle. Knowing Isla was using the guest bedroom, I decide to check on her.

"Isla?"

The door is slightly ajar, so I take the liberty to push it farther open, and I find my friend sitting on the edge of the bed, wiping a tear away.

Instantly, I'm concerned. "What's wrong?"

"Hadley, I need to tell you something," she sniffles. "I can't keep it in anymore."

"You're scaring me," I inform her and sit next to her, touching her arm in comfort. "It's okay. If you don't like my attempt at a charcuterie board, you can tell me. Is that what it is?"

She smiles through her tears. "It's delicious, just my stomach didn't agree."

I frown. "Oh gosh, I can't afford to poison people at

dinner tonight, not when a hockey team is relying on two of the guys present."

"They'll be fine. It's me. All me. I'm pregnant."

My eyes wash over her body to study if she is joking with me, but she isn't. I'm frozen from shock. "W-what?"

"A few months, actually."

"Huh?" I'm speechless. "How."

"A hurricane," she hiccups.

My eyes drive side to side as I register the timeline. "As in…"

She blows out a long breath. "Nobody knows. Not even…" She can't seem to muster the name.

But I can, and this is a twist. "Vaughn Madden," I croak out.

And she nods.

BONUS SCENE

CONNOR – 5 YEARS LATER

Opening the door to my hotel room, I sense my wife's presence instantly. I wasn't planning on Hadley being here, but when I left the stadium thirty minutes ago to find a text from her that I had a surprise in my room, then I knew it would be her—she's my sixth sense.

While she doesn't travel with me for away games since it isn't allowed, she does attend the random game in destinations that are fun and warm and stays in my room, which is allowed. Which is why I'm slightly puzzled that she showed up here in Denver at the end of January. It's the opposite of warm.

I've stayed with the Spinners my entire career so far, which means Hadley traveled from Illinois. But here she is leaning against the desk in the hotel room with a peculiar look on her face.

"Couldn't wait another week to see me?" I tease her and walk straight into her arms.

My fingers weave into her hair and bring her in for a deep and warm kiss. It's been days since I've touched her, and the feeling never fades. That reunion moment after time away, it keeps us alive.

When I pull back, I can see that she has a shy smile and she peers down.

"You okay?" I smile to myself, as she is kind of adorable.

"Yeah, just since you have to go on to Detroit, it would be next week when I see you for bye week," she explains.

I'm looking forward to mid-season bye week for a few days off. A bunch of guys are heading down to Mexico, but I just want to relax at home with Hadley. I'll catch Wyatt's varsity hockey game too and check in with Alex who decided hockey wasn't for him at all.

My wife nibbles on her bottom lip, debating something.

I take her hands in mine, determined to get to the bottom of this. "What's going on?"

"I couldn't wait to tell you something…"

Squinting my eyes, I'm not a clue further on the mystery.

She gathers where my brain is at and continues. "Remember Christmas?"

My brows raise, as I'm shocked she would even question that. I had three days off, and we didn't leave bed except for family dinner on Christmas Day. We even pulled over on the side of the road at one point. That's our rhythm during hockey season; days away from one another, contrasted by days that I live inside her.

"Up there on my list of best days of my life." I walk her to the bed to sit down.

"Yeah, so, uh, we also decided that we would… you know… try the baby-making thing…" She's waiting for me to catch up, and the glimmer in her eye informs why she might be here.

"Prime window when we need to try is now?" I wonder.

She shakes her head. "We're kind of already a few steps ahead."

Shit.

Didn't see that coming. But damn, my smile beams. "You're pregnant?"

She nods before happy tears pool in her eyes. "Found out yesterday, and I'm going crazy not telling anyone."

Pulling her into my arms, I kiss the hell out of her. This is wonderful news. Great news is exactly what I needed, it was a rough game and loss tonight .

"Well, this is amazing." I'm nearly speechless.

"I didn't have time to find a cute little jersey with your number that says baby, and the dog kind of buried the pregnancy test somewhere in the yard, I'm not even joking. But I did take three more tests at the airport for fun." Hadley shrugs her shoulders, and she's adorable.

I hold her close and fall back, keeping her tight against my chest. "We're going to be parents," I breathe out as I take in the news.

"Yeah. I guess I'm about six weeks. I called the doctor and demanded that we have an appointment next week since you'll be home."

I squeeze her tighter and kiss the top of her head. "You know, a week might be enough time to get little jerseys. I think we have some people who would appreciate them."

Hadley looks up to meet my gaze and splays her palm against my chest. "Our parents are going to flip."

STANDING outside the door to my parents' house, Hadley fidgets with the presents in the bag.

"Will you relax?" I place my hand on her upper back. Normally, we just walk right in, but we stalled when Hadley had a nervous freakout when my hand hit the door handle.

"Sorry. It's not every day we tell our parents that they're going to be grandparents." She's a little sassy, but I'll take it. She had her head over a toilet most of the morning.

I also know that she's been dying to tell our moms, and I want her to, even though it's early. She needs a support network until I'm back at the end of season.

"Who do you think is going to combust first?" I ask.

Hadley throws me an entertained look. "My money is on your mom."

I wiggle my long finger side to side. "Nah, I'm betting on your mom."

"We shall see."

The door flies open to my mother on the other side. "Oh, hello. What are you two doing out here? You never come to the front door." She looks at us peculiarly.

"Oh." I scratch the back of my head. "Felt like shaking it up since there is a pile of snow over there," I lie. As proven by the fact my mom peeks her head out the door to examine the driveway that was clearly shoveled earlier today.

"Right." Her tone informs me she doesn't believe us. "Come in, you two. Both of your brothers are starving, and your mom, Hadley, went overboard with dinner and wine."

I guide my wife inside and whisper, "Showtime."

After a round of hellos, we all find ourselves at the dining table where we left presents on our parents' plates. Since it's a school week, our brothers just grabbed some food and went to go work on their homework.

Hadley leans in to speak softly into my ear. "One of the moms are on to us."

"How do you know?" I whisper back.

"Wine. Blue cheese in the salad. Things I can't consume." She's overreacting, but it's cute.

I rub a soothing circle on her back. "Ugh, common ingredients at a dinner."

Hadley throws me a death stare. "Presents. Now."

I laugh and lazily hit my wine glass with a knife to grab everyone's attention. All eyes are on me, and I stand up with wine glass in hand.

"Good to be back for a few days," I begin. "As you can see, we left you each a present, so perhaps open them?" I'm not one for speeches.

"At the same time," Hadley adds and touches my arm.

Our parents glance at one another, curious yet with gentle smiles on their faces. I notice April squeezing Spencer's hand for dear life on the table.

Slowly the tissue paper finds its way to the floor, and everyone is lifting little hockey jerseys up.

My mother is the first to gasp before she beams a smile.

April coos and grins. "This is wonderful. I mean, I'm going to be a young grandma, but this is awesome. I'm so happy for you both. I was picking up the vibes." She nudges Spencer's shoulder. "Didn't I tell you she had a glow the other day at lunch?"

"Not a glow. Just post-vomiting color," Hadley states bluntly.

"How are you feeling? How far along?" my mother begins to list.

Hadley squeezes my arm and returns to sitting to be close with her as we take in our parents' faces. "A lot of morning sickness. I'm about eight weeks, and we had an ultrasound yesterday since Connor is home for a few days."

My eyes drive to my dad who claps his hands together. "This is great news. Like *really* great news. My son is going to be a dad." He blows out a breath. "Crazy but amazing."

All our attention turns to Spencer who seems to be transfixed by the tiny shirt in front of him. He's awfully quiet, and his face is neutral.

April rubs his arm. "Alive there, *Grandpa*?"

Then it happens.

Spencer Crews cracks. A tear, then he swipes it away.

Everyone is surprised by his clearly emotional reaction to our news. It would be entertaining to most, but it feels somewhat fitting considering his relationship with Hadley.

My wife stands up and circles around the table to kneel down and hug him. "Yeah, Dad, you're going to be a grandfather. If it's anything like your dad skills, then you're going to be an amazing grandfather."

They share a moment together and hug.

"You're going to be a great mom. My daughter is going to be a mom," he reflects, with a smile spreading.

"There is kind of one more little detail," Hadley informs him, with fingers coming up to indicate a smidge in length.

"Oh?" he says, curious.

Hadley stands again and walks back to me, taking a seat next to me. We interlace our fingers on the table and prepare for the gasps about to hit our ears.

"Twins skip a generation," I inform the table and wait for someone to get the hint. I see that little detail beginning to register in our parents' heads. I decide to add fuel to the fire. "Due date is right before season starts, but we're going to need all the help we can get."

"Twins?" Spencer's jaw drops.

It's a total myth that twins skip generations, but I'm not about to highlight to my father-in-law that either his daughter's eggs or my super sperm decided two babies would be in our cards.

"Surprise," Hadley announces.

The table erupts in a lot of comments and sounds of celebration. It's good to see everyone happy. But the best part is watching my wife completely elated by the scene in front of us and the fact that she's carrying our children.

Really, though, I didn't factor twins anywhere into our game that turned into more. No, like, this is coming from the blindside, but really, it's the perfect play.

Leaning in, Hadley's and my foreheads touch, and I have to grin because I'm going to rock this dad thing with her, because I only play to win.

THANK YOU

This was a story that was in my head from the moment that I started the Lake Spark world. Thank you to everyone who has been along for the journey of this small little town. To all of the ARC readers and social media sharers, a big thank you. You are key for readers discovering Hadley & Connor's romance.

Autumn, is there a thank you to the moon and back? You deserve it for putting up with me and keeping the rocket ship moving.

My editor Lindsay who has been with me on every book. Are you tired of me saying thank you again? Well, thank you.

Rachel for beta proofing, thank you for catching what my eyes don't.

Lindsey, it is such a pleasure to work with you on our special covers!

My family…yep, we're still doing this. Thank you for letting me hide away and disappear to cafes to write.

Made in the USA
Columbia, SC
25 October 2023